Love, truth, death, and

SEAN CONNERY

The Untold Story

Lynda Graham-Rowe

Infusionmedia
Lincoln, Nebraska

Enjoy!
lynd?R
in Bethany Beach!
8-9-2?

Infusionmedia
2124 Y St #138
Lincoln, NE 68503
https://infusion.media

Printed in the United States
10 9 8 7 6 5 4 3 2 1

First Edition

ISBN: 978-1-945834-26-4

Library of Congress Control Number: 2021913224

This is a fictionalized account inspired by real events. All names used in this story, except for those of public figures, have been changed and are the product of the author's imagination.

This book is intended for **mature readers only.** Adult subject matter and some explicit content.

Cover photo from the Dutch National Archives, donated in the context of a partnership program to Wikimedia Commons, with all rights waived. Photo taken November 23, 1983, by Rob Bogaerts/Anefo.

This book is dedicated to the late "Frank Mitchell." Without him, without his friendship, there would be no story. I hope you are watching from the other side, Frank, and that you are proud of me for finally sharing your adventures with the world, just as you wanted. I am picturing you reunited with your finger and sipping cocktails with Sean; shaken, not stirred, of course.

Also, I would like to acknowledge my firstborn, Jennifer, as the creator of the perfect title for this book, a title that beautifully captures the essence of its content. Also, a huge thank-you to all of my children—Jennifer, Catherine, and Christopher—for their unwavering support and advice through all the ups and downs of this incredible journey.

Contents

Introduction

"We discussed it last night and again this morning over break-fast and all four of us agree. You will write our story."

"I'm so honored, but, as much as I love to write and have dreamed of publishing a book, I never have. I think the four of you should write it yourselves or get someone with experience to do it."

"We don't want anyone else. I have already told my pub-lisher that we want you. You will be the sole author... There will be no ghostwriters... That is our final decision, Frenchie. More later, 007 (I only sign that to my friends.)"

It began as a shocking yet tender and intimate story of love, one that would stun the world with its uncensored revelations. That itself would have sufficed to create a best seller, but as time passed and trust grew, the stories evolved. No longer was this merely a unique and candid love story. It became a cleansing of the soul for all involved, true confessions of a most unexpected nature.

So how did a French teacher living in Lincoln, Nebraska, get involved in this magnificent story? It all started with a substitute teacher named Frank Mitchell, one phone call, and the sharing of cancer stories.

Prologue

Frank Mitchell called himself the world's oldest living substitute teacher, yet he was so much more than that. He was an amazing individual in his own right, and this story illuminates his talents and incredible adventures, one of the greatest involving his friendship with Sean Connery. This was a friendship kept secret for over fifty years, with only those in their closest circle being aware of it. Then, in November 2008, Frank joined my colleague Nancy in the teacher's lounge, where he received a phone call. After a short conversation, he stated, "I have a great story, but it requires my telling you that I'm personal friends with Sean Connery." The flood of stories began shortly after his confession. Eventually, I had over three hundred pages of email correspondence from Frank, his wife Loretta, Sean's wife Micheline (Mickey), and finally Sir Thomas Sean Connery himself. After fifty years, they felt it was time the world know their story—in intimate detail.

The four had chosen me for the honor of writing this tale for a most unusual reason. I am a cancer survivor, diagnosed with breast cancer in August of 2007, then treated through surgeries, chemotherapy, and radiation. Shortly after that day, when Frank told Nancy of his friendship with Sean Connery, I explained to Frank why I needed him to replace me so often. I was finishing all my treatments, having my port removed, seeing doctors. His response shocked and saddened me greatly. He said he had guessed that I was recovering from cancer treatment because he knew the signs. It is no secret that all who have known the struggles, heartbreak, and pain of cancer share a unique and unbreakable bond. I was in the middle of my fight while Frank was slowly succumbing to the disease. He had been diagnosed with chronic myelocytic leukemia and had been given around eighteen months to live. For Frank and me, this unfortunate cancer bond led to the trust necessary for my involvement in the project. I began by merely collecting and organizing their emails. But by the spring of 2009, I felt, as did the other four, as though a book was the next natural step. It became a labor of love for me, and the project was progressing beautifully, or so it seemed. Sean wrote:

> I believe I have a good nose for business. I think this book will be a HIT!! But Loretta has a saying, "beware of the shadow." I'll explain that later...but for now...I don't see any shadow. One has to be so cautious in this unread world of film and publications. Having said that, my publisher and producer feel we probably have a gold mine under our feet... Stories this week. We know you're out there. We know what time you're using. None of this is lost on any of us. Thank you for this work. S.

As I continued to write, still without compensation, I began to doubt how serious they were. How far would this project go? Would I see the gold mine they kept mentioning? Finally, in March of 2009, I inquired about the possibility of a retainer and a contract. Sean emailed me the following response:

> My dearest producer friend and dearest film director friend have read almost all of the email that has been written. They've read it many times. We've told them the only ground rule is - Lynda Graham-Rowe is the one and only writer!! No help, no ghostwriter...all of it will come from you. So, to answer your question on a practical basis. Knowing how slow it all goes, especially at first...you should think of

working one more year. You probably won't need to finish next year, but I'm guessing you will want to. You will be given a retainer so that you can afford to just write!! That's how it works. If all of this goes as it seems to be... I suspect the real money will be in hand within a year. I can't promise anything. I've seen many projects evaporate before my eyes...so keep Loretta's shadow in mind at all times. It can always appear. But, so far...it looks like gangbusters. I hope this answers your questions. Patience Frenchie, patience... it will come but not soon. S

With that, I continued to work, trusting in their friendship and honesty. Yet my excitement and trust were cut short one heart-breaking day in the spring of 2011. Just as I thought all my hard work would pay off, when I informed Sean that the long-awaited manuscript was complete, he told me that they had changed their minds and would not agree to publication. The dream was shattered; no book, no film, nothing. I was cut off and devastated. Time passed as I attempted to digest this insane turn of events. My best seller had become a pipe dream, and all communication with the four had ceased following Sean's abrupt halting of the project.

Eventually, my sadness turned to anger and frustration. I met with some attorneys to see what legal paths I might take to request compensation or to go ahead and publish regardless. It was at this point that reality hit me full force. Sean, Micheline, and Loretta had communicated with me exclusively through email. I had met and spent time with Frank, of course, but I had no proof that the stories came from Sean and the others. Therefore, I was told I had no recourse.

Many tell me I was duped, that Frank played a joke on me, that he did all the writing himself, and that it was all an old man's eccentric fabrication. But to what end? In my heart and mind, I know that Frank did not fabricate his friendship with Sean, if for no other reason than the sheer volume and complexity of the correspondence I received. I also know that Frank wanted me to share his story with the world. I saw in him an amazing man who told me fantastic tales, ones that are fascinating and truly captivating, no matter if they are real, embellished, or fiction. Through this journey, I have come to realize that if Frank somehow did miraculously create all of these stories himself as some sort of personal challenge in his final days, he was even more brilliant and tenacious than I gave him credit for. Therefore, proof or no proof, I present to you the story as it was told to me: the story of love, truth, death, and Sean Connery.

1

The plan

Frank's cancer was diagnosed in 2004. One of the first things he started to plan for, even while still in shock from the diagnosis, was Loretta's future without him. He remembers calling Micheline Connery to tell her the news. The first thing she said was that she and Sean would take care of Loretta. Then unbelievably, about two months later, Micheline was told that she had ovarian cancer and that it had metastasized. Her cancer was also determined to be terminal. When she finished telling Frank the horrible news, there was a slight pause in the phone conversation, and then the two of them started talking at the same time. They talked about and agreed immediately to what came to be known as "The Plan."

First, some background by way of explanation. Loretta (Welch) Mitchell and Sean Connery dated from February of 1958 to into 1961—three and a half years—until he met Diane and knew that this would likely lead to his marriage. Though they were very much in love, Loretta sensed that she and Sean would never marry. He didn't want children at the time, and she very much did. Though they tried living together, again and again, they would find themselves fighting after just a few days. If they spent more than three or four days together in his home, it was just a matter of time before one of them wanted to kill the other. Nonetheless, their deep love and attraction for each other continued, undetected by the rest of the world and often right before their eyes.

At this time, Frank was also living in California and was a highly respected singer with the Robert Shaw Chorale. It was 1959, and Sean Connery was not yet the famous 007 but was about to become so. Loretta met Frank when she went to hear the renowned Robert Shaw Chorale rehearsing. He noticed her afterward, how stunning she was, and asked her out to dinner. Loretta agreed and soon told Frank that she was seeing a man named Sean Connery, who also loved the Shaw Chorale and would want to meet him. The three became very close friends and would often dine out together or just spend time talking. As time passed, Frank said, "Sean knew I loved Loretta. Loretta knew I loved Loretta. I knew that I loved Loretta." So Sean told Frank to "get off his duff" and ask her out, which he did. At this point, Sean was seeing Diane, and they were married in 1962. In 1963, Frank proposed marriage to Loretta, and he was surprised, he says, that she actually took the ring.

Sean married Diane, Frank and Loretta were married soon after, and the four continued to be close friends. Diane and Sean Connery were divorced around 1972. Then he met Micheline Roquebrune, a French artist, fell in love, and they were married in 1975. As fate would have it, Frank and Loretta's friendship and love for Sean continued with Micheline. The four became fast friends and more and have remained such through all these years, their love for each other growing over time.

So, when Frank and Micheline discussed their fates that day, even through the great sadness and pain they were feeling, their focus was on the ones who would be left behind; on how they could help ease the pain Sean and Loretta would be feeling from their loss. Thus "The Plan" took shape. By November of 2008, since they had both been told that they probably had about eighteen more

2

months to live, a time frame they would both somehow far outlive as it turned out, they decided they should discuss their ideas with Sean and Loretta. They just needed to find the right time to tell the other two.

Thanksgiving weekend, 2008, Sean and Micheline Connery were spending a few days visiting Loretta and Frank Mitchell at their home in Lincoln, Nebraska. It was a Saturday night. Sean turned to Loretta and said, "Take me out for a drink. We need to talk." Loretta and Frank looked at each other, and then Micheline said, "You and I have to talk too, Frank." Once Sean and Loretta had left, Micheline said to Frank, "We both have about eighteen months left. You are worried about Loretta, and I'm worried about Sean. We need to clear the air for them so we can all enjoy the rest of our time together."

Sean and Loretta returned, and all four sat down to talk. Micheline and Frank told them that they always knew that Loretta and Sean had never really given up their relationship, that they were still very much in love with each other, and that that was just fine. Then they added, to the shock and amusement of Sean and Loretta, that they too had fallen in love and started a romantic relationship. Sean and Loretta were relieved that their secret was out, yet quite surprised to discover that the other two were also in love. Loretta said to Frank, in front of everyone, "If you knew that Sean and I had continued our romance, which by the way has nothing to do with our love for you, why didn't you two tell us?" Frank responded, "It was more fun to watch you two trying to be discrete and feeling guilty! At any rate, if you had told me that you and Sean had returned to being intimate on your trips to Las Vegas, which we sanctioned, I would have said, 'That's nice, but did you win anything?' Micheline and I knew all along and were giggling over your discomfort when you returned."

3

Frank and Micheline then explained to Sean and Loretta what "The Plan" was. They said, "We know you still love each other very much. We don't want you to have to hide that anymore from us, and when we are gone, we want—in fact, we insist—that the two of you be together. We want you to be married, finally, and we want you to love each other freely from this day on. If you travel somewhere together, we want you to get one room. No more hiding, no more pretending."

They all cried a lot, hugged a lot, and before the evening ended, they all knew just how much they loved each other, truly and profoundly loved each other. "The Plan" was, if Frank were to go first, Loretta would move in with Sean and Micheline, although she would also have a cottage of her own down the beach from them about a half mile so she could have some private time if she wanted. If Micheline passed away first, Frank and Loretta would live in the cottage together, but Loretta would divide her time between him and Sean.

Frank explained further,

I suppose some might call us "selective swingers," but though that term might be catchy, it is misleading because it does not make clear how profound our love is for each other. We share a bond, and it is difficult to put into words just how strong it is. There is no way we would have anyone else a part of this. It's all about the fact that we each love two people at the same time. Yes, you can! You can love two people! Each of us is different. If she is with him, it is not a betrayal to me in my mind. It has nothing to do with me. Same as when I'm with Micheline. It has nothing to do with Sean or Loretta. "It is what it is," as they say. We love our world. We do not expect many people to understand or approve. But we want to tell everyone who wants to know what our thinking is and what our feelings are about what's happening. It has to come out. It's one thing for an elderly Nebraska peasant such as myself to be involved in a lifestyle such as this. No one would take notice. It's another equation altogether if the name Sean Connery jumps off the page. That opens up an entirely new situation. And it will come out someday. So, while people may not want that kind of life for themselves or even really condone this lifestyle, they can at least have our explanation and try to understand how very unique our situation is. Then, when Micheline and I are gone and Sean and Loretta are together, perhaps they will not judge them so harshly. It is what we want.

2

Love at first sight

Loretta Elizabeth Welch was born in North Dakota on June 1, 1938, and was one of twelve children. Her father was a bus driver in Fargo, and her mother was a stay-at-home mom. In high school, her only interests were choir and art. Her family had a very cold streak in their emotional makeup, she said, and so she never had the usual high school boyfriend crush or the terrible breakups that can go with them. She just never got that wrapped up in any particular boy. If a boy wanted to date her, she would go out, but if not, fine. She explained, "I never understood the girls who screamed and cried and moaned because some idiot high school boy dropped them. To hell with them, I'd say." She didn't drink or smoke or ever take any kind of drugs, and she was a virgin even after high school.

Loretta was an average student with a huge interest in art and design, especially in clothing from different historical periods. Since her counselor knew she had no interest in college whatsoever, he suggested that Loretta work a year, save some money, then head for the film studios in Los Angeles, which she did. Loretta graduated in 1956. Early in 1958, she took a bus to Los Angeles and applied to movie studios to work in sketching and costume props and design. She was hired almost immediately. One day, during her first month on the job, she was in the costume room sorting when in walked the most gorgeous man she had ever seen. He was a movie actor by the name of Sean Connery. She hadn't seen him in anything, but what did she care. She recalled, "The Hollywood types had hit on me from the first day I arrived, but I wasn't interested. I only cared about my job... that is until... he... walked into the room! My life changed forever in that moment!"

In 1958, Sean Connery was in Hollywood working on the film *A Night to Remember*. At that point in his Hollywood career, he had only had a small role in *Lilacs in the Spring*, a movie he suggested I *not* rent, and a role in *Action of the Tiger* in 1957. In *A Night to Remember*, he played a deckhand on the Titanic and thought his career might just take the same plunge as did the boat itself. On a positive note, during the filming of this movie, he met Honor Blackman, who would become his Bond girl "Pussy Galore" in *Goldfinger*, and above all, he met *her!* Sean said it was fate. If he had already been the famous James Bond, none of this would have happened. He was still a struggling young actor. He continued, "If I had already made a Bond film, the money would have been there, and no way would the director have told me to run over to costuming to get an outfit. I wouldn't have met her. I wouldn't have met Frank Mitchell. Thank heaven the gods knew I had to know and love both of them!"

When he walked into the costume room that day for a fitting, there she was, the stunning woman who would quickly become the secret love of his life, Loretta Welch. This incredible love affair went on quietly for over fifty years, unnoticed by reporters, unseen by the world. His life, like Loretta's, changed forever at that moment. As she finished fitting him for his outfits, he asked her out for that evening. He picked her up at seven p.m., closeout time for her, and they went to dinner and for a long walk. By midnight, they were in his apartment. Loretta was twenty-one years old at the time.

She told me,

I was a virgin until 2 AM on my first date with Sean Connery. My sexual experiences up until then were very limited. I was proud of that. But, that meant I didn't know what I was doing. We were sitting on his balcony, and he picked me up and took me to his bedroom. I was as scared as I could possibly be, but no way was I backing out of this. Now, I had always imagined a sexual experience to mean I should perform oral sex on the man, and then when he got another erection, we would have intercourse. That is what I had heard and what I thought he expected. Not with him! He took the longest time to undress me. He massaged me as he did so.

Then he slowly undressed, and there we were. So then I thought it must be time to move down on him, but he stopped me and laid me back, and I felt the pleasure of his mouth on me for a wonderfully long time! Then I finally took my turn on him. After that, we showered together and talked for a while, never rushing anything. Then he began to pay attention to my breasts, and finally, we came together—not once but several times. It was now 6 AM. He picked me up at 7 PM for the next four nights, and then I started staying at his apartment. He gave me a section of his closet for my clothes. He had two bathrooms, so I had my own place to 'girl up.'

Sean added to the story at this point, saying, "Loretta's recollection of our first time together is completely accurate, but I would like to mention that I had not planned the sex for the date. I'm sure people think I take women to bed and then never call the next day. Not true! Believe it or not, I did not date much as a young man. I always concentrated on my careers, though I must admit that in the '50s, during my bodybuilding days, I was a bit of a playboy. This was long before I met Loretta. There were one-night stands in those days. We did not have to worry about AIDS then, and I always used protection." He added, "I would guess that back then I went to bed with at least three or four women per week. I'm embarrassed to say... but it's the truth... I suppose it would be silly to say I was raped at times, but in reality, it felt like it. I can remember having intercourse when I didn't want it. I did it just to get away and get home. I don't think the 'poor me' stamp will hold up, so I'll get off the excuses. But when I started my acting career, things were different. I really didn't date much. That first night with Loretta, it's just that I had the most wonderful evening with her and she was so beautiful and sexy... and, well... it happened. I did not know she was a virgin. We don't have virgins in California!"

Then came the fourth night of them living together. Their fights became legendary. The police were called during their very first fight by a tenant who lived next door to Sean. They didn't arrest or ticket them; they just said to quiet down. Loretta asked him if he wanted her to move out, and he said no way, so they worked out an arrangement where she would spend three nights at his place and the rest at hers. This worked splendidly. They were able to live together part of the time and then not. Over time they discussed the future. She wanted children. He did not; his focus being on his rapidly growing film career. And so, between the fighting and their different views about family, they came to the sad conclusion that they would never marry.

Loretta described their early relationship this way:

Our dating was strange. He was always working or trying out for parts in upcoming movies, etc. It was strange, yet I loved it.

I loved him. But it was peculiar. We were both so stubborn that we got into the silliest arguments and ended up yelling at each other. But then there was always makeup sex, which was terrific and so, what the heck! When we talked of marriage from time to time, we knew that it would be a disaster of a union, so we just went along, knowing that one of us would meet someone one day who would fill those needs. I do think, though, in looking back, that I would have married him in a New York minute if he'd asked me to—children or no children. I was in love up to the last hair on my head. We would have periods when we were together daily, and then he'd be off on a movie, and I wouldn't see him for three months.

He called every day, sometimes twice. During the away times, our phone conversations would be that maybe we could marry after all, but then he'd come back, and after about five days under one roof, I'd almost be throwing things at him ... although I never did ... and he never, ever hit or slapped me at all. He sent me flowers every week, and he gave me jewelry, which I still wear to this day. When he was in town, our dates were usually concerts, art galleries, or driving to interesting places on the West Coast. We enjoyed just being together. We adored each other. I should mention that now that we have matured and we can spend extended time under one roof without fighting, our love for each other has grown even more intense.

I asked Sean if he was faithful to Loretta during those years. His career was taking off, and women were constantly throwing themselves at him. As Loretta noted, he was often away on location. Temptation was everywhere. I need to explain here that Sean and Loretta make a clear distinction between sex for the sole physical pleasure of sex, and making love or having an affair. To them, the former is not being unfaithful. The latter would be, since there would be the intent or desire to continue a relationship with the other person.

So Sean answered my question in this way:

As to being unfaithful to Loretta, I did it less and less. My rationalization stems from my never ever being with another woman in our world of Los Angeles. I did have sex from time to time on location, mostly with leading ladies and supporting cast members. Many times we would end a section of filming and party somewhat. Pack on the tired feelings and alcohol, and you just ended up in someone's arms. But in LA, I was a good boy. I came home to her after working, and we would spend the evening together. So, in my mind, I was being "faithful." She knew what was happening. I would just tell her. I think I was so honest with her because she would never ask. She never tried to spy or to listen in on phone calls, or try to catch me in a lie ... nothing like that. So, I just felt I should say that we partied after a film shoot and it got a little personal and she would laugh. Our dating was erratic as I was gone so much. But when I was in town, we spent every moment together. I was so in love with her that I really never wanted to be with anyone else.

Then I asked Loretta the same question: Were you faithful to Sean during those years? Her answer was much the same as his. She said,

When Sean was out of town, I would have sex now and then at the studio. Since I couldn't leave town because of my work schedule, I felt that, since I only had sex when he was out of town, that constituted the same kind of strange loyalty or fidelity as his, if you will. Masterful rationalization! I also told him when it happened, and we both considered these as sort of "asides," as they say in the theatre. I was never serious with anyone, and neither was he. The kind of sex I would have at the studio could best be described as "quickies." There were crew members that I really liked as friends, and so, at times, we would just do it now and again for the sexual release, but no affair.

So from 1959 until Frank and I were married, I had sex with Sean and Frank and occasionally a crew or cast member. I've mentioned my obsession with oral sex. From time to time, I would just have oral sex with a friend of mine. It was just a way of life out there. The sordid Hollywood stories you read about are usually true.

Where did these "quickies" take place? Loretta said that sometimes she and her crew member friends would come across a bed on the set that had been used in some sexy scene in movie history, and they would have sex on that same bed. She recalled one specific time when, she said, "I had a *ménage à trois* on the very bed on which Clark Gable made love to Vivian Leigh in *Gone with the Wind!* I was so excited about it I called Sean that very same night and told him. He thought it was very creative."

From 1958 forward, this incredible story of love continued essentially without interruption, through Sean's marriages to Diane and then to Mickey, through Loretta's marriage to Frank, with their knowledge and blessing, I might add. Yet, it remained utterly hidden from the outside world. How could this be? Sean rose to fame while with Loretta, and not a single person took note of it. He spent time with her in public places all through these years, and no one asked a single question. As Sean was nearing eighty years old when they began telling me their story, he decided that it was time he reveal the truth about his life and loves. He told me that it was time for all to know, that he wholeheartedly endorsed this project of ours, and that he was pleased that the writer was someone who "gave a shit" about who they really were; some of the highest flattery I could have received. When he told me such things, there was no way I would ever have predicted the abrupt change that would come down the road.

Sean said he never understood why the press never noticed Loretta, never asked who she was, why she was with him so much, but "the idiots in those days would just walk right by a sinking ship just to ask me what I had for breakfast!" Loretta added that she often had a reporter or photographer ask her to step over to the back so he could get a better picture. She always just said yes, of course, and moved away, holding her breath, waiting for them to slowly turn toward her with a "who are you?" look. But they never did. In today's world, someone would have caught wind of Loretta and later Mitchell (Sean's loving way of referring to Frank). Some-one would have eventually noticed the foursome, first with Diane involved and then with Mickey in the picture. Sean remarked, "I've seen some of the same reporters and photographers stalking me for over twenty years. Why, in all that time, did not one of them pick up on what was a very peculiar scene? It amazes me to this day."

There was a point in Sean and Loretta's relationship, when each was married and they were living in different cities, that they began occasionally meeting in Las Vegas for a few days at a time. In the early Vegas days, Loretta would stand behind Sean at poker tables, rubbing his back. Never did a reporter ask him who she was. "I guess they thought I was paying one of the Casino's girls to do it," he notes. "Loretta is more beautiful than those girls, so why not take a second look at this attachment to my right arm?"

On one occasion, a reporter followed a maid into their room to get a scoop. This was common practice. They would give the maid money to "accidentally" open the motel door as though coming in to clean, and then they would charge in behind. This time, Sean happened to be on top of Loretta in bed, and they couldn't see her, as he was so much bigger than she. He guessed it must have looked like he was sleeping. He calmly turned to the reporter and cameraman and asked them to step out; that he would talk to them by the pool in about an hour, something he rarely did.

Of course, the reporter was thrilled and complied, not wanting to blow his chance for a rare interview. He and Loretta were actually "engaged" at that moment but had blankets over them in a way that blocked her out. That could have been the picture of the decade, but it just happened to be a chilly morning. Usually, they would not have had covers on them at all. Loretta had just asked for the blankets when the maid, the reporter, and his cameraman came barging in. Sean commented, "Wouldn't that have been something? I always laugh when I think about that moment."

The maid, in this instance, knew what was happening and didn't say a word. Loretta said, "I think she saw—maybe my foot from the angle at which she was standing. I could see her looking down that way, and she had this little smile on her face." The reporter and his cameraman left so as not to screw up the possible interview, leaving the maid standing there alone. Sean also knew she had seen something to tip her off as to Loretta's presence and what they were doing. She started to leave, and Sean said to her, "My dear, would you hand me my billfold on the dresser?" Without withdrawing from Loretta or losing his erection, he took out five one-hundred-dollar bills and handed them to her with his many thanks. She really could have blown their cover, and it would have been a terrible predicament for both Sean and Loretta. As the maid was leaving the room, Loretta said thank you in a quiet little voice. The maid doubled over with laughter and thanked them both before closing the door.

Sean later told the front desk that this maid was to be the only one to be in their room for the entire four days. She made a small fortune off of Sean. They also got excellent service from her during that week. Once, Loretta came out of the shower, and the maid was cleaning the room. That was the first time she had seen Loretta's face. The maid was a Hispanic woman in her early forties raising two teenaged sons, she later told Loretta. She said the money was a lifesaver for her. After that, Sean and Loretta asked for her every time they stayed at that hotel, and that became their only Vegas hotel. She was their maid for several years, and as you can imagine, no reporter ever got past her to get into the room. Loretta had told Sean about her two sons, and so he gave her an enormous amount of cash during that time.

This was far from the only story about Loretta and Sean in Las Vegas. They told me there were so many more that there could probably be a separate book filled just with these tales, and all of them went undetected. At the MGM Grand Hotel in Vegas, Sean and Loretta were on the elevator and were involved in a little foreplay when a woman in her early thirties got on. She had a deformed leg and needed crutches to get around. She saw without looking directly what they were up to and asked, "Do you want me to keep this elevator going nonstop? I'll not turn around, Mr. Connery." Sean explained that you could do that with elevators in those days, but you can't now. So, Sean looked at Loretta, shrugged his shoulders, and said, "You are so kind."

She kept the elevator going, and the two of them had intercourse standing up. Loretta added, "We must have been a little drunk to have done that, I think!" Then Sean asked her to take them to the fifth floor. She did, they spruced up a tad, and then Sean gave the woman one thousand dollars as they got off. There were several other times in Vegas when similar scenes could have been captured on film. Since Sean and Loretta saw each other alone so little during that time, they took full advantage of those moments together, no matter where they were. If they found themselves in a quiet place together, they jumped at the chance to be intimate, even if for only a few minutes. They were quite literally like animals. Sean said, "No class whatsoever. It was much fun."

The fun wasn't only in Las Vegas, though. It was also in the studio. When Sean did love scenes in his films, he demanded that only the cameramen, the director, and his lady in waiting (helper) be allowed on the set. He didn't want some random photographer grabbing extra shots, especially since many times Loretta was substituted for the actress. The actress was happy, and so were Loretta and Sean. They would film the actual scene, and then Sean's leading lady would slip out of bed, and Loretta would slip into the bed, and they would both be undressed. Then the crew would leave with the cameras rolling. Sean and Loretta, since they always wanted to fall into a bed anytime they could, would then, as Sean put it, "finish the scene as told in real life." He continued, "My lady in waiting would not leave, but would move a little distance from us. We would need a robe put on us as we got out of the bed since the cameras were still rolling. This took place after I'd left Loretta for Diane, so we weren't seeing each other as often, and our hormones for each other were off the charts, so to speak. We never, uh, mentioned this to Diane or Frank, although it would not have mattered to either of them. We were very embarrassed at our animal behavior and our tacky way of not controlling our-selves, so how could we tell them without dying of shame?"

"Funny thing, though," Sean reminisced, "the film crew would later edit those films, and they would always, intentionally, find scenes like this to include in each movie, but that would not betray the fact that another woman was in the film. They would inject scenes that were pretty intimate, as a matter of fact. Some even had to be cut. These kinds of shots were included in 'Dr. No,' 'From Russia With Love,' and 'Goldfinger.' There was a time when Diane and I had just watched the outtakes of 'From Russia With Love' and were driving home. Diane was giggling. I asked her what was so funny, and she said, 'Isn't that strange! Tatiana [the leading lady] does her toenails in multiple colors just like Loretta!'" Well, Sean thought he was going to lose control of the car. By the time they got home, they were laughing so hard he could hardly park in the garage. He immediately called Loretta and told her to see the film and watch for that particular love scene. She and Frank saw it later that month, and she called back yelling at Sean, saying, "What idiot film editor left that in?" Really though, she loved it, of course. Sean at times also had Loretta have bit parts in his films, as an "extra." When Frank and I were watching *Goldfinger* together one evening, he paused the movie during a scene poolside where sev-eral young bikini-clad beauties were running behind Goldfinger, giggling, and pointed out one of them. "That's Loretta," he said, "the one in the blonde wig. They made her wear it even though her own hair was far more beautiful." We watched the scene several times over, as I got quite a kick out of seeing it.

After recounting all these incredible and often humorous tales, Sean and I were discussing the writing of this book, and he exclaimed, "Imagine what people will read here; a romance that the world has never known about, a romance that the reporters never ever realized was right under their very noses! I think this book will put me in a much different orbit than what was thought of me up until now!" I must say I wholeheartedly agreed. At this point in the project, all four were extremely enthusiastic and so excited to tell their stories to me, and through me, to the world. I naturally mirrored their emotions. As the months passed, however, attitudes slowly began to change, as either Mickey or Frank and sometimes both simultaneously were getting sicker and weaker, I was told. There would be periods during which suddenly no one would write, and then just as quickly, the jovial mood would return, as the two bounced back.

3

The three

Life is often an unpredictable journey, and for Sean and Loretta, that was an understatement. Whether separate or together through the years, their adventures were so amazing and at times unbelievable that they begin to sound surreal. These stories of love and hidden romance began in 1958. Returning to that year, when Sean and Loretta had just started their romance, and when the name Sean Connery was not yet known to the world, one can only wonder how it was possible that with a love so strong and a passion so intense, their paths could separate. How could they possibly have left each other?

Nineteen fifty-eight was an eventful and life-altering year for Loretta Welch and Sean Connery. He came to Hollywood to make it in the film industry. She came to design costumes for the actors. Both reached their goals and then some, but their falling in love, something completely unplanned, something that certainly must have been fate, as Sean called it, was the highlight of that year and many years to come for both of them. They were living life to its fullest and loving with a passion beyond measure. Sean was slowly heading for fame, and Loretta was right there with him, but life is rarely simple, and choices needed to be made.

In 1958, a young man named Frank L. Mitchell arrived in Los Angeles, having been selected through auditions to sing with the prestigious Robert Shaw Chorale. In 1959, Loretta went to watch one of their rehearsals, as previously mentioned. She had sung several of their arrangements in her high school choir and felt compelled to see them perform. After the rehearsal, this strong, interesting man came right up to her and introduced himself. She loved his directness. They talked for a while, exchanging the usual information, and then he said, "May I take you for a drink?" and Loretta agreed. He took her to a terrific lounge, where she told him she was dating a man by the name of Sean Connery but that it was not "etched in stone," as she put it, and that they both dated others from time to time. Of course, this contradicts what Loretta had explained earlier when she told me that she and Sean had sex with others on occasion but not relationships. Then again, their definitions of fidelity were not those of the majority of society, so one can only assume that this encounter was not a problem for either of them anyway. Frank continued, "I'd like to be one of the others." Loretta and Sean had been dating for over a year at this point.

A few nights later, Loretta was having a drink with Sean, and he asked what was new in her life, so she told him she had met a fascinating man who sang with the Robert Shaw Chorale. Sean went crazy. He loved the Chorale and insisted that Loretta bring him along to meet Frank. The two men hit it off right from the start, and from then on, the three would often simply all go out together. As their friendship evolved, they spent more and more time together, and Sean and Frank became the closest of friends, more like brothers. In the beginning, after an evening out, the three of them together, Frank would break away, and Loretta and Sean would go home. As they all drew closer, Loretta told me she started fantasizing about having both of them in bed at the same time. She said she even hinted at it, but they just ignored her.

Loretta explained,

I met Frank in 1959, over 50 years ago. I had been dating Sean for over a year. Sean and I loved each other. We were in love with each other. That never changed. But I knew it couldn't last. From the beginning, I could sense that we were not meant to be a committed couple for the long term. He didn't want children, and that was very important to me. As I explained earlier, we even tried to live together, but after three or four days, I would go back to my apartment so as to not "kill" him. I knew that at any given moment, he would tell me he had found someone, and it would lead to marriage. I loved dating them both. This was not a conflict in any way. The three of us were young and involved with our new professions. None of us was really thinking of marriage with anyone.

Sean was not yet the famous 007, but he was the most gorgeous man Loretta had ever seen. Frank was what she thought of as a fascinating man to be with. He was mysterious. You never knew what he was thinking. Loretta found him incredibly sexy but differently from Sean. He turned her on even after forty-five years of being together. In his day, Frank was an incredible singer. Being in the Shaw Chorale meant you were a master of serious music. Although they did record some Broadway tunes, spirituals, and folk songs, they mainly performed music from the Masters. Loretta said that Frank was not only a talented musician but that a date with him was just "a great fun-and-laugh time." He was also really in shape and very muscular. He was a black belt in judo and karate and took excellent care of himself.

Sometimes, Loretta and Sean went to karate and judo matches to watch Frank compete. Frank had a great body, but he had no more hair on his head then than he had when he and I met, according to Loretta. Sean was also almost bald and always had been, she added, just to be fair. He wore hairpieces in his films. Loretta didn't care about those details regardless. She told me that both of these men were so considerate, so careful of others' feelings, and very, very intelligent. What more could she ask for? Sean was much more serious, but he could joke with the best of them. Frank would often converse in terms of analogies or metaphors, humorously. He couldn't just give you a straight answer. People needed to listen carefully to his responses or they would miss a great comeback or funny line. He didn't care if you missed it. It was just the way his mind worked.

Loretta, therefore, found herself dating two men who were both, in her mind, fabulous. She told me, "I was excited to hear the doorbell ring, and I honestly didn't care which one of them was standing there." About three months into their casual dating, Loretta and Frank knew they were headed toward an intimate relationship. But Sean was the kind of lover women dream about, not only how he looked but his lovemaking prowess. So when the night came where Frank and Loretta knew the kissing and fondling were now a prelude to making love, she could tell that he was nervous and tentative, and she was also worried about how *she* would react. To ease the tension, she whispered to him that she wanted to be with no one else but him now, and she said the most amazing thing happened. Frank regained his composure and confidence, and Loretta discovered that his lovemaking technique was, as luck would have it, almost identical to Sean's. Loretta couldn't believe it. She had worried needlessly. Loretta told me it was as if they'd both attended the same "Ivy League School of Love-Making." She said that, naturally, there were a few differences, but overall it was about 75 percent the same, and all of it was wonderful.

24

Loretta provided some insight into this technique she described as so similar.

These two men had a much more lady's pleasure first technique that was refreshingly different from so many other men. As we both heated up in both cases, I would make the usual woman's move to go down on them, but both of them would stop me. Almost word for word, they would say something like, "You just lie back and relax," and then both would begin a body massage, then move to kiss me everywhere and make their way slowly down to pleasure me for a very long, wonderful time. I think I had three or four orgasms before they even had one! Then it was my turn, and then they would start all over again, and then finally we would end with intercourse. Each episode was long and unhurried and was always, always directed towards my feelings, not theirs. They never ever afterward jumped up to go to the fridge to get something to drink, or light up a cigarette, or worse, to leave; neither of them. We always, even to this day, spend a long quiet time just holding each other.

Loretta continued,

Now, believe it or not, I'm a very private person. I've never ever described this scene to anyone until now. Can you imagine how many times I've been just flat-out asked the question of who was a better lover by the few who knew I had dated Sean Connery? Some would try to be subtle, but there really is no subtle way. I'm not going to apologize for this somewhat graphic story. I've done the best I can here to explain how Frank Mitchell could walk side by side with the great Sean

25

Connery, and this is what is on people's minds the most, I'm sure. At the very least, the way I see it is, Frank will read this, and I've never even told him exactly all of it. This will be the first reading for him also. He doesn't need it now, and after our first night in bed, he never really needed it. He knew he could provide the chemistry I needed, and I knew I could do the same for him. Sean didn't matter.

Throughout Frank and Loretta's more than forty-five years of marriage, the few people who knew that Sean and Loretta had been lovers before Frank came on the scene looked upon him like, as Frank called it, "some poor schmuck who was taken for a ride," because they figured she must still be in love with Sean. Frank said his response to them would always be, "Well, of course, she's in love with him. He's in love with her too. But you should see how Sean adores and loves his wife as well. And you should see how Loretta adores me. Sean and I are two different people, believe me. There is little similarity between Frank Mitchell and Sean Connery. It's just that we both love the same two people." Frank continued, "Then I would say to them, 'How do you know I don't love someone else also?' It's not a matter of infidelity as far as our foursome is concerned. We all four love each other. It's not that she is doing something behind my back.' It's at this juncture that they would just shake their heads and look bewildered. I would then close that conversation with something like, 'You just have to understand we don't think like Walt Disney sometimes.' That generally ended that talk, and you can just picture the look on their faces at that point."

In November of 1961, when Sean met Diane, Loretta said she sensed something was different, and Sean didn't wait long to confirm her suspicions. He told her as soon as *he* knew it that he was going to propose to Diane. "I was just knocked over," Loretta recalled. She had never felt such sadness and cried for days. She told Frank, who was a great comfort. He was there for her but did not attempt to take over Sean's spot in her heart. He even backed away from intimacy with her for a while, which she said helped a lot. Yet she continued to enjoy their dates, and she found herself growing fonder of Frank each week. Soon she realized that what she felt for Frank was true love. Was it the same as her love for Sean? No, but it was real love nonetheless.

Loretta recalled, "I never thought Frank and I would move our dating to such a high level. At first, he was a terrific fun guy but really, I was dating him for a diversion. I've told him that. I never thought we would go to bed. I never thought I'd fall in love with him. A person could see why I thought that. After all, I was dating 'The Man'! Even if he wasn't the famous James Bond at first, he was the talk of the film world. The different actresses I would outfit would sit around and talk about this Sean Connery, and I was practically living with him. I knew I was his 'main squeeze' as we used to say. I never said a word to them, of course."

As Loretta recounted this story, she digressed for a few moments to tell a humorous tale from this time. At times, she said, Sean let it be known that they were a couple, and Loretta reveled in those moments. One day, for example, Loretta was working with four women from *The Price is Right* show with Bob Barker. All they talked about was Sean Connery and how they wanted to go to bed with him. Loretta says she just kept her mouth shut and hummed and brought out different clothes for them to try on. Then, in he walked, Sean Connery in the flesh. The girls went crazy, of course. They really made fools of themselves, Loretta said, screaming and dancing around him.

He was very polite and visited with them for a few minutes and then excused himself and went over to Loretta. Of course, they thought he was there for some article of clothing, but no. He wrapped his arms around her and gave her a big kiss. Well, Loretta recalled it got pretty quiet in there at that point. Then Sean said, "See you at seven," turned, and greeted the girls, saying, "Ladies, a pleasure." On his way out, he turned back to Loretta and said, "Oh, you forgot your watch this morning." He gave it to her, kissed her again, and left. One can imagine the jealous glares she got from those four women. Then came the not-so-subtle questions and insults, frankly, such as, "Oh, were you his girl last night?" and that sort of thing. Loretta told me she just smiled and said, "Actually, I live with him," and they turned around and left. She said it was one of those moments in life that goes in the "classics" bin. She added that Sean always made sure there were several scenes like that when she was being looked down upon or treated as inferior.

As wonderful as all of this was, Loretta had to accept, late in 1961, that her life with Sean was to end—or at least change course drastically, as it turned out. Sean remembered that in that year, he was in *Frightened City* and *The Longest Day,* and he also began the filming of *Dr. No,* the first Bond film. His film career was genuinely taking off now. It was during this time as well that he had met Diane and decided he would need to leave Loretta. Sean remembered, "'Dr. No' was released in 1962. My life as the popular James Bond began in the same year that Diane and I were married."

As time passed and Loretta spent more time with Frank, she realized just how deep her love for him had grown. She was still madly in love with Sean, of course, but the two were not mutually exclusive. She realized that she was capable of being very much in love with both of them simultaneously. So, when she and Sean were talking one day, before his marriage to Diane, he said to her, "You realize that Mitchell loves you, right?" Loretta answered without thinking, "Yes, and I love the hell out of him too—as well as you!"

So Sean told Frank to "get off his duff" and go after Loretta. Strange as it sounds, things slowly evolved into Sean and Diane and Frank and Loretta. Diane was also a huge fan of the Robert Shaw Chorale and had already asked to meet Frank. The four of them remained friends throughout Sean and Diane's marriage, and Diane remained in contact with Loretta and Frank for many years after that. Remarkably, Loretta said that she and Diane got along well. Diane took Sean away from her, but "what did it matter?" she concluded. It was going to be someone eventually. Why not her? Loretta said the funny thing was Diane would always say something like, "What the hell is he doing with me? You are much better for him, and you both love each other. When he and I split, you two should get it right and stay together!" Loretta told me Diane never said "if," always "when." She decided that that must have had something to do with their ability to be friends.

4

And then there were four

During that time, Sean, Diane, Frank, and Loretta occasionally all went out together. *Dr. No* had just been released, and Sean had now become the famous James Bond, 007. He was recognized wherever he went. Here he tells an ironic story about the great James Bond being rescued by none other than Frank Mitchell, musician. Before recounting the story, Sean wanted to give some background information. "Let me begin by explaining that Frank held a third-degree black belt in judo and second degree one in karate, both from the Sobukan Japanese School of Martial Arts. This story took place on March 17, 1962." Having set the scene, Sean recalled,

Diane, Loretta, and I were walking along our favorite beach just above L.A. It was a beautiful spring evening. We'd just come from a St. Patrick's Day party given for charity by some of the Irish movie stars. The beach was not far from there, so we decided to drive over and go for a walk. Mitchell was familiar with this beach and knew that Loretta and I had gone there often together. We knew that Mitchell would soon be back to town after a Shaw tour that went through the major cities of the East Coast, but we didn't know exactly when he'd be back, so we didn't hang around waiting for him at the house. We just knew he would be home any time.

So there we were, Diane, Loretta, and me strolling along the sand when we all hear someone say, "Let's be the first to beat the hell out of 007." We turned to see two large men coming at a good speed right toward all three of us. My first reflex was to push the girls together and then to the ground out of their way. I knew it would be too late for me to recover my balance and deal with them, so I got the girls to the ground and was waiting at the same time for the first blows, but they never came. It seems that walking above us, looking for us, was—Mitchell! He had seen the men approaching us at high speed and headed for us immediately. So down went the girls, but at the same time, Mitchell reached the two men from behind, and within seconds they were on the ground. He then turned on the first one he came to, picked him up, sliced him two or three times with some kind of karate move, picked him up again, twirled him around, and threw him down hard. The guy never moved after that. Within seconds, he was on the second man, who had apparently realized they were in trouble and was trying to get away. But Mitchell had him and bent him in ways I never knew the body could bend, and looking at the guy's condition after Mitchell was through with him, well, I'm guessing that I was right—the body shouldn't bend in those directions. The entire event couldn't have taken more than two minutes. I just stood there stunned. Same with the girls. They were still on the ground, and we all just stared at him. You know what he said? "Hi, guys, sorry I'm late." He then picked up the girls, dusted the sand off of them, especially concentrating on their breasts and groin areas and rear end, then said, "I'm starved! Let's go eat."

Postscript—Mitchell had me take the girls to the car, which was right above us, while he dealt with the shore police, who had been called. Apparently, someone had taken film of the entire event, and someone else took a series of pictures. So there was no problem for Mitchell, and I was never identified in the film, as the quality in those days was not very good. He said later that the police just took down his name, the names of the two guys who had tried to attack me, and asked Mitchell if he wanted to press charges against them. He said no. The guys, who were not doing so well, had to be taken to the hospital. This story never made the papers because my name never came up. Mitchell didn't use it, and I guess the two guys didn't want to admit attacking me, so they didn't use my name either. All the way through dinner, we ate and stared at Mitchell. We knew he could do those things in a regulated contest, but I guess we never thought it really worked that well in the real world. We thanked him all night, which truly pissed him off! He hates to be complimented. So now, I'm old and gray, and it doesn't matter, so this story can and should be told.

Frank finally proposed marriage to Loretta, and she said she was so happy she jumped at him. At this point, she knew without a doubt that this was the man she wanted to marry. However, an important conversation was still to be had, the one about Loretta's love for Sean Connery. Frank said, "Um, we do need to discuss the 800 lb. gorilla in the living room." Loretta replied, "Look, I love Sean. I always will. But, there's no way I'd marry him. I cherish the time we had, but now I'm going to turn my attention to you. I love you and am completely in love with you. I don't want you to think about him in that light anymore."

Frank's response was amazing. He told Loretta,

I believe you when you tell me your feelings for me. I believe you because I truly, with all my heart, believe that you can love two different people at the same time. I accept your love for me. I don't doubt it for a minute. But, and I'll only say this one time, at no time are you to pass up any kind of relationship with Sean Connery. If you find yourselves thrown together for whatever reason, I want you to make love. You don't need to tell me. You can, but you don't need to. I don't know if you can believe this, but if you are happy in his arms in bed, it will give me joy because I love you, and I want you to be happy. I could even watch you in bed with him without a trace of jealousy. Believe it! Believe it all! There is no dismissing a love like you are so fortunate to have. You will always love him, but it has nothing to do with me as long as you love me too. If the time comes that you can't deal with our marriage, you are to let me know. Never suffer because of me. That would hurt me the most.

Frank attempted an explanation of his way of thinking. He told me,

Not many people have our strange ideas of life and love and death, at least that's the way it seems to me. Much like the two men in "Paint Your Wagon" who shared the same woman, it makes all of us happy. It fits our idea of life in general. All three of them loved each other, as do the four of us. (Now, I want to be clear about this—Sean and I share a brotherly kind of love, and we absolutely refuse to be in the same room with each other when there are sexual activities. The ladies have asked and continue to ask, but our answer is always the same—"NO WAY—EVER! Deal with it!"

34

So the following was Frank Mitchell's way of thinking:

As far back as I can remember in my early life, I never had the usual American dreams—wife, children, home, job, retirement, etc. I never saw myself in those movie endings. I have always just thought of a person as someone to love, hate, admire, make love to, whatever. I never put them or myself in some kind of slot in the life cycle. Sometimes this philosophy has caused me a problem with the interpretation of the ten commandments, but you know what? Then and even now, I don't give my actions a second thought. I'm sure I'll have to answer for that. So, for example, when my dear, dear friend Sean Connery calls on the phone, so sad and missing my wife-to-be, I don't get insulted or indignant, since I know she loves him also. In every corner of my mind and soul, I want all of us to live life together, share each other, be with each other in every sense of the word—to be happy! And now I'm getting my wish.

About a week after the eight-hundred-pound-gorilla conversation, Loretta was back in bed with Sean and repeated what Frank had told her, word for word. Sean looked at her for the longest time, and then he said, "You and I have been honored to meet one of the most unusual and rare people on Earth. We must cherish him always." Loretta, of course, agreed. Two days later, Loretta told Frank that she had relayed their conversation to Sean. Soon after that, the three went out to dinner together and had a wonderful time. At the end of the evening, Frank made a toast. He said, "To a rare friendship! Sean, I now officially invite you to join me in my life with Loretta. You are welcome to see her, talk to her, write to her, love her, and make love to her. You will do me the honor to accept this most unusual request." Sean and Loretta just stared at him, and then they drank their toast. Loretta turned to Frank and said, "I love you. You are the most unusual and interesting man I've ever met, and I mean even over what's-his-name here." They laughed. Then Sean said to Frank, "You have taught me a great lesson in life. I owe you a great service. We shall always be friends." Sean added,

Mitchell has always known. He has always been indifferent to our love. He just doesn't think about it. Amazing. To this day, he regards himself as Loretta's other husband, and now that's the way I look at it. On one of Loretta and Frank's first visits to California this past winter, when we had all just started to make it a foursome openly, we were just sitting around the fire one evening, Loretta and I looking at each other, Mitchell and Mickey looking at each other, and Mitchell just said to me, "Which bed do you and Loretta want?" Well, much laughter ensued, and that's the last we saw each other that night. Mitchell is not an irate husband. He has never been. Loretta and I are lovers, and now, adding to that, Mickey and Mitchell are lovers. And we all love that it's this way, so that's where we are.

Frank and Loretta married in November of 1963 and moved to McLean, Virginia, a Washington, DC suburb. At least four times during Sean's ten-year marriage to Diane, Loretta visited them in California. During these visits, she was intimate with Sean by himself and later with Sean and Diane together. She would tell Frank about it when she would return home. He always had a joke for a response, and Loretta told me she never, ever saw hurt in his eyes.

5

A real-life OO7

Frank L. Mitchell was, without a doubt, the most unique, exceptional human being I have ever met. He was so many things, did so many things, and had so many talents that it would take volumes to recount them all. When we first met at Lincoln High School, my immediate impression was, "What a kind, sweet man!" The students all loved him (of course, he *did* always bring them candy when he came to substitute teach), the teachers all loved him (he brought them candy too), and it never bothered him at all if a teacher had an emergency and couldn't leave him lesson plans. He would just "wing it," often by teaching the students sign language, which he had also "picked up" somewhere along the way—at a proficient enough level that he would interpret for the hearing impaired from time to time.

When Frank and I discussed his singing and teaching one day, he explained how much he admired, despite all *his* talents, my colleagues and me for speaking more than one language. He said,

Obviously, I am not a man of languages. All I have other than the usual two-year requirement taken years ago are the pronunciation courses for my choral music literature. But I knew the importance of languages. When parents would ask me why we sang in so many languages, I would say, "Oh, that's called education." Another of my favorite answers was, "Vivaldi did not speak English." It was difficult to explain to people that the translation is never the same from the language to English.

The chorister would see the English translation under the original and wonder why we just couldn't use our own language. I would then bring in a specialist in that language and interpret what the French or Italian or whatever actually said compared to the English translation. This helped me get my point across. I would go on to say that the romance languages (aptly named, may I say) were so much more beautiful to listen to than English, German, or Russian, all of which I also used. I must admit that, as much as I love this country of ours, I am—sometimes—embarrassed to be an American. I get in so much trouble when I say, "America's greatest problem was being settled by the pilgrims." Our lack of understanding of different cultures, the gay community, the philosophy that you and I carry, and so on, well, the average U.S. guy thinks it's his duty to show how disgusting those thoughts can be.

Many of "my people" need to get a life. I don't care if my neighbor slaughters a goat to begin their worship service. (Now I'll have the animal people on my tail—I would give the goat a stiff drink, though.) I taught for years at McLean High School in northern Virginia, a suburb of D.C. Most of my parents and students at one time or another went to school in other countries. On more than one occasion, at the close of my Christmas concert, many parents would bring down bottles of excellent wine and place them on the stage for my wife and me to take home. Imagine doing that here in Lincoln. (Those were clearly not the parents who complained about the different languages. Indeed, they expected such. It was when I came back to the Midwest that those complaints began.)

Frank was never one to mince his words, that's for sure.

As I was preparing for parent-teacher conferences one evening, Frank was in a very humorous state of mind. He told me he had some lines I could use when speaking with parents about any "problem students" I might have. He said, "I'll be thinking of all of you at parent-teacher conferences tonight. Here are a couple of lines I used in the past. Feel free to borrow any of them:

"Is everyone in your family slow?

"Have you ever thought of having your son neutered?

"I apologize for using the words *dimwit* and *nincompoop* on his last report card. That was tasteless of me.

"What are your thoughts about having her put to sleep?'"

What a sense of humor he had!

In his thirty-three years in the classroom, not counting his thirteen years of substitute teaching with Lincoln Public Schools, Frank was asked to be godfather to four babies born to his former students and act as father of the bride to three of his former choir girls. He continued to correspond with students dating back to his first year of teaching at McLean High School in 1963 until 2008, and he was a guest speaker at over ten reunions over the years, as requested by other former students. Loretta said she had never seen anything like it. "Talk about 'Mr. Holland's Opus'!" she said. He was a very lovable kind of guy with so much to tell you that you could listen for hours and not be bored for an instant. From November 2008 until his illness made it impossible, we spent many hours talking and became quite close. My first impression never changed. During our time together, it did not seem real or possible to me that he might be gone before too long. In the time he had left, however, I can say without a doubt that he lived life to the fullest, the way he wanted to live it, and that he wanted his story told in as much detail as possible. What a story it is, and it was kept secret for so very long.

Frank was born in 1936 in Lincoln, Nebraska. He attended Capitol grade school, which is now McFee Elementary School, by the Capitol. He then went on to Irving Jr. High, Lincoln High School, graduating in 1954, and Nebraska Wesleyan University, graduating in 1958. His parents divorced in 1940 when he was four. His mother was the bookkeeper with the five Wagey Drug Stores until she retired in 1974. When he was eight, his mother remarried to Robert Hunt, who owned the 17th and Washington streets service station. After their marriage, they bought the house around the corner on H Street, now a parking lot. Robert died in 1974, and Frank's mother died in 1992. He had one sister and two stepsisters.

The story of Frank's mother is a fairly typical one for that era. The story of Frank's father, however, definitely is not. Emmett Mitchell was born and raised in Albion, Nebraska. He was one of eight children, and every one of his brothers and sisters stayed in the farming business except for him. Emmett moved to Lincoln, graduated from a pharmaceutical school, and was a brilliant pharmacist in the late '20s and early '30s during the Depression. He and Frank's mother married in 1929. Emmett could be a great family man, could be a wonderful man in general, but he was also a terrific poker player, which wasn't necessarily a good thing for his marriage. In the early '30s, there wasn't much of a salary even for pharmacists, so Emmett would often stay all night in the drug store where he worked playing poker, and he made quite a bit of money at it. In large part because of this constant association with these low-life characters, Frank's mother eventually decided to leave Emmett. His father then moved to New York and met some even less savory folks. Through them, Emmett discovered that he could make a great deal of money—not playing poker but rather by taking a very different path—as a contract assassin for the Mafia.

6

Emmett, the Mafia, and the CIA

When Frank was eight years old, he began spending summers with his father, either in New York, Chicago, or Pittsburgh. Emmett had apartments in all three cities. Frank explained a little about this *business* his father was in. "A little history. First," he explained, "there is a difference between a Mafia hitman and a Mafia Assassin, believe it or not, albeit a silly one. A Mafia hitman does all kinds of work in the organization: burglaries, murder, fencing, extortion, gambling, you name it—all of the fun things that endear them to the heart of society. Murder is just one of their jobs. The Assassin, on the other hand, works alone. He does nothing else but carry out contracts on any Mafia or organized crime enemy. He is known to few people for what he truly does. For example, Emmett's friends thought he was an accountant for the organization, what they called 'the easy side.' He was very personable, well liked. He could hold court for hours at social functions. Everyone thought that Emmett Mitchell was really fun to have around. Only a few knew his real work."

Emmett told Frank about his real line of business when he was fourteen years old. Up until then, he honestly did think his father was an accountant. Frank didn't know but wondered who the tough-looking guys were in the back rooms of taverns, though. He said his father was also an officer in the Fraternal Order of Eagles, a service club much like the Elks and the Shriners. The Eagles didn't know it, but organized crime was using their club to launder money throughout the world. To this day, they don't know it, Frank told me. He adored his father despite his line of work and always spoke highly of him. He said they were a great father/son combination. His dad often repeated to him that Frank was not to even consider this way of life; if he did, it would be the saddest thing that could happen to him. So that, and the fact that Frank couldn't hurt a fly in those days, kept him on the road to finishing school and becoming a singer and a teacher.

By way of explanation and perhaps in an attempt to justify Emmett's occupation, Frank said, "My father never killed a child or a woman. He never killed anyone who would be missed by decent society. His work dealt with vermin. At times even the CIA would request his services to eliminate people whom they deemed a 'problem.' One of my father's favorite contracts was to 'eliminate with extreme prejudice' pedophiles that the government couldn't put away for lack of evidence that would hold up in court. A great line used by the CIA was, 'there are no swans in the sewer.' This doesn't necessarily make it right, but it gives me room to forgive his ways."

Due, in part, to his pharmacy training, Emmett had developed several *magic potions* that, if you were unfortunate enough to be its recipient, killed you. He was also a fantastic marksman, giving him various options for ridding the world of his mark. Frank would go out in the country with his father at times, where Emmett taught him to fire a pistol with accuracy. He also taught him the psychology behind different scenarios; for instance, how to respond in a gun battle and how to survive mass hysteria, confusion, and panic by those around you. While Frank never needed to use these skills specifically, he said it served him well in confrontations of all sorts during his life. With every lesson, his father would say, "This is only for your entertainment. For you to consider what I do as a way of life would destroy me. You will not even think about it!" It is estimated that his father completed over 150 contracts in his thirty years as a contract assassin. That's about five per year. Frank said, "If I sound so blasé and prosaic, two of my favorite words for some reason—what else can I do? I loved him beyond measure. He was my idol, not as a killer, but as a father. I just did not give it a thought." Emmett Mitchell died late in 1975, at age sixty-eight, from complications related to diabetes that today would have been considered minor.

Frank himself never became an actual member of the Mafia. He just grew up knowing them. His father could not be a full Mafioso because he was of German origin, but that didn't matter since he was a highly skilled assassin. Still, Frank would play with the gangsters' children his age and sort of grew up with them, at least during the summers. Most of them followed in their families' footsteps and became full members of the Mafia, but at no time did they try to have Frank do so. His *civilian* status was honored by them all, and they seemed to love the little guy from Nebraska. He was a favorite with many of the godfathers of the '40s through the '70s and, later, with their offspring.

Sean and Mickey were treated to meeting gangsters as far back as 1975. Sean and Diane, and Loretta, were introduced to them as far back as 1960. Frank hadn't mentioned his connections with the Mafia to them the first year of their friendship (1959), but one day in Los Angeles, Frank, Sean, and Diane were dining and a well-known Mafia godfather from Detroit came walking into the restaurant. Sean says he turned to Frank and Diane and told them who the man was. As the godfather walked by their table, he stopped, turned, looked down, and said, "Frank?" Sean says Frank immediately got up and bowed to him and took his hand as he bowed, which is a sign of respect to a godfather. To Sean's amazement, they hugged each other, and Frank introduced Sean and Diane. Sean was still not the famous James Bond, 007, so the godfather just shook his hand, and then they parted.

Frank picked up the story from here. He recalled, "Sean kept staring at me and didn't say anything. He just kept looking at me over dinner. I looked up and said to him, 'Is something wrong?'" Sean then asked Frank if there was something he wanted to tell everyone. Frank then said something like, "Oh that, uh, um, he was a friend of my father's." Later, they went back to Sean's apartment, where they sat for three hours as Frank told them the story of his early life in his father's world. As the years passed, Sean and Diane and later Mickey met and dined with, and entertained in their home, some of the most notorious gangsters in United States history. It fascinated them to listen to Frank talk about his father. How could the father of such a sweet boy/man be such a cold-blooded killer?

Frank was, for sure, quite lovable on the surface. Everyone who met Frank loved him. People didn't just like him. They loved him. And so it was with the godfathers and their children. Frank would never brag about this information, but until his death, he was still so well thought of that several of the Mafia families would have considered it an honor to do him a favor. It seems that when Frank spent summers with his father, he would often watch over the younger children, at times taking them to ball games at Yankee Stadium or to see the Cubs in Chicago or the Pittsburgh Steelers playing football. The young kids loved Frank. The godfathers never forgot this kindness and sincerity from him. Frank never asked them for anything and would refuse money from them when he returned from an outing with the young people. This was the highest compliment that could be paid to a Mafia family—not asking for anything. So, even though Frank never followed in his father's footsteps by becoming part of the Mafia, he was known to quite a few of them, and he knew that if he ever needed their help, all he had to do was ask. All his life, Frank had the power to have most anyone killed. He never exercised his power in that fashion, but it was always there.

One example in which Frank probably *did* use his influence was as follows: There was a rather highly publicized incident in the late 1950s that almost got Sean killed. He was on set doing a love scene with the great American actress Lana Turner, who was in real life dating a Mafia hitman named Jovani Severino. Jovani got jealous and stormed the movie set, threatening Sean. Sean, given he was no weakling and certainly not a coward (he had, as those who know his history may recall, taken fifth place in the Mr. Universe bodybuilding contest in the early '50s), didn't miss a beat. With little effort, he took the gun that Jovani had pointed at him, beat the hell out of the guy, and threw him out of the building. After that, it was feared that Severino would have some of his Mafia family members take revenge against Sean. For some reason, however, they never retaliated. Did Frank make a call and use his influence? Though he never admitted it, I would guess that he certainly did.

In 1977, Frank left teaching for five years to manage an exclusive lounge in Minneapolis. It was owned by the Mafia but only as a legitimate moneymaker. They held many businesses that were on the up-and-up. They paid their taxes, had the proper licensing, all of that kind of thing. From time to time, Frank scoffed at the idea that our government officials were most always squeaky clean, honest, law-abiding folks, though he still agreed that this is one of the best republics on the planet. His cynicism came from several years of witnessing the contacts, meetings, etc., that his father had with such officials. When he was older, Frank sat in on some of them with his father and other organized crime members. He often found himself near—not at, but near—a table full of Mafia assassins, along with state governors, senators, congressmen, local mayors, and city council members, you name it, and in all different combinations.

Frank said there was a two-edged sword analogy; on the one hand, the government was chasing after organized crime, and on the other, they were working hand in hand. He can talk about it because most are gone one way or another. The events involved are no longer of importance, but most of all, because when he once asked a godfather why he was allowed to walk the streets with this kind of knowledge, the godfather just smiled and said, "Who's going to believe you? "Frank added this thought-provoking commentary: "Before we all jump on organized crime, and that doesn't mean you must like or agree with what they do, take a few minutes to think things over and do not judge blindly. Organized crime cannot exist without the public wanting whichever of their services appeals to them. They cannot exist without the help of financial institutions and parts of city, state, and national government. Believe the stories you hear about the U.S. government in concert with organized crime when it comes to enemies of the state. My father received many, many contracts from Uncle Sam himself to rid the world of certain problems."

During this same period, when Frank worked as a manager for this lounge in Minneapolis, Loretta and Frank and her entire family were invited to a wedding for Loretta's niece. They had booked the reception in advance with the park department at Hiawatha Park and Lake. Loretta, Frank, and their children were all there, along with the entire Welch family—Loretta's folks. All was going well. The guys were playing baseball, the kids were swimming nearby, and hungry folks were eating. Frank had gone to the car to sleep. He was exhausted and didn't really like wedding receptions. Suddenly, Loretta was tapping on the window of the locked vehicle. Frank woke up to hear her say, "You've got to get over to our area. Tim is shouting insults at Mario Cosimo," who was one of the most feared godfathers in history. It seems the park people had made a mistake and given both receptions the same area. Tim, a hothead, would not even give Cosimo and his people a chance to work it out and divide the site, which Cosimo would have been willing to do. Tim and Loretta's brothers and brothers-in-law were ordering them off and out of that part of the park. Cosimo's daughter was at this point crying, the wives were distraught, and the men were beginning to stare. When a Mafioso stares at you, that's a bad thing.

Luckily, Frank was very close to all of this family. He had cared for their kids when they were young. He had gone to many social events with all of the gangsters that were there. So, he went running over and took care of things in this way. He walked up to the loudest and most abusive of Loretta's brothers and said this:

"John, Tim, if you've ever, ever listened to anyone in your life, it is very important that you listen to me now. It is too late now to reason with these people. They are past that. You are to go around and get everyone to pack up. We've been here long enough anyway, and we were going to leave within a half hour regardless. I want all of you to stand still." I said this to all of them once I got them to shut up. I then turned toward the Godfather, who had now recognized me. They all had, and they were grinning at me as they watched me try to calm my people.

I reached over and grabbed a bottle of very good champagne and walked over to the Cosimo family, who were now looking at me with great amusement. They sized up the situation and did not let it be known that we all knew each other. I bowed, kissed the Godfather's ring, and said in a way that my idiot relatives could not hear it, "Godfather, I'm asking a favor. There is no good reasoning behind it. These people have no idea what they have just done. I'm going to have them out of here within fifteen minutes." I turned to Margo, the daughter who was now, thankfully, smiling at me. I had taken her to movies when she was young. I bowed to her and kissed her hand, and begged forgiveness for this group of people. She kissed me on the head and laughed. I turned back to Cosimo and asked him to spare these people any harm even though their actions were unforgivable. He smiled and waved me off and said to go and be well and to call him for coffee the next time I was in town. I told him I would, and believe me, I did.

Frank got his relatives out of there and back home. When they got there, they all wanted to know what Frank had said to the park people. He just told them that he had apologized. They made fun of him for years for having been too soft on them and not standing up for his family, and they said that the only reason they left was that the kids were there. Only John and Tim looked at Frank differently from then on. He never told them how close they came to perhaps not death but undoubtedly terrible retribution, but they must have sensed something.

On another afternoon while still in Minneapolis, Loretta took their son and three of his friends to Carter Lake outside of St. Paul. There, they were terrorized by a motorcycle gang. Loretta remembered Frank's father talking about what to do if she ever found herself in a possible abduction or assault situation, either sexual or just being attacked. She began to just talk with the gang leader.

She asked him questions about his girl and if he had children. The guys had not moved to attack, but they were talking very rough and moving closer and closer. So, she continued to work her way into his good graces. Bottom line, he became friendly and finally helped her to her car as the others watched. Loretta got in the car and cried and shook all the way home. She told Frank about it, and he took her to see some of his friends. They asked her to describe everything she could remember.

Off to the side, Frank made one request. He did not want anyone killed or permanently injured. Six weeks later, Loretta showed him a newspaper article in the *Minneapolis Tribune.* It seemed a motorcycle gang had gone skinny-dipping in Carter Lake. When they returned to their very expensive motorcycles, they found them destroyed, bent beyond recognition, and of no use whatsoever. Frank said this was one of the few times in his life that he had used his connections with his unusual friends. He often wondered what he would have ordered if Loretta had been assaulted or worse. When he was honest with himself, however, he told me he knew the answer to that.

Jumping to the 1960s, Frank recalled another instance when his Mafia friends used their power for good, or at least to avenge wrongdoing by others. When Frank and Emmett were in Cicero, a suburb of Chicago, they went to a Mafia-owned lounge and were in the back meeting room. Frank was sitting in the corner watching TV and eating popcorn. Emmett was meeting with a man named Panzanos, a Mafia chieftain. Their meeting was interrupted by a couple of newlyweds whose motel room had been robbed of all of their wedding gifts. "Now, believe it or not," Frank told me, "in those days, you would get better food, drink, and service in a Mafia-run entertainment area, such as Vegas. They wanted you to spend your money and have a great time without the worry of being assaulted in any way. Vegas and other such places were much safer when they were controlled by organized crime than they are now. At any rate, this couple was brought in to see Panzanos, who listened to their story."

Frank continued:

When they had finished with their tale of woe, he gave them $1,000 and told them to go out on the town as his guest, including being driven around in a limousine and not to go back to their room until about 2 AM. I asked my dad later what would happen, and he said that the thief would be found in no time trying to hock the gifts and that these would be returned to their room along with an envelope with apologies from the management and several hundred dollars, which in the early '60s was a great deal of money. Now, realize that not only would these people naturally return to that establishment in the future, but they would also pass that story around and bring in more business. Those days are long gone. You were very safe in major cities' entertainment areas run by the Mafia in those days. Now, I'm not saying that's the way to run our country, but how is it going for the average citizen these days?

Frank had many stories about his father and the Mafia, all of them fascinating and incredible. He said that he would sit for hours when he was older and listen to his father's stories and talk with him about what happened that had transformed him from pharmacist to assassin. What Frank had noticed over time was how his father would, on occasion, turn in an instant from being very social, fun, generous, and caring to being the most frightening man he'd ever seen. He was the proverbial Dr. Jekyll and Mr. Hyde. "The transformation was terrifying," said Frank. "No grimace, no snarling, no showing of teeth, no growl." Frank said his eyes would just cloud over from their blue to a dark gray, or at least it seemed that way to him. Frank said Emmett was a brilliant man who could have positively contributed to humanity, yet he could always tell that Emmett was not happy with himself. There was a sadness that surrounded him, due at least in part, Frank believed, to how he had decided to negotiate his life. It will never be known if he genuinely regretted his career choice.

Frank always wondered what it was that had been triggered in his father's soul that allowed him to take lives. He added that though his father was an assassin, he never tortured anyone, "if that counts." In tremendous contrast to Emmett the assassin, he was simultaneously a very devoted family man. He never missed a birthday, Christmas, graduation, or the birth of grandchildren. His dedication to his family was noteworthy. When he was in social situations, he would become someone else. He spoke differently and would appear to be having a wonderful time when in reality, he was reticent and almost nonsocial. He never told anyone except Frank about his real career, and to this day, people would think he had been an accountant. His parents never knew who he was, and he was glad about that. His wife, Frank's stepmother, never knew. Frank was the one who finally told his half sisters the truth, and they believed him right away. They had always known something was *off*, and they had wondered if he was some kind of government agent. Well, in a way, he was at times. What an enigma Emmett Mitchell was.

While we were discussing his father, Frank recalled this story concerning his grandparents when he was about sixteen years old. He said,

I never really knew my grandparents on either side. I met my father's brothers and sisters a couple of times. But there was one most memorable occasion when I went with my father up to Albion for an anniversary party for his parents. We got there to find my grandparents in great distress, crying and terribly worried. Here's why. The Mitchell farms were extensive. My grandfather was able to give out large plots of land to his three sons who had stayed in Albion and farmed. One of his sons married, and he and his wife settled down to live their life on the farm. This son, Emmett's brother, of course, made out a will giving the land to his wife, who then turned around and made a will giving her belongings to her family. Emmett's brother died in an accident. Six months later, his wife died of whooping cough or some disease that today would be cured in no time. So now their section of the farm, which was right in the middle of the Mitchell landmass, went over to her parents, who knew nothing about farming and couldn't have cared less about it. Grandfather Mitchell tried to buy it back from them but to no avail. On top of that, they did not cultivate or work the land in any way and forbade any of the family to touch it. So their land grew out of control and began to wreak havoc on other sections of land. As we sat in the room listening to all of this, I could see my father [Emmett] listening intently. He always rested his head on his hand, just like Vito Corleone in "Godfather I" when he was thinking. I knew their troubles were over. They did not. They did not know who he was.

When they had finished their story, he gave everyone the following orders and requests: First, he asked for the names of these people and where they lived. Second, he told them that they were to all take a vacation to Loveland, Colorado, a favorite spot for the family even then. He told them to be prepared to leave with 24 hours' notice and that he would let them know when it was time. They were to remain in Colorado for a week. As we drove back to the Omaha airport, I said, "That's really rotten of these folks to do this to Grandma and Grandpa." He nodded and said, "It's all going to work out well. I'm going to encourage them to take the offer." He never told me what he said to them, although we can all guess. When the Mitchells returned from Colorado, the deceased wife's parents took a check for only $5,000 and never bothered the Mitchells again. The cost of that land even in those days was over $100,000, and they had been offered $75,000 to start the bidding.

Sean added another story to the tales of Emmett Mitchell. It was 1961. Diane, Sean, Frank, Loretta, and Emmett were dining at a French restaurant in Los Angeles. Sean recounted,

At the table across from us sat a father, mother, and a darling little girl about seven years old. The child was not eating her food, probably due to the heavy seasoning of high-class cooking. The father yelled at her to eat it or get hit right then and there. The wife protested, and the guy struck her with the back of his hand. The child started to cry hysterically, of course, and her mother was on the floor bleeding. The father, in an obvious rage, picked up the child and threw her towards us. I caught the girl, and Frank's father had the man on his back while the women went to attend to the wife. All of this happened in about fifteen seconds from the moment the husband struck his wife. Frank's father, when it was all over, had dislocated the guy's shoulder and his jaw and broken both of his wrists, all with about two moves. The police came and took him away and took the wife and child to a hospital as her jaw was broken. It was a horrific scene, as you might imagine.

That night Sean asked Frank how his father could disable someone so quickly with such precision and so few movements. He answered that Emmett was a martial arts expert and could do that any time he felt it necessary. Later that night, Frank went in to say goodnight to his dad as they were all staying at Sean's house then. He was reading in a chair when Frank came in. They talked a little about the abusive husband and father. Frank said he didn't even get to help since Emmett had been so fast. He smiled at Frank and handed him a plastic cover, which contained the husband's name and address. Frank asked him what the punishment was for such an animal as this guy, and all Emmett said was "extreme prejudice."

It was one of the few times that Frank knew in advance that someone was going to die. Los Angeles is a major city, and a murder such as this didn't even make the papers. Frank recalls that he did look up the name in the obituaries for a while, and one night he read about that man's funeral. Cause of death: suicide. He was found in his car, in the garage of his business, motor running, cash, credit cards placed on a table nearby, making it look like he was the lone participant. Frank never asked his father about specific events. If he wanted Frank to know, he would tell him. Frank thought that these kinds of eliminations made his father feel better about himself, and Frank could see why. He concluded, "To rid this world of pedophiles and abusive husbands and fathers is maybe not all that bad. But hey, now I'm venturing into a world of morality that I dare not discuss, especially me."

During his career, Frank's father did far more than just help his own family and innocent victims of abuse when he encountered them. Of course, he took care of the contract killings his Mafia friends ordered, and he also, as already mentioned, at times helped the United States government, notably the CIA. The government didn't know or contact him by name, of course. They would contact organized crime directly. It was a love-hate relationship. One branch of our government was chasing them, and the other half was contracting with them. In his over thirty years of taking contracts, Emmett was never arrested, the police never questioned him, and he never had a close call. It was as though he did not exist. He paid his taxes, appeared to go to work for the Eagles club, and raised a family—his wife and Frank's two half sisters, and Frank, at least in the summers. Frank was the only one in the family to know what he did at that point. About a week after Emmett Mitchell's death in 1975, Frank's stepmother called him from Pittsburgh, Emmett's last real home, saying there were some men there to pick up his private file that he kept in a small safe, and what should she do? He told her simply, "Give them the safe. They know the combination and will only take the business that does not affect you." And so she did.

7

The early years

By now, it should be clear that Frank's childhood was at the very least extraordinary. Very little was what one would consider typical, though, of course, things were relatively normal during the school year with his mother. Yet even when he was with his mother, there were some unusual events, and this one in particular also had a lasting impact on Frank's life. In 1945, he was nine years old and lived at 717 South 17th Street between G and H streets, which is now a parking lot. Frank told me this story:

I would leave my home by the alley on 17th Street, turn right and down the alley to 16th Street, and go to school. As I passed by the back of a house that would have faced G Street, I would observe a family of four practicing judo and karate in their backyard. I often stopped to watch them through the fence.

One afternoon, they invited me in for tea. We were all served a cup, but I had learned that, to be polite in Asian culture, I needed to wait until the parents took the first sip. In part because of this show of respect, I believe, I was then invited into their circle to study martial arts. The family was Hunan Nishiyama, brother of one of the most famous karate instructors in the world, Hidetaka Nishiyama, his wife and son, and daughter. My affiliation in karate was the Shotokan Academy, which was founded by Hidetaka. The affiliation for judo was the Shobukan School of the Martial Arts, which was run by the Nishiyama family. I studied both with them until I left Lincoln at the age of 22 to study at the University of Colorado, and the skills I learned have served me well all my life.

In high school, Frank also had a less-than-typical career. He had a different way of thinking about life than most students, as one would imagine, given his father's lifestyle and line of work. He said that when a teacher would ask him, for example, "What do you want out of life?" his answer was not what would be expected. He remembered saying something like, "I know I don't want to mow my lawn on Saturday mornings. I don't want to stay in the same job all of my life, or the same community, or keep just the same friends." He even recalled saying, "And furthermore, I believe that sex is a nice way of saying good morning." Now, in the early '50s, and even today, you didn't say that kind of thing at school, and Frank got into a bit of trouble with his teacher, who probably at that point much regretted posing the question in the first place.

I asked Frank if he dated much in high school and when/with whom he first had sex. For Loretta, as formerly noted, it was at the age of twenty-one with Sean, though she had dated a bit in high school. For Frank, his answer once again threw me for a loop. He told the following story of his first sexual experience: "A Lincoln High School teacher seduced me. It was the Spring of 1953, and we were preparing for Joy Night, which is a sort of talent show put on by Lincoln High at the end of each school year. This teacher asked me to meet her in the costume room at the back of the auditorium to look for something for me to wear in a skit that she was sponsoring. It wasn't exactly a room, just a partitioned-off area where we piled high what limited costumes we had. That area was then cleaned off during a production.

"You can imagine my sadness now as I walk up the beautiful stairs from the front door and see the auditorium being reamed out. I performed so many times on that stage; in musicals, singing groups, plays, you name it, and now it was being changed in the twinkling of an eye." Frank told me this story as Lincoln High was undergoing a major reconstruction, including the total gutting of its auditorium as he knew it. Had he been able to see it when the reconstruction was complete, I am sure he would have been amazed and thrilled at the transformation, but that never came to pass. Indeed, he would still have felt the nostalgia for what was now gone, but he would have been excited to see and hear productions in the new state-of-the-art theater, dedicated to and named for the famous Ted Sorenson, who was a Lincoln High alumnus as well.

Frank returned to his story after his short digression, saying,

The point of this is that not only did I perform musically there, but thanks to her, I performed sexually for the first time in my life! I was 16 in April of 1953, 17 in May. We met at about three thirty, right after school. The main doors were locked. There was no one in the auditorium. She told me to take off my shirt so we could try on different articles of clothing. I was such a stupid boy. I'd never even touched a girl's breast before. I'd kissed a few girls, but think about it: In those carefree years, we were not very worldly young people, and I had no idea whatsoever what she had in mind.

With my shirt off, she began rubbing my back and shoulders and telling me what a nice body I had. I honestly thought she was just complimenting me. Well, I still wasn't getting the picture, and then she told me to slip off my jeans to try on some sailor pants. At this point, I was getting embarrassed but still didn't think anything improper was taking place. DUH, DUH, and DUH. Color this idiot stupid!!! So there I am in just my undershorts, and she says, 'I think that top would fit me,' and she slipped off her blouse and took off her bra. I was frozen in time ... not breathing very much ... and then she slipped her hand into my shorts!

Well, I went from age 16 to age 35 in about a nanosecond! My body reacted accordingly, and then I couldn't help notice she was completely bare, and we were falling back onto a mattress already on the floor. HMMMM, how did that get there??? I called her my teacher for sexual advancement instruction. I must not have been a good student, as I had to keep having sex over and over, trying to get it right. I apparently did so poorly that the lessons extended into and through my four years at Nebraska Wesleyan University, although my work in that field does not appear on my transcript. Probably an oversight. When I moved away, I never saw her again. She also left Lincoln in 1958, moved to the mountain states, and my last correspondence from her was in July of '58, I believe. Her final words to me in a short note were, "I loved it all, Frank, thank you. Have a good life." I never saw or heard from her again after that.

After finishing almost all of his music degree at Nebraska Wesleyan University in 1958, Frank headed for the University of Colorado at Boulder. During the summer, Frank was taking an astronomy class at the University of Colorado because he was short one science class for his Wesleyan University diploma. NWU had agreed he could take it in Boulder and then receive his diploma in August. He was to begin his studies for a master's degree in music in Boulder in the fall. While Frank was there studying astronomy, the Robert Shaw Chorale came to the university for a four-day workshop. They were also auditioning for two new members that they needed, a bass and a baritone.

Frank recalled that life-changing episode in his life like this:

I was a senior at Nebraska Wesleyan in Lincoln. I was a music major with minors in history and psychology. I walked with the graduating class of 1958 in May but did not receive my diploma until August. It seems I was short a science requirement. So, I took a summer session astronomy class in Colorado, where I was to begin studying music in the fall. I do remember that you need to look up to see the stars ... after that, it's hazy. In June, while I was lying on my back at midnight with my class look-ing up and listening to a wonderful professor talking about those little bright shiny things, my music buddy told me that the Shaw Chorale was coming to the University of Colorado for a four-day seminar, workshop, and performance and that they were holding auditions for a bass and a baritone. He and I decided to sign up for the audition.

The auditions were very intense in nature, lasting every after-noon from four p.m. until around seven p.m. They were held in a large room—no piano. Sitting in a corner was Shaw himself, but he did not speak much. It was Frank's turn. He was brought in and sat with five of their singers, who had perfect pitch, naturally. He explained to me at this point how the auditions worked:

I was given a pack of audition music. Selection no. 1—pitches were given, and we began to sing, I on my bass part and the oth-ers covering the rest of the harmonies. Now, what I had heard was, the first audition, you begin to sing. If you are asked, you go to the next piece and so on, with the music getting harder and harder. The longer you stayed, the better you were doing. I lasted the entire three hours. Day two—me, the other five, and new people to audition. This time, I and the others who had lasted the first day did the singing, and so on and so on, building each day with the original five Shaw members, those of us who were passing the audition so far, and the next auditions. Came day four, and it was me and seven others who had lasted the week. We were taken through some of the most excruciating singing challenges I'd ever known or even heard of. At 8:30 that night, Shaw got up, walked over, shook our hands, and congratulated us for lasting this long. Then thank you, goodbye, and we'll let you know.

Midnight after all the auditions, I'm on the football field again looking at the stars with my class when we hear a huge voice, "Frank Mitchell? Frank Mitchell? Please come here." I thought to myself, "Well, Frank, the sheriff's finally got you!" I walked over to two of the Shaw singers who had been with me during the entire audition. Here's what they said: "Go to your room, grab enough clothes so as not to be arrested, and come to the music building audition room. Also, bring personal items. You're flying out tonight for Cleveland. We have a performance with the Cleveland Orchestra in two days with George Szell."

Frank explained that Szell was a famous American orchestra conductor.

In a daze, I stumbled to my apartment, got my stuff (I didn't own much anyway), and went to the building. We were congratulated, taken by van to the airport, and I was in Cleveland the next morning. Since I'd already sung the Verdi "Requiem,"which was what the program was, I just had to go through five final run-throughs in two days, get the tux that they fitted me for on the plane, stash the $500 they gave me as upfront money ($500 was big money in 1958), and we performed that night.

Things settled down. I signed the necessary tax papers and information sheet, was given my folder and the music, and flew to California, which was home base. As you know, that changed my life forever. One year later, we were recording in Los Angeles, and I saw this beautiful woman leaning against the wall listening to our rehearsal. I found her after the practice and took her out for a drink. It was Loretta, of course, my future wife. Here I am, 50 years later. I've had a glorious life. I'm the luckiest man I know.

In 1962, Sean and Loretta were separated by his marriage to Diane. Loretta and Frank then became the main two of the threesome, as previously mentioned, but Frank says that Diane or no Diane, they remained a threesome. Most of it was long distance, but there were always phone calls and the US mail. Sean and Loretta were comfortable remaining friends and sometimes lovers because Frank insisted on just that, beginning with the already-mentioned toast he had made at dinner. Frank and Loretta stayed in California until they began to prepare for their wedding. He then resigned from the Shaw Chorale and signed a contract with McLean High School to start teaching and directing music for the 1963–64 school year. They moved to McLean, Virginia, a suburb of Washington, DC, in August of 1963, but their wedding took place in Fargo, North Dakota, Loretta's hometown, on November 1, 1963.

In McLean, Frank was a very busy man. Not only was he the director of choral music at McLean High School, but he was also directing the DC Community Chorus, and he was minister of music for a huge church in Washington, DC. He was "working his ass off," as he says, hell-bent on establishing a future, like all young married couples. He was proud of his work and trying so very hard to bring in money and establish himself as a well-known choral director. He was often gone, and Loretta was always supportive, never giving him the "you're *never home*" speech. He was directing performances at such prestigious places as the Smithsonian Institute, the US Senate, and even the White House. And at that time, they were expecting their first child. They were happy and busy building their future together.

Their daughter was born on July 30, 1964. They had a marvelous life situation and were seemingly on their way to a successful, happy future. Loretta and Frank were living in an apartment at the time, and she had become close friends with her neighbor from across the hall, whose husband was in the military and also rarely home. This neighbor became a caregiver for their daughter and was available whenever Loretta needed someone to watch over her.

Loretta often volunteered at her church, a Lutheran Church in downtown Washington, DC. Loretta was raised in the Lutheran Church, and it was her favorite. She had decided not to attend the church where Frank was minister of music partly for that reason, but also because she was no longer interested in singing. She knew that she would feel pressured by others in the congregation to do so if she was in the church where her husband was directing the choir. This decision of hers to join a different church didn't turn out to be a good one, though who could have known? Because of her involvement in this particular Lutheran Church, when their daughter was just nine months old, a yearlong, unfathomable nightmare began for Loretta.

8

The year

Loretta began, "I was repeatedly raped starting in April of 1964. I was 25 years old.

On that fateful day early in April, I was at church and had spent the day working on some charity baskets when the Pastor (Marco) asked me to stay for a visit. When we were tucked away in his office, he sat me down and said, in effect, that he was related to Silvano Vitale, one of the famous godfathers of the Mafia in Miami, Florida. He then produced pictures showing Frank and me at what looked like a Mafia meeting. In effect, it was a social gathering, and since Frank and I were civilians, we were not considered to be a part of organized crime in any way, but who would have believed us?

The Pastor then said that he could place this information in the hands of the newspapers and that by the weekend, our lives in this area would be ruined. In those days, being associated with the Mafia was far more detrimental than today. Frank would have immediately lost all of his choral directing positions and would have been banned from teaching permanently. The Pastor then told me to take off my clothes. I asked what kept me from telling everyone what was happening. He said he would take the chance that people would believe him over me. He was very popular and loved by his congregation, and I was almost new to the church. He then physically took off all of my clothes for me and had me perform oral sex on him. Then he raped me twice in the next hour. I was so afraid that Frank would lose everything he worked for that I said nothing. I was frozen with fear. I did everything he asked. He went on to tell me that I had to be on call when Frank was away at rehearsals or performances or whatever. He knew the music schedule at Frank's church. He knew his school's program schedules, and so on.

For the next year, Loretta was raped by this pastor at least once a week and sometimes more. Many times he would have her "service" him before the church service began. Disgusting. By this time, Loretta knew she was in deep trouble, as she would certainly appear to be a willing participant should she try and tell anyone. She knew she could no longer charge him with rape. It would not look good for her. He took many pictures of them having sex. He filmed them. It was humiliating for her, to say the least.

Loretta compared her sexual assaults to the type usually described in the news. She explained that the circumstances in her case were, on some level, less horrific. Her attacker was a professional man. Marco was very clean and well-groomed. He did not throw her to the cold ground somewhere. They almost always used the bed in his back office. Strange that he would have a bed in his back office, no? She was never forced to have intercourse in extreme weather conditions or "terrible settings," as she called them, and she was never caused any lasting physical injury. But she *was*, by definition, being raped. It just happened to be by a very nice-looking, clean, educated man of the church, who might have been very likable in other circumstances. Many women in the congregation found him quite attractive. Nonetheless, Loretta essentially felt kidnapped, and she was without question being sexually abused. Personally, I doubt I would have continued this scenario for a year. I would have had to figure some way out. I could not have coped. But life for women in that era was, of course, quite different, so though I find Loretta's decision a bit faulty, to say the least, I am truthfully in no position to judge her at all.

Loretta kept a detailed journal that entire year. She shared the contents of her diary with me in extremely graphic detail, some of which I will spare the reader. She kept track of every aspect of every rape, counted each episode, and noted explicitly what it entailed in what I would term a very compulsive manner. She would go home and fill out her diary after each assault, dates, times, and what precisely he did to her or made her do. It was her way of coping, perhaps of confessing, but to no one else, and therefore to no one who could help her. The very first time happened very fast, she recalled. He sat her down and talked about the picture of Frank and her with the Mafia godfather. That took only fifteen minutes, and then he forcibly removed her clothes. He took off all of his. Loretta said he was very rough with her. He seemed to have very little idea what he was doing, so the assaults would often cause Loretta pain.

Loretta would try and talk to him. She said things such as, "Can't you be a little more tender about this? Can't you at least calm down and let us do this in a controlled manner?" And, "Do you have sex with your wife this way?" That made him angrier, and he said, "Shut up and keep your legs apart." This, by the way, was getting harder and harder to do after the third hour, Loretta told me. When he finished that first night, he told her to get dressed. Then he sat her down again and went over the rules. His main concern was that Frank not be alerted to her coming to the church so often. He was frequently worried about Frank's observations.

Did Frank notice her absence? Did he ask about it? Anything that would show he was suspicious. She was to come over when he called as long as it was possible in her lifestyle. If she couldn't, then she couldn't, but they would have to make up the time later.

April through September were the worst months. In addition to the trauma of the continuing rapes, Loretta would, of course, go home to Frank, who would sometimes want to make love within hours of her being abused by the pastor. She said, "I was sore as hell, and I had to pretend nothing was wrong, and sometimes it was almost impossible. Frank and I would generally spend at least a couple of hours making love. I was very sore, and sometimes even walking hurt. Those six months were pure hell, not only psychologically and emotionally, but also physically." And to top it all off, Loretta had a baby who wanted and needed her attention. Luckily for her, in a sense, it was Frank's busiest summer so far in their young marriage. He was directing a musical at the Arena Stage in Washington, DC. He also had his church choir and was putting together some special programs for a six-church choral concert that he was going to direct. He did not have the time and the energy for the usual lovemaking they had had the first two years of marriage. Loretta added, "It's strange to think about it now, but he would apologize all of the time to me for being so absent, and I assured him not to worry that I understood. In reality, of course, it was a godsend. The nightmare was always how could I possibly continue this double life for months or even years? I was distraught."

To make things even worse, she and Pastor Marco were having sex even more often because *he* wasn't as busy, and she never had the time to heal. She knew she had to change his brutal ways. She just had to, she insisted when relating her nightmare to me. During the first episode and the first four months, Loretta said she had to run to the sink and throw up many times. Sometimes Marco would make her shower, as he had everything in his room/office—again, something I found very bizarre. She would throw up all over herself and then would have to clean up. This couldn't continue, she told me. He was so rough. Over time, to better survive, she talked and talked to Marco so that he would think of her as a person. She worked him into conversations like they tell kidnapped victims to do, she said, and there is no doubt that she felt kidnapped. Over time, she got him to slow down his savage, aggressive techniques.

She taught him about foreplay. Even though she still hated him and what he was doing, at least the sex act itself started to feel good. She began having orgasms, creating a strange and powerful psychological contradiction for her. How does one reconcile having orgasms with a man you hate and who is raping you? Loretta said, "A person cannot calculate the level of hatred I had for that man, yet he would manage to make me come!" Loretta said to him once, "You do realize that there is a chance I'll get the last word on what you're doing to me, and you will be ruined for life?" He did not believe it. "The longer this went on," Loretta confessed, "the closer I felt to a major psychological breakdown." She asked him how long this was to continue. He said she could quit the church, but it would not affect the meeting times. If they moved away, then that would end it. Other than that, he saw her as his sex partner for an indefinite period—no time limit—just on and on. She asked him if he did this to other women, and he said no. He had just gotten the idea when he saw the picture at that Mafia family reunion in Florida. He recognized them immediately. He thought Loretta was beautiful and that he had to own her, and this was the perfect plan. He said he had worked it out in his head for several weeks prior.

The fourth time he tried oral sex on her, she started to laugh. She said she couldn't help herself. He, of course, asked what was so damn funny. She remembered what she had said, "I've had that done by experts. You are not even close. You have no idea what is going on down there with a woman. I suggest you either read up on it, ask some guys who know what the hell they're doing, or better yet, stop it." And so, amazingly, he did stop it, she said. She couldn't believe it. Maybe it embarrassed him so much that he didn't want to try it again. She was shocked that she had said that to him, but by that time, she knew he wanted no marks on her body, so she would be physically OK. He took hundreds of pictures, graphic pictures in humiliating and embarrassing positions and poses, and he would always say, "Imagine if these got out to the public!"

Months passed. Loretta was in a terrible situation. Then, in July, things got even worse. Marco wanted to try something different. At the beginning of July 1964, Marco knew that Frank would be at a five-day workshop in Roquebrune, Virginia, so he had big plans for Loretta. He told her to be at his office at eleven a.m. When she came into the office, there was a very nice-looking young man talking with Marco. They were introduced, and Marco said, "Dear, this gentleman is from an escort company, and I've arranged for him to have sex with you for a few hours."

Loretta didn't know what to make of this change of pace, but by now, she was entirely under his control, and without giving it much thought, she went into the room, they undressed, got into bed, and had sex for a couple of hours. Time was up. He left. She showered and was told to take an hour's nap. About three p.m., she was awakened by another man. The same ritual, then shower, then nap. About six p.m., another man. Now she was asking herself why this was happening. What the hell was going on? It seemed Marco got a kick out of watching. Then it was nine p.m., another man. Midnight, another man, the fifth one to have sex with her. This continued until three a.m., a total of sixteen hours of on and off again sex. Marco filmed each session with the date and time showing. He arranged for the same thing also in August and September. Loretta was becoming more and more despondent. Marco could see the effect on her and finally stopped. He didn't want Frank to ask questions, which he had started to do. Loretta was reaching her breaking point.

Then, in October, Loretta underwent an extraordinary and almost complete psychological transformation that allowed her to keep her sanity. She became two different people: one who hated Marco beyond measure and loved Frank deeply and one who was acting as if she loved Marco and wanted to be with him. Thinking that you are in love with your captor when there is a long captivity period is a relatively common psychological phenomenon and is considered a survival technique. For Loretta, that was certainly an accurate description of what happened. Her voice patterns changed when she was with Marco, and her behavior also changed dramatically.

Not long after this transformation took place, Loretta was parking her car at the Lutheran Church to see Marco. She remembered noticing all of a sudden that she was walking quickly, as though with great anticipation. She was not dragging along with her usual sullen, dreary attitude. She was excited. She said, "I almost stopped in my tracks. The next thought that hit me like a bombshell as I walked into the church was, MARCO HAD NOT CALLED FOR ME! I was going there on my own!"

Pastor Marco was a sports nut. So, that day in October, he was in his office watching a World Series game. He had this look of surprise on his face when Loretta came into the room. She could see him thinking, "Did I call for her and forget?" Then came the realization that no, he hadn't called. It was a World Series game, and he never missed them. He looked at her, puzzled, and she said she walked around, got down on her knees, and went down on him. He stared at her, and in a soft voice, he said, "Would you teach me how to make love?" Loretta said, "I took him to bed. I showed him what I was used to doing. He brought me to several orgasms in that hour. He was so proud of himself, and I felt so sorry for him for the first time. He was a little boy now. He was no longer barking out commands or insulting me like in the first six months. Three hours later, I knew that on some level, I owned this guy. I tried to find the hate that was usually there, but I could not feel it for now. We increased our "love-making" time together, sometimes at his request, sometimes at mine. He told me his wife was shocked at his change in the bedroom. By way of explanation, he told her he had been watching porno movies to learn. They had only had sex once a week, her choice, in the past, but as he showed her his new techniques, that increased quite a bit." He would joke with Loretta that he was having trouble dealing with two women at the same time. Reading this story puts into question Loretta's state of mind and whether she at this point was now simply having an affair with Marco. How could that not be the case? But events would later shatter the fragile illusion that permitted her to cope and rationalize and continue.

Months into this new routine, Marco was getting bored again. His next fantasy was sex with three or more people. After Loretta had taught him how to change his sexual techniques, he had begun to cooperate more casually in their encounters, at times observing rather than participating, and he hired his first big-time prostitutes. The sexual episodes now consisted of Loretta having sex with multiple men *and* women.

Loretta recalled,

The first woman was beautiful, regal even. Her clothing was high-class. She was nice, quiet, and gentle. Marco had us undress. Then he had us both relieve him with oral sex. Next, I was told to start oral sex on her. I had never in my life considered having sex with another woman before. I had always found the idea repugnant, being very devoted to the Lutheran Church's traditional teachings.

Marco thought this would be yet another way to debase me and make me suffer. I had become such a seemingly willing participant, and now he wanted to be back in control. I was disgusted by it, but he wouldn't let me stop. He made sure I did it the same way I had taught him to do it. This went on for quite some time, and then it was her turn, and at this point, I actually began to enjoy it! Ever since then, I have sought out and enjoyed lesbian sex. Marco's plan had backfired. It was supposed to be an awful experience for me. When Marco saw I was enjoying it, he became enraged and had us change positions.

Next, a male escort came in and was directed to have sex with me. He was very handsome. I'm so grateful that the people I was thrown up against were at least nice, pleasant people to look at and be with. He was a terrific man, very pleasant, and careful of my feelings. This man and I became particularly good acquaintances over the next few months. Marco used the same three women and two men, not all at once, but alternating them. One of the times I was with him, I whispered in his ear that I had been abducted and threatened with exposure, but I told him not to tell the police. He said the most important thing to me, and I'm sure it saved my life! He said, "You must go to a psychiatrist as soon as possible. I can see two personalities in you. I've been wondering if you were somehow deranged, and now this explains it."

The male partner went on, "Kelly, one of the women partners with whom I am friends, and I have discussed the thought that you might be mentally impaired because of how your voice changes from one sound to another. One minute you seem to be having the time of your life, and the next minute we can feel tears on our skin—your tears. What you've told me now makes sense. I won't go to the police, but I'm going to give you my name and phone number. You are to contact me if you ever feel in danger or if I can help." I had a friend, and Samuel was his name. I had someone who might help me. I knew then that things might turn out in my favor. I thanked him for being so gentle with me. I was having so much intercourse that I was beginning to get sore.

After that, sometimes he would fake it if he could. I kept thanking him over and over again, very quietly. Marco never heard us. We had our conversations in sex sounds. My very next partner a week later was his female friend, Kelly. She would whisper in my ear and ask how I was doing that day and how I wanted her to perform. She told me that she and Samuel were going to keep watch over me. She also gave me her name and phone number.

There was now hope, but the abuse went on. At several of these encounters, there was Loretta plus two men and three women. Marco had her pleasure the men first while he watched. Then it was the women's turn in a variety of combinations and positions. During another of these sessions with multiple people, Pastor Marco went a step further, adding blasphemy to his list of other endearing qualities. Loretta recalled that the last time there were six of them, Marco ordered them to go into the main sanctuary. There were cameras there. Marco could watch the proceedings from his office, which is precisely what he did. He directed them to go to the sanctuary naked. Over his microphone, Marco would call out instructions, such as forming a cross with their bodies. The men were told to urinate in the master communion cup and throw the urine out onto the black carpet—what a sick man he was. Loretta recalled,

> I remember all of us being so disgusted, but he was paying the others so much that they didn't refuse. Then he directed us through different scenarios, several of which took place under the central cross. I felt emotionally ill afterward. This was my place of worship, and I was very religious in my early years. To do this was beyond horrible.
>
> Marco remained in his office the entire time and never came out there that night. I guess he simply enjoyed watching. That was the last time all six of us were together. Another time, Samuel, Kelly, and I also had to do a threesome under John the Baptist's painting. I remember it so clearly now. Marco could not see, but Kelly and I were crying, and Samuel just kept apologizing to God and Jesus to forgive him/us. It was an awful time!

As December rolled around, Loretta continued in her state of almost psychotic confusion. Though there were times like those just described when Loretta could feel the hatred for Marco seeping through her, she was such a mess psychologically that she went back and forth between Frank and Marco as if she were simply having an affair. She would still write in her journal each time, but the script's tenor was much different. She was no longer so sore, so she could get back to her normal speed with Frank in the bedroom. His free time had returned enough that they had resumed a more normal sex life. Loretta said it was actually a happy Christmas for her somehow. She said, "Frank, the baby, and I had such a great family life. My love for Frank grew and grew. I was a happily married woman, believe it or not. I had to force myself to remember how huge of a lifestyle problem I had. How could I ever stop what was happening?" Loretta didn't realize it at that point, but she had been so transformed that she had little idea of what was happening to her. Because of this transformation's nature and depth, there were times when Loretta wasn't even sure whether her *affair* was with Marco or with Frank.

By March, Frank was starting to suspect that something was going on. He was becoming more and more sullen. He kept more to himself. Loretta could see him studying her, and she knew he thought she was having an affair. Who could blame him? And in a way, he was right. She had to slip away from the house for no apparent reason at least once a week. Frank was so easy to live with and never asked where or why she was going out, but sooner or later, he was going to start asking questions. During this same period, Marco was changing too, which was not a good thing for Loretta. He was beginning to realize what he had done. He was thinking more clearly about how it would end, and he was therefore becoming more dangerous than ever. Loretta was probably in mortal danger now, and she was beginning to sense it. She had asked him how long this was going to go on, which had caused him to focus on the end game, and that was most likely to kill her at some point in the not-too-distant future. What other solution would there be for him?

Loretta began thinking about how she could escape from all of this. She certainly couldn't call rape. With all that she had done, and with all of it having been filmed, that would never hold up in court. Who would believe her? She remembered what her escort friend Samuel had told her, and she went to see a psychiatrist. She had several sessions with him, telling him everything. He explained that, despite her seeking out Marco, she still hated him subconsciously, and she was still his prisoner, just with different rules. She was headed for a tragedy if she didn't wake up and rethink her feelings.

When she started to do that, she was slowly taken back to the beginning, to her real self. It hit her hard. She kept saying to the doctor, "What have I done?" He said, "You changed into the person you are now out of necessity. It's called survival, but we are going to bring you back." As time passed and Loretta began to put the year back together, her hatred returned. She began to realize what had happened and was what was happening to her. She also realized that, if this continued, it would undoubtedly cost her her marriage, and very likely her life. She knew all at once in early April, one year after this had all begun, that she wanted more than anything to break loose. She wanted her life back. She wanted this man out of her life for good.

Finally, Loretta called her best friend Mary Sue and told her what was going on. Her fear was now at its highest point, and she needed to confide in someone close to her. She told Mary Sue everything, and Mary Sue believed her. She said she always had a strange and uneasy feeling around Pastor Marco, and one time he had put his hand on her hip a little too close to the *off-limits* area, as she called it. Loretta was pretty sure that Mary Sue would tell Frank, and she was right. Frank was most often thought of as a "warm-and-fuzzy" kind of guy, liked by all, but Loretta knew that he had a dangerous and dark side as well, and she knew about Frank's father's past, so she wondered what might happen. Still, she couldn't go on with things as they were. Though at times she asked herself if it had been a mistake to confide in Mary Sue, she had reached her breaking point, and she had felt compelled to tell someone who would understand and believe her. She had come to terms with the fact that she had, at least in her way of thinking, few if any other options for ending this hell of hers alive.

9

Like father, like son

Washington, DC, April 1965. Frank L. Mitchell sat staring blindly at the kitchen walls, tears rolling down his cheeks as he listened to the story unfold—the story of the horror his dear wife Loretta had endured for one very long year—and he had not even noticed that anything was wrong. How was that possible? He had been so busy with his music that he had been completely oblivious. As his wife's closest friend, Mary Sue, recounted almost word-for-word what Loretta had told her. Frank's disbelief evolved into furor—a furor mixed with the guilt of feeling that he had let Loretta down somehow, that he had failed her as the husband who had promised to watch over her always.

His eyes turned a cold steel gray, and he could feel his heart breaking. Mary Sue's first statement to Frank had been, "Loretta has been a sex slave to Pastor Marco for exactly one year..." As soon as Frank heard these words, the question was no longer whether Pastor Marco would live or die, but rather when and how he would die. This would not be the first time he had killed a man, nor would it be the last. You see, Frank, over the years, and despite his promises and best intentions, had become more like his father than he ever imagined he would. Killing was not new to him, but this would be the only time in his life that Frank L. Mitchell would plan to kill a man purely out of revenge.

Frank stayed only half an hour listening to Mary Sue. That was all the time it took for her to lay out everything that Loretta had told her about Marco—the entire year presented in condensed form. Loretta had spent hours telling Mary Sue almost everything that had happened to her, and she had written it down as Loretta talked, as she had asked. When Mary Sue had finished, she gave Frank her well-written notes. Then she said she had nothing else to report. Frank simply got up, numb and in a state of shock, and walked out the door. He drove around for about an hour, not knowing how to handle this without putting Loretta in an embarrassing or humiliating position. He went home. Loretta and their daughter were in North Dakota visiting family and weren't due back until the next night. That would give him time to think. Frank called his father, read him the notes, and he simply told Frank that he would be there in the morning.

Frank's father pulled into the driveway around eleven a.m. They went out for lunch, and Frank gave him the notes from Mary Sue. Emmett read them several times. They picked up Loretta and the baby at the airport that evening. Loretta had a feeling Emmett would be there when she got home. She felt so relieved and safe to see him as she got off the plane. They sat around for the evening and talked and cried. There was never a mention as to what would happen to Marco. It was not an issue for discussion. Emmett asked Loretta to tell him as much as she could about Pastor Marco's habits, his way of life. She knew a lot, of course. What caught Emmett's interest right away was Marco always getting up at four a.m. to work out and then stepping outside to get the paper. Knowing this part of his daily routine would be very helpful. Even though it was uncomfortable, Emmett asked Loretta to go over everything several times. He wanted to hear it all: the humiliations, the threats, the escorts, all of it, and the details that went with it all. He apologized for putting Loretta through that, but she knew it was essential to Emmett and Frank. That was Saturday night. At this point, Marco had thirteen more days to live.

Tuesday, Wednesday, Thursday, Friday, Emmett and Frank drove around town, around Marco's neighborhood. On two occasions, they were outside at four a.m., watching his light go on in the house. They had also found out by this point that Marco's wife was leaving town on Sunday. Emmett selected the following Saturday morning as the day Marco would die. Frank didn't want to wait that long. He picked Thursday morning. Loretta knew nothing of any of it. Plans were made, and the waiting began.

That Sunday evening, the same day Marco's wife left town, Frank told Loretta he had a surprise for her. They were also going to leave town for a few days, and they were leaving Monday morning, the next day. He had made arrangements to take off work at his three positions. Monday morning, they piled into the car and took off for the Atlantic Ocean, which was only a few hours' drive. There they spent three glorious days swimming in the ocean, dining in nice restaurants, and going to parks where the baby could play. Loretta told me, "It was wonderful. Frank was upbeat and back to his old fun self." They returned to DC on Wednesday evening.

All day Thursday, they just relaxed around the house. Frank had an afternoon rehearsal from two to four, but other than that, nothing was planned for Thursday evening. Frank never really went to sleep that night. They all retired around midnight. He got up around three a.m., dressed, went to his dad's bedroom, took his pistol, the silencer that went with it, a full clip of ammunition, a killing knife his dad carried on occasion, and some tools that he'd learned to use when he was a kid. Then, he left the house. Loretta never asked a thing. She was used to Frank going to take a walk or drive at times during the night when he couldn't sleep.

Frank recounted the night, telling me,

I parked about a block from Pastor Marco's house. I walked in the street next to the curb. This takes away suspicion from a middle-of-the-night walker in your neighborhood. Dad once told me that you never walk the sidewalk after midnight. Walking in the street close to the curb gives the appearance of someone who has a specific destination. He said to walk the sidewalks looks suspicious. I mean, a bad guy wouldn't be so apparent as to walk out in the street, now would he?

With the help of the special tools, I was in Marco's house within thirty seconds. At this point, I remembered reliving stories my father had told me. [He never went into details about an actual event, but he would go into precise detail about entering a home or wherever and getting the occupant's attention.] Back to Marco's house. I was now in his living room. I turned on the TV very loud and sat in the farthermost corner away from the set. He came charging down the stairs, wondering why the hell the TV was on. He couldn't see me. I was just sitting quietly in the far chair. He went directly to the TV as I knew he would do, turned it off, and stood there wondering why it had just come on like that.

Dad had also explained that no one at that minute thinks of themselves as being in danger. I mean, why would an intruder make that kind of noise? So the victim has no fear at all at that moment, just confusion. He stood for a minute or two, and then he heard my voice. "Good morning, Marco." He whirled around, trying to focus on my whereabouts, and then could faintly see the outline of me sitting in the chair. Sitting is intentional. Once again, you remove fear from a victim if you're sitting. I mean, if you're there to attack, you'd be standing in a threatening mode, not sitting down where you look incredibly vulnerable, right? Well, in this case, wrong, of course!

He flicked on the light and recognized me immediately. Now that brought on the fear. He had before him the husband of the woman he had terrorized for over a year. And yet, I knew that his arrogance would return. I knew that seeing me just sitting there would give him and his very athletic body renewed courage. I was right. His emotion changed from fear to indignation, and he said, "What the hell! Who do you think you are to come into my house at 3:30 AM and confront me this way? You don't realize who you're dealing with! You are in so much trouble, I don't even know where to start!" I remember most of his words, I think, exactly.

He finished his bravado speech and started towards me. At that point, I raised the pistol and shot off his right kneecap. As he fell screaming, bewildered, incredibly shocked, I put a cloth in his mouth and duct-taped it into place before he could take enough of a breath to scream again. The pain from such a bullet wound has to be unreal. He lay on the floor writhing in pain, holding his knee, rolling back and forth, and looking up at me with anger and terror written on his face. I walked over to him and wrapped the wound to stop most of the bleeding. He only had about a half hour to live anyway.

Then, I pulled up a chair next to him. He was sitting on the floor holding his knee at this point, and I said, "Hi, Marco, I'm Frank Mitchell, Loretta's husband. I'm going to give you a series of commands. If you fail to comply immediately, I will shoot off another part of your body, and believe me: You will surely miss it. Now, Marco, first things first. I'm going to help you up to your safe. I want you to bring out all pictures of my wife. I want to see the films. And I want you to do this now." He looked at me for a moment as though he might refuse, but I brought the pistol up again waist high, and he, with my help, got to the bedroom safe. It was already open, which saved a great deal of time.

I told him to bring out everything I'd asked for. There were two large photo albums and packets of photos. There were two large film canisters also brought out. I told him I wanted to see the film and got him back to the living room where he inserted and began to play what he had filmed. I pushed him to the floor again, sat down, watched the film, and looked through all the pictures. I became physically ill. My sadness was so overwhelming. I could even hear myself moan like an injured animal. I was destroyed inside, and he knew it. I fast-forwarded through the two films, glanced at all the photos, and then set them down on the couch. I took the film out and placed it in the canister. The other film I had already replaced in its canister.

Then I turned towards Marco and pulled up a chair. I ripped off the duct tape and pulled out the cloth. I had already told him that to cry out would be his last sound. I then began to ask him all kinds of "why"-type questions. «How could he do this to a human being over and over again for so long? The humiliation, the pain, all of it—did he have remorse of any kind?" Well, of course, he said he was sorry, but I began to realize that I had asked stupid questions, and there was no way he could give me honest answers.

Then he asked me what I was going to do. His bravado was returning; I guess because he was still alive and probably thought I was just going to beat him up or something like that. Then he threatened me with the influence he had with the mayor of our suburb, the police, the largest church in the area, all of that. What did I have? Nothing. He said I would never allow those pictures to be shown. He began to get an indignant look on his face once more. I quickly put the cloth back in his mouth and put fresh duct tape on his face. Then I began to talk to him.

I pulled my chair up close to him and said something like this, "Marco, what you have done will stay with Loretta and me for the rest of our lives. I don't know how extensive the mental damage will be. Loretta and I are very strong people and will survive most of it. You, however, Marco, will not survive the night. You are in the last half hour of your life." At this moment, the realization struck full force, and he believed me. He tried to talk but couldn't. His eyes did the pleading. I then pushed him down and stripped off his robe and pajamas. It should be noted here that I had been wearing special gloves the whole time.

I told him I wanted very much to cut off his manhood and shove it down his throat. I said that I needed to sit and think about that for a minute. Did I want to do such a barbaric act? After a few minutes of thought on that subject, I told him I would not do that, but the bad news was that his form of execution would be the kind known among the Cosa Nostra as "Buckwheat." It is a most excruciating way to die. I told him I was going to place the tip of the silencer into his rectum and fire only one shot. The result is too hideous, but what else could I do, I thought, after all he had done to Loretta? I told him that the bullet fired at that angle is known to deflect off the bladder, stomach, lungs, and probably lodge in the upper torso. It never reaches the brain. Death only comes after about thirty minutes of indescribable inner pain. You bleed out, of course, but very slowly, and your insides have been ripped and mangled, creating such agony. The fear in his eyes said it all.

Some form of civility somehow returned to me then, and I knew I couldn't do this. I just couldn't live with myself if I went through with such a savage act. What I was doing was bad enough. So I sat there thinking to myself about my decision not to cut off his private parts nor perform the barbaric "Buckwheat" method of execution, and I decided I would simply put two bullets into his brain. As I was thinking about it, I realized that he had not made a sound in about a minute or so. I looked down at him and saw that he was already dead. His fear had been so great that he had swallowed the cloth into his throat and had strangled himself to death. I felt that this was indeed punishment enough. The fear and pain and anguish that I'd just caused him over the past hour was surely enough, wasn't it?

I gathered up my belongings, the film, the photos, put them into a cloth that I'd brought with me, and left. Over the years, I've thought about that night so often. I'm very relieved that he was actually and literally "scared to death." Can there be a worse way to die? I wasn't cheated. It was a classic ending. I do not regret that night. I challenge anyone to look at those pictures and the film, put their own loved one in Loretta's place and then tell me I was too rough on the poor guy. But what does it matter? I did it. It was over, and we went on to a beautiful and exciting life. And, I'm proud of myself. I didn't mutilate his body, and I didn't perform the barbaric "Buckwheat" form of execution. If he'd lived, I'd have just shot him.

Loretta's revelation to me about her year with the pastor had caused her to revisit, almost relive, a very dark time in her life and had clearly reopened deep psychological wounds for her, which she would need to address with professional assistance soon after she confessed to me. She told me, "Revisiting 1964 and bringing out the Marco events has really thrown me for a loop. I'm going to need a little time. Be patient with me." Likewise, Frank's reliving the story of Loretta's "Year" and the pastor's death weighed heavily on him. Loretta described his behavior after he had told me what he had done to Marco. "Frank is in a little bit of shock from writing you his story last night." (This was in April of 2009.) "I don't think he has allowed himself to think much about it for some time. He sat there last night, and we could see him in deep, deep thought. None of us attempted to intrude. Later that night, I found him standing by the window around 3 AM, just staring out at the ocean. Then he went for a walk along the shore. I just left him alone. I saw that Sean and Mickey were watching him from the other room. I went out to them, and we turned out the lights and just watched him by the shoreline. If ever a man had to review a part of his life, well ... this was certainly dramatic enough."

A few months after Marco's death, Frank realized that he needed to confess to Marco's Mafia relative, Silvano Vitale, that he was the one who had killed him and deal with the consequences. It was a matter of honor to him. Loretta learned of Frank's trip to Florida to meet with Vitale some time after the fact, through Emmett. Loretta recounted,

Frank was in Roquebrune, Virginia, with his high school choir. It was an exchange program with Roquebrune High School. Frank's choir would sing there, and then the next week, they would come up to McClean. Emmett was staying with me.

So, sitting around one evening, I wondered aloud why Vitale hadn't been seen at Marco's funeral and did he ever suspect that he or Frank had anything to do with it?

Emmett told me that a couple of months after Marco's funeral, Frank flew to Miami and asked for an audience with Silvano, which was, of course, granted. Frank was very close to him and the family. Emmett then related the visit they had that evening. Frank had told him that it was just Silvano and him sitting in the living room together. Now, this may seem uninteresting, but one has to know that no high-ranking godfather or chieftain would ever be without protection in any room in the house other than the bathroom and the bedroom. So, to meet him alone was the highest respect that could be paid to a civilian.

Emmett continued telling me of Frank's trip. Silvano asked why the formal visit? Frank just said to him, "It was I who killed Marco. I need for you to hear me out." Silvano gestured with his hand for Frank to continue. Frank then took Silvano through the entire year, step by step. He showed him some of the pictures and put the film in, showing an obvious rape scene. The whole presentation took no more than an hour. When Frank had finished, Silvano thought quietly for a few minutes while Frank just sat there. At last, Silvano looked up, got up, came to Frank, and hugged Frank's head against his leg. Frank got up, and they embraced.

Silvano offered his apology for the behavior of a family member. He said that Frank had had no other choice and that Frank was a true warrior in his eyes. He had protected his family. They had a few drinks, and then Frank was driven to the airport, and he came home. There was never any other mention of it anywhere except that Silvano let it be known in the

Mafia world what Frank had done. They reacted as Silvano had, saying that Frank had done the right thing. He was kind of a folk hero to them for years. That's why they bestowed upon him the need to do something good in their name from time to time, which Frank has done.

Returning now to the day after Marco's demise. On the Friday morning after Marco's death, Loretta went over to the church for a group meeting only to find hundreds of people gathering around the sanctuary and classrooms. People were crying and talking and hugging, and she asked what had happened. It seemed that Pastor Marco had been found murdered in his own living room. The police speculated that he had only been dead for about two hours, which put the time of death at around three a.m. They also said it appeared to be a professional killing. She went home and told Frank and Emmett the news. They both kept eating their eggs and didn't bat an eye. Loretta remembered that Frank, in a calm and emotionless tone, simply said, "Could you pass the pepper, please?" It was a bone-chilling moment, but Loretta said nothing more, and neither did they.

Later, details of the assassination emerged. When the police entered Marco's home, they found his safe open and found that the only papers left behind were legal, such as insurance. There were no pictures. There were no films. The money was also still in the safe. This was one of the reasons that the police concluded it was a professional hit. To leave the money in the safe after an assassination was seen at the time as an insult to the victim and often as a sign of Mafia involvement. Neither Loretta, Frank, nor Emmett was ever questioned about the case. There was no reason for them to be, as Loretta's frequent comings and goings to see Pastor Marco had gone entirely unnoticed, just as Marco had wanted. Also, the church was so large that if anyone had noticed her frequent comings and goings, they probably would only have thought she was a staff member or going for counseling.

Loretta recalled how she felt when she heard Marco had been killed. She said, "I must be honest, of course, and say I was delighted. It couldn't have happened to a nicer guy. I was finally free. My normal, real thoughts and feelings had returned, and I realized how deeply I hated that man!"

Now that he was gone, it was time for Loretta to try and put this nightmare behind her and to rebuild her life with her family. She and Frank remained in DC for another eleven years. Loretta reconsidered her original decision and started going to Frank's church and joined the choir. His choir adored her, and she ended up loving the church. As for Frank, he never forgave himself for not realizing that something had been very wrong. He felt such guilt for not even having noticed how often Loretta was gone. He was too involved with his performances at the White House, Senate, Smithsonian, his own church, etc. He said, "I took no notice of Loretta's absence. In fact, I was not even aware of most of it." He felt that he failed her. He was supposed to be her guardian. He was supposed to be there to protect her, and the fact that he wasn't continued to haunt him for the rest of his life.

He told me, "You can give me all the reasons and examples of 'How could I have known?'—that kind of thing, but it doesn't help.

"I asked Loretta over and over for forgiveness, and she has always said I was being too hard on myself. There was no way for me to know. But the thought of her having gone through something like that just rips my heart out!" Loretta and Frank grew back together over the next few years and, of course, remained so until the end. Loretta told me that many times over the years, she wanted to talk to Frank and ask him what had happened, but she just couldn't. She could tell that he also wanted to talk at times, but they would just stop the sentence almost in mid-air. Someday there would be the right time and place for this talk, but not yet. For now, it was time to try and heal and to "forget," time to concentrate on their love, their relationship, and their family. That time, of course, would come right after Loretta and Frank shared these stories with me.

Sean told me later he also felt his share of guilt for not having asked Loretta outright what was wrong. During Loretta's horrendous year, he and Loretta did not see each other, as he was far too busy with his newfound stardom and his own family, but he phoned her almost every week to stay in touch. Throughout that year, he could sense that something was very wrong. Loretta seemed depressed and distraught. He could hear it in her voice. But since she didn't volunteer any reasons for her unhappiness, Sean very wrongly concluded that she and Frank must be having marital problems. He felt it would be wrong for him to intrude. It was not his place. Unfortunately, he actually backed off his contact with her to leave them the space he thought they needed to resolve their relationship problems. Looking back, he obviously wishes he had said something, either to Loretta or to Frank. "Perhaps the abuse would not have lasted for so long," he told me.

10

Killing in three-quarters time

In December of 1967, two years after Loretta's nightmare had ended, she was sitting and talking with Emmett. She told me of their conversation. "Emmett and I were very close. I was to him, I think, a daughter. I could get him to laugh. He was such a sad man, at least most of the time. He would talk about how he wished that his life would have been different. He always talked about not killing any nice people but would then add, 'I don't think that's for me to decide.' His eyes, his mannerisms, speech patterns, all were given over to Frank. While they didn't look alike, they were in many respects very much alike. Knowing this to be the case, I said, as we listened to Christmas carols being sung nearby, 'Well, I am glad Frank didn't go into your world.'"

It was the second time I'd said that to Emmett, and once again, I got the same result. He looked away from me, he looked down, and then he looked away again. But this time, I didn't let it go. So I backed up and asked, "OK, what is that look? What should I know?" This was his answer. "My son is not me. I never wanted this for him. I always thought of him as a teacher, a musician, or a businessman, but never anything like me. For the most part, my wish has come true—with some exceptions." I continued my assault. "What are you saying?"I got this response to my question. "Frank is revered by many powerful men and families in the underworld. Over the years, he became the favorite of sons, daughters, nieces, nephews—you name it—he was family to them, and is until this day. [Frank was thirty-one at this point.] He is now considered the most powerful civilian in the world of organized crime. In just those short 23 years that he roamed with me from New York to Chicago, Pittsburgh, San Francisco, Los Angeles, and so on, he stacked up more friendships and loyalties than one can imagine. He even saved the lives of two children belonging to the Cosimo crime family. He threw himself out into the street, scooping up a Cosimo grandson, threw him in the air, and took the brunt of a car that had gone through a stop sign. The average person simply cannot imagine the impact of someone saving the life of the grandson of Cosimo, one of the most feared Godfathers in America.

"Then, on Frank's 21st birthday, in 1957, he was visiting the Panzanos family and took Panzanos's daughter to a school dance. His instructions were to leave her there and then her date and his father would bring her home. Frank didn't like the situation. He said later that it just didn't feel right. He didn't like the kid at all, so he stayed outside in his car. Around 11 PM, he saw the school's side door open and the girl being carried, fighting and screaming, to a waiting car. He could see that there was a driver plus the two guys who were carrying her. Frank followed them to a quiet park about three blocks from the dance. When they took her from the car, she was naked and seemed dazed and almost unconscious.

"Frank slid out of his car, walked parallel to them on the other side of the trees, and when they threw her to the ground and took off their pants, he was on them. They were unconscious within seconds, and she was back in Frank's car with his jacket around her. He grabbed her clothes and purse from their vehicle and took her home. Imagine the gratitude of the Mafia world over Frank's intuition, bravery, and rescue. It was legend within a month. The third time that Frank saved the life of a Mafia child was very much the story of being in the right place at the right time, but still, it meant the world to the Marcello family. The Godfather Marcello had a very immature daughter who had gotten pregnant when she was only sixteen. Marcello did not believe in abortion and had the child born to the family. One night at a lawn party, the daughter went berserk in the upstairs bedroom and threw the six-month-old baby out the window. Guess who caught the baby? Yes, indeed, my son! Well, you stack up these kinds of markers for people like these, and they will do anything for you.

"So, Loretta, what I'm leading up to is that one of the Godfathers, and many other important family leaders, brought Frank before them at the end of that summer of 1957. He was told to remain a civilian, with one exception. The families always wanted to do good along with what they know to be bad. So, they told Frank to go through life in his civilized world, but told him that if at any time he should come across a situation where some innocent, or especially good citizen was being destroyed, hurt, put upon, anything like that, that he was to call upon their help and save these people from this unfair or terrible injustice, and Frank agreed."

Loretta listened carefully and thanked Emmett for their conversation, but she did not probe further into any specific details as to what Frank's agreement with his Mafia friends had entailed to that point. Unknown to her, as time passed, Frank had begun to feel the desire to take a more active role in righting the wrongs in this world. He evolved into a sort of Robin Hood of the under-world, guided by his father and contracted by the CIA to help elim-inate some of the most notorious drug dealers and pedophiles one can imagine.

In July of 2009, Frank revealed his involvement with the CIA and told me about his first contract hit. There would be many such stories, each of them incredible, as one can imagine, each of them presenting a stark contrast to the Frank Mitchell I thought I knew so well. I learned over time that there were several Frank Mitch-ells. He was an excellent and dedicated classroom teacher and a fantastic musician, yet he could so quickly become a terrifying human being. He was a man of many worlds, but one who was never to be feared by his loved ones. In fact, those he cared for controlled him in a sense, as he loved them so much that he would never allow any harm to befall them. I was honored and deeply touched when he told me that I now fell into that category.

Those closest to him at times referred to him as "The Ghost." His thoughtfulness, gentleness, and kindness blended with the predator lying just under the surface to create a unique human being. All people get incensed when a wrong is perpetrated on a loved one. That is an expected reaction. We can all become overwhelmed with hate or rage when a loved one is harmed. Yet some, like Frank and his father, were able to feel those dark emo-tions even when it was not their own loved ones who were being harmed, but any innocent human being—especially a child.

Emmett once told Loretta, "I have seen, under certain cir-cumstances with Frank, a mental change come over him—a cer-tain look—that even frightened me a little—because I could see myself in him." Sean commented, "Frank may seem like a warm and fuzzy bear, but I wouldn't want him mad at me. At times he seems more dangerous than some of my Bond enemies." He was

100

indeed an enigma. Those who met him could immediately sense his inner strength and were cautious of him. In the year I knew him, before his confession to me about his hidden career, I grew to love him as one of my dearest friends, and I would never, ever have surmised that he would be capable of even hurting a fly. The only side of him that I and others involved in his teaching and music worlds ever experienced was, in fact, the warm, fuzzy bear that Sean described.

Frank wrestled for a long time with whether or not to tell me about this other career of his and feared I might not want to speak to him anymore if he did. When he had finally decided that I should know, he sent me a very humorous yet mysterious note of introduction to pique my curiosity and make me feel like begging him for an explanation, as he so often did. He wrote, "It is obvious to me that another can of worms is about to be opened. Those wiggly little guys will soon be all over the place. One of them will carry with it the possibility that my involvement with my father's world was more tangible than first presented to you. We have gone out of our way to show you that I am such a great and friendly member of society. But what if there are some 'flaws' in that description?" He then promised me an explanation the next day, and so began the tales of a Frank Mitchell I could never have imagined existed.

Frank began his first story with a brief explanation.

A "mark" is the person to be eliminated with "extreme prejudice" (meaning, of course, assassinated). In 1960, I was 24 years old. My father introduced me to a branch of our Secret Service that deals with "problems that cannot be solved through mutual discussion." Now that isn't their official name, obviously, just my way of presenting their project descriptions. This branch was officially referred to as the Assassin's Corp.

This was five years before the untimely demise of Pastor Marco. I was already a paid Assassin for our government when I was told of Loretta's horrific experience. First, there was a training period during which I received firing range practice with my Beretta 9 mm friend. I learned procedures for pricking the skin with a small needle containing a drug that indicated to a pathologist simply that the person died of a heart attack. I also learned the uses of other poisons, but I never used them. Then, I was provided with false identifications, credit cards, cash for incidentals like travel and hotel, etc. Finally, I was introduced to Anton Panzanos, Sergio Marcello, and Luciano Cosimo.

These three men would become my lifelong friends. We worked a total of 177 "events" together. My personal account, including these 177, is somewhere over 240 marks. Our main targets were drug dealers, pedophiles, and severe domestic situations where the husband, usually the husband, was so abusive as to threaten the wife and children's lives. Nonetheless, there were three women who fell into that category—believe it or not. By the way, when you read that someone important has died of a heart attack, well, take that with a grain of salt. Most of the time, that's true, but there is a 25 percent chance that our government actually eliminated them.

Frank continued:

My first assignment was with the above three friends in New York City, downtown Manhattan. We were to act as if we were delivering a valuable order of morphine and cocaine. We were kept waiting by the drug dealers for about an hour. Then, in came three men. One stood by the door, one by a row of windows, and one at a desk. Cosimo placed the stash on the desk.

I stood behind Cosimo. Panzanos placed himself between the door and window men, and Marcello remained seated over in a far corner. Our instructions were to eliminate all of these "gentlemen."

As the discussions and supposed negotiations dragged on a little too long, we knew that they had no intention of paying up, but what did it matter? As I stood behind Cosimo, I saw a pair of shoes sticking out about an inch under a window curtain. I made eye contact with my two men who could see me, who then silently transferred my message to Cosimo, who was looking away from me. This look indicated that there was someone else in that room, and the responsibility for that person fell to me. As the main guy blabbered on, I made a start signal, followed by me shifting my weight. That shift was the signal to begin a ten countdown, and then we drew our pistols. I took out the man behind the curtain and the one at the door. Cosimo took the man at the desk, and the man by the window was taken down by all of us. The entire action took approximately 15 seconds. We then scooped up the stash as well as the money and sauntered out of the bar. We used silencers on our weapons, always, of course.

Strange as it is to say it, I enjoyed every minute of it. I was especially proud of myself as I got into the car and lit Cosimo's cigar. My hands were steady as a surgeon's. Thus began my life in this underworld that I cherish to this day. I was part of a team that eliminated some of the worst scum on the planet. I do not have any remorse, guilt, or sadness concerning any event in which I had a part. These people most likely would have escaped the law. We have a very poor track record in this country of prosecuting the bad guys. Their lawyers are too good. In some cases, we took out the lawyers as well. Two days later, I was back home directing Bach's "Cantata 150" featuring some Northern Virginia Churches' combined choirs. All my working life, transitioning from assassin to teacher, choir director, and family man allowed me to be a human being again. Over the years, I found I could move from Dr. Jekyll to Mr. Hyde with ease and have loved every minute of it. I do not apologize. I claim that the good Frank makes up a little for the bad Frank. But then, that's my rationalization.

Frank explained that the US government had become very distressed with pedophiles in America, as they or anyone should. It was so difficult to prove it in those days. These people were not the random, sick individuals we hear about on television or in the newspapers. These were the ones who were known to abduct children and abuse them or sell them as sex slaves internationally. They belonged to groups so organized that to catch them at it was almost impossible. Also, even if they were caught by chance or luck, they had so much money available to them for lawyers that a conviction was often out of the question. There were no DNA tests, kids wouldn't testify if they were found alive, or their families wouldn't let them do so out of embarrassment or fear, so the CIA turned to organized crime for assistance.

The elite few that they hired to rid the world of this scum of the earth became known as the Assassin's Corps. They were paid at least ten thousand dollars per contract, with the Mafia getting a percentage of it. In those days, that was big money. Nineteen fifty through 1967 were the busiest years for those contracts. Frank would receive cash and pictures of the victims—often children— often badly bruised or torn or beaten and sometimes dead. He would also be given the name and address of the pedophile. Once he had the information in his hands, the pedophile had approximately two weeks to live.

After the hit, the body would often be left in the home of another pedophile as a warning, much like the guy in the film *Godfather I* who woke up with the horse's head in his bed. The child abuse was horrific, as it goes without saying. When Frank was in his twenties, Emmett had shown him pictures of some of the little children who had been assaulted. Frank told me simply that he wouldn't want me or anyone else to see them.

For over thirty years, Frank was a paid assassin, hired, through his Mafia connections, by the CIA. As it was revealed to Loretta in a special private meeting in 1994 with President Bill Clinton, Frank was considered the most prolific assassin in organized American history, averaging about six marks per year. His weapon was usually his 9 mm Beretta pistol. He was an outstanding marksman. His other method of execution was the needle capsule that, when poked into your leg, for example, caused an apparent heart attack within thirty minutes. He loved his work. He hurt no innocent person, ever. He was not sadistic. Seldom did he torture. He would be given a profile of the mark, shown photos of the little children who were the victims, and be given all the information he needed to find his mark. He was flown to each city or country. He was provided with and kept for the rest of his life four valid identification packets—credit cards, driver's license, etc.—so that he could at any moment become someone else.

Loretta told me that Frank was never a danger to others in the "normal" world, only to "filthy pigs," as she called them. She said that Frank would just become a different man in certain situations and that though he was slow to anger, seeing him that way was a terrifying event. Frank gave me his thoughts on this subject. "In my strange way, I am at peace with my other being. I think these people should be 'dismissed' from society, but I know many feel that people such as myself don't have the right to make that choice of life or death and to be sure, that is a valid argument. But tell me, how many little girls grew to womanhood because I made that decision for them? The world does not miss these folks. Think of your darling grandchildren." That instantly sent chills down my spine.

As soon as Frank spoke those lines to me, I began to do some in-depth soul-searching, and frankly, I continue to struggle with this dilemma. I had always been a staunch pacifist. I had firmly believed that there is a peaceful solution to any problem and that to hurt another human being or animal, for that matter, intentionally was very wrong. To this day, my children tease me that they were not even allowed to play with toy guns, such as water guns, and that I would search to find them squirting ducks or fish instead. "How embarrassing!" they would tell me. Teaching for five years in a Quaker school had only reinforced my beliefs that there is always a peaceful way to resolve a conflict.

Now, here I was, trying to imagine how I would feel and how I would behave if someone even tried to hurt my children or grandchildren. Would I be capable of killing another human being? The frightening thought was that yes, perhaps I would indeed. That realization then brought into question so much of my belief system. I still consider myself an adamant pacifist, but now I understand that there might be limits to my peaceful ways. Indeed, my pondering has led me to realize that these issues are not black and white. I have discovered that I understand entirely Frank's ability to rationalize his acts as morally sound, his lack of remorse for what he did, and his loved ones thinking of him as a hero rather than a monster.

Frank explained that so many people could not fathom the US government subcontracting assassinations to the underworld, but he assured me that it was true and that such power existed. They could and did do so. He added that many Americans are naïve. They believe even today that our form of government would never condone assassinations. This naïveté made Frank want to laugh. He said that it is now and has always been one of our government's preferred forms of solving a problem. Dead means you're gone. Problem solved. He and his father were hired to "eliminate with extreme prejudice" for that reason.

As mentioned previously, Frank had already helped with a few contracts for the CIA when he killed Pastor Marco, but he was not yet considered an official member of the Assassin's Corps. That would soon come to pass. After Frank dispensed of Marco in 1965, he changed, Loretta said, or rather, he seemed to shed his outer skin. He underwent a sort of metamorphosis. She asked him many times if he always knew who he was, that he would, in fact, follow in his father's footsteps, and his answer was always "yes." No explanation, just "yes." At about that time, Emmett received a plethora of contracts from the CIA, which he would find challenging to complete independently, even though they gave him all the time he wanted. So, he went to Washington, DC, for a sit-down face-to-face with two men from a secret branch of the CIA. He told them about his son—said to them that Frank had the nerve and psychological makeup to work with him and that he had already killed more than one man. Within a month, Frank and Emmett were sitting together with the same two men. At that point, Frank came to be officially considered an assassin for the US government and worked under the code name Black Sabbath from October of 1965 until May of 1997.

When Emmett had come to him with this offer to assist the government, Frank had jumped at the chance. Over the next year and a half, he and his father assassinated more than forty-three men and women in charge of a worldwide pedophile ring. These people would have children kidnapped—often off the street—and sell them to pedophiles worldwide for large sums of money. The children would then be locked up and used as their sex slaves until they got too old, at which point they were often killed. The idea was to eliminate as many of the ring members as possible, hopefully sending a message to others that they had better change their ways or they would meet the same fate. After Emmett's death, Frank continued to work with the government to rid the world of as many of these "vermin," as they called them, as possible.

All of Frank's marks were monsters, without a doubt. As I heard his stories unfold, my black-and-white sense of morality, and the validity of the commandment "Thou shalt not kill," to which I had always clung without question, came into serious debate, as I just noted. I began to ask myself what I would have done in Frank's place and did I think it was wrong for the federal government and these hired assassins to take justice into their own hands and eliminate these people from our world. I still struggle with my answer. I know it would not be possible for me to carry out hits as Frank and Emmett did, even of the most hideous of criminals, but I now wonder how far I would go to defend myself, my family, or some other innocent victim. Hopefully, there will never be a need for me to find out.

What follows are a few examples of the type of justice Frank carried out on some very despicable characters he was asked to "eliminate with extreme prejudice." Most times, Frank simply tracked them down and shot them, but there were some instances where that just didn't seem to be enough to him—times when the marks had caused such horrific suffering to others that he wanted to "even the score" at least to whatever extent was possible.

In the mid-1960s, a "dear husband" made his wife have sex with multiple other men and women while he and their ten- and twelve-year-old daughters watched. Then later that same night, he would sometimes have sex with his own daughters. On occasion, he would kidnap a young girl who would then be sent overseas to a wealthy businessman to be his child sex slave. These horror stories had bothered the US government for years and continue to do so to this day. When apprehending these criminals seemed impossible, or when they were caught and tried but the government could not seem to convict them and send them to prison, even though they were 100 percent sure of their guilt, the federal government would at times contact their underworld "assistants" and have those individuals permanently removed from society.

In this particular case, Frank had been provided with a file on the man, studied it and the man's habits for a month, then one night went to find him in a hotel room. He rendered the man unconscious in his room and tied him securely. He had plans that went beyond merely a bullet to the head for this particular case. Frank then drove to the wife's house and introduced himself in this manner:

Good evening, "Mrs. Jones." My name is not important. I am a paid Assassin whose job it is to kill your husband this evening. I have him tied up at a local hotel, and he is heavily sedated for the moment. I know this seems difficult to believe, but if you would accompany me, I will take you to see his sorry ass all bundled up. I've decided to tell you this because I've noticed over the past month of surveillance that you seem to hate his guts? I was wondering if you would like to watch the event, or better still, shoot him yourself?

Frank continued:

The woman grabbed her coat without a word—not a word. We made it back to the room just as her "hubby" was coming around. His mouth was duct-taped, and so he could only listen as I explained to "Mr. Jones" that he was about to die and that I had invited the "Missus" to watch, or better still, to shoot him herself. Hubby looked over at the wife with much hatred but no fear as yet. Marks usually refuse to believe at first. But then, out came my 9 mm Beretta, and I handed it to the wife. It had a silencer, and now the husband was getting quite concerned, to say the least. She calmly walked over to him, gave him several personal thoughts, and told him that the first shots would remove his genitals. She removed his pants, lowered the pistol, and fired three shots, taking out his family jewels. Then, as he rolled around on the floor, she shoved the gun into his mouth and fired three more times, taking off his head. Then I drove her back home, and we never talked again.

New York City, 1968. One of Frank's dearest friends, Paolo Lazzaro, a single parent to his beautiful daughter Angel, age eight, called Frank from his hospital bed. He had suffered a heart attack when he was told that Angel had been abducted, raped, and murdered. The man who had taken her was a known pedophile. The authorities knew who he was and that he was guilty of at least four such crimes, but no proof would stand up in court. Frank described what happened next.

At his bedside, Paolo had me promise to find the man and avenge Angel's death. Of course, he knew he didn't even have to ask. I was devastated and incensed. Angel had always called me Uncle Frank. We were very close. With my dear friend Cosimo, we found the man in his bed at 2 AM.

We took him to a warehouse in Long Island and bound and gagged him. Then we pulled him up so that his arms were straight over his head. His feet were taped together. We cut away all of his clothes. Then we cut off his testicles and penis. Portion by portion, we fed them to him, making him swallow all of them. We then put a rat inside a glass jar and strapped it to his lower waist, and we left.

"I realize that this kind of behavior does put me in league with a psychopath, I suppose, but think about it," Frank concluded, "he would have gone free to continue torturing and killing innocent children. He was very wealthy and had great lawyers. It is doubtful that he would have ever been convicted. You could say I could have just shot him and achieved the same results but, but somehow that didn't seem enough to me."

Manhattan, 1972. Frank received a file on a husband who routinely beat his wife and children. In addition, the federal government also knew that he molested young girls and that he had killed at least two that they knew of. There was no proof, but there was also no doubt. Two witnesses had already been declared ineligible. After doing surveillance on this man, as they always did with their marks, Cosimo and Frank followed him to a hotel where he had rented a room for one night. This was downtown Manhattan, and they knew the area well. Keep in mind that one of their favorite "dropping-off" places was under the Brooklyn Bridge. So, they watched their mark get high at the bar—not drunk, he was too smart to do that. Then, they watched him solicit a prostitute and give her his room number. He went up ahead of her.

Frank and Cosimo had in their possession pictures of the two little dead girls that they knew for sure he had killed. The prostitute was to go up a few minutes later. As a brief digression, Frank told me he had a philosophy about the words *prostitute, whore,* etc. He didn't believe in those concepts or definitions. "Why is the man not a whore?" he asked. Good point. Now back to the story. Frank and Cosimo went upstairs before the woman and knocked on the door. He opened it, of course, expecting her, and got a surprise. They took him quietly down the stairs to the garage, put him into the car, and drove to the Brooklyn Bridge. They placed him inside a large waste barrel, showed him the little girls' pictures, and explained why they were there. They then secured the top and pushed the barrel off of the pier. It bobbled a few feet and then disappeared. Frank ended this story by telling me, "The world will not miss him."

Scenarios such as these happened an average of six times per year during the years Frank worked as Black Sabbath for our federal government. Most of the time, he preferred to use his Beretta and work quickly, but there were exceptional cases, like those just described when Frank felt the need to use other means—means that would cause his mark to suffer at least a little as compensation for what he had done.

When the idea of publishing this type of delicate information came about, it was necessary, the four told me, to get clearance from the current administration; that is to say, permission from President Obama's federal agents. Frank explained to me that one of Sean's attorneys had contacted the proper authorities. A private meeting had been held with some of them to discuss whether or not the Obama administration wanted the Assassin's Corps' existence and their activities made public. I was told that the response had been that yes, they did. They wanted this story to educate citizens about the kinds of people who were removed from our world in this manner. They also wanted to have them understand that the Corps still exists, though even more secretively than during the time Frank worked with them. Frank also told me later that, without my knowledge, they had done a background check on me, though I'm not sure what the "Feds" would have been looking for. Good that I don't have anything to hide!

All of this naturally sounded quite far-fetched to me—I was having trouble believing that our president's agents would bother with such a thing, first of all. Secondly, it seemed to me that the Assassin's Corp's existence on some level was already public knowledge. At any rate, this is what I was told, and I was also told that I was clear to continue to write about Frank and Emmett's secret line of work, but with one stipulation—Frank had to be gone before this story could be published, and sadly, that is the case.

11

Promises and Quentin Tarantino

Once Frank and Loretta had spilled their secrets about not only Loretta's year with the pastor but also about Frank's involvement in his father's career as an assassin, there was a spell of much rapid writing activity on their parts. In addition, all of them excitedly agreed that now there should be not only a book, or two books—but also a film. When they broke this news to me, I was ecstatic! Well, that is an understatement, to be sure, since Frank added, "You will have all copyright laws in your corner."

Nonetheless, Frank seemed to alternate between the excitement that his story was finally being told and a sort of sorrow or regret that he had told me so much. At one point, I asked him outright if he wanted to stop. His response was, "No, no ... we play it to the end ... no matter how many books or films. And no, I'm not sorry I put this into motion... I just get moody at times:))))) For example, after talking about it tonight, I'm back in the mood:))" Then the news just seemed to keep getting better, as Loretta told me that Sean had spoken to none other than Quentin Tarantino about directing the film, and of course, he eagerly agreed. She said he would be writing me soon. I laugh at myself about my almost giddy reaction to being told I would hear from Tarantino. I suppose the fact that I was emailing routinely with Sir Thomas Sean Connery had become old news for me by then? Things were heating up now, and I was on cloud nine.

Once the four decided that a film would be based on my book, and Tarantino accepted to direct, Frank next told me he had come up with the film name himself, and I thought it was brilliant. It would be called *Killing in 3/4 Time*. His message read as follows:

"Quentin Tarantino came to see us, and we talked about the book and the film. You will get to meet him, of course. I love his work. I'm glad he's going to do it :))"

Not too long after these revelations about my book becoming a film directed by none other than Quentin Tarantino, I opened my mail and found the following:

5/30/10
LGR, Quentin Tarantino here. Hello.
I've read all pages, and they are terrific.
We will meet by the end of the summer
to discuss the projects ... book first ... then
film. Thank you for your work and your
patience. I've waited as much as five years
to get a project started. We won't have to
wait that long. Great work... QT

I remember having trouble breathing for just a little while and reading and rereading his message. What a great feeling that was. I was ecstatic but frankly a bit intimidated about responding, however. What should I say? How should I address him? It's Quentin Tarantino! When I answered, I began by asking him how he preferred I call him. His response immediately put me at ease and made me smile. He also updated me on Frank and Mickey's health and a few exciting details about the film.

6/1/10

QT is just fine. I've seen Frank a few times. They take him on car rides to get him out, but he is quite ill. Mickey does better and will probably live longer than F. I know they plan on flying you out mid-summer ... BTW... I've been talking to Anthony Hopkins, to be Frank in the film. I think that would be a good match. I'll visit more later... Be well. QT.

I got quite a chuckle out of QT—how clever. Anthony Hopkins! Wow, that would be an excellent match for Frank! I asked who had thought of Mr. Hopkins—him or Sean or Frank himself. QT's response was as follows. In addition to answering my question, QT provided quite a bit more detail concerning not only actors for the film but proof of Frank's secret career. (Apparently, Mr. Tarantino has a penchant for initials):

AH was my choice. Frank never got used to the idea that anyone would make a film about him. It will be in documentary form. With the help of the "Feds," we now have pictures of some of the debris he left behind. One of his "Marks" was a world-known assassination and will amaze even the strongest of hearts. His mistress will play herself. Loretta will be played by Jennifer Tilly, at least at this writing. I will send along bits and pieces of this kind of information for you to enjoy. I can't reveal the mystery "Mark." just yet. QT

While I had Quentin's attention, I decided to ask him more about how business works in his world since, despite all my excitement concerning the film, I still had no contract and no compensation. His insight was quite helpful and appreciated.

6/2/10

In our business, it can happen tomorrow or next year... never resign anything until you see our contracts. As I mentioned, I've sometimes waited up to 5 years to start something I thought would happen next month. So just continue your life as though we don't exist until the phone call comes. It's a tough way to live, but we endure.

It can be a heartless and brutal business. No one cares about a person's timeline. Kill Bill 1 and 2 took seven years to begin filming, cost me a bundle... I made it back, but boy, it was tough.

Later that next week, I found myself torn and intimidated again—no longer about merely talking to QT, but because he had mentioned including Frank's mistress in the film. At that point, I had had no intention of mentioning her existence. Now that I am recounting the story of the story, she will be included, but at that point, I was strongly opposed. Could I tell the legendary film director that I didn't want her mentioned? Yet, I felt I must if we were going to be working together. I wrote and explained my reasoning. This was Quentin's response:

6/7/10

I wasn't clear ... no selections other than Tony have been made. It is your book. You put in what you want, and we follow what you write. No mistress??
Then no mistress. I hadn't given it much thought until you spelled it out. I liked your thinking. Just go with your instinct.:)) Never mind us ... you just write.

I was delighted with his thoughtful response. It had been quite a week, I must say, as just a few days prior, I had opened my email to find the following:

Anthony Hopkins <************************>
06/04/10 at 10:41 AM
Lynda,

Tony Hopkins. Your address was passed by Quentin. I've read [the introduction to] your manuscript, and I found exciting reading. I had met with Frank before his illness took control. I had time to watch and listen to him. He is a very interesting man. The story is incredible, thanks to your writing. You can't believe how many silly scripts are wandering about the countryside ... yours was refreshing.

It will be some time before we meet... But meet we shall. The pleasure will be mine.

Enjoy your summer... regards... Tony

What? An email from none other than Anthony Hopkins now? And such a sweet, kind email! I responded, expressing my joy and surprise about finding his message. I asked if he would be interested in reading what I had written to date, which was far more than what he had in the introduction, and if he would be kind enough to critique it for me. He responded with much humor, and I liked him immediately.

To Lynda Graham-Rowe
06/05/10 at 9:50 AM
I chatted with QT about your manuscript. Both of us have a ritual of dealing with one project in our mind at a time. We are not as smart as women who can think of several subjects at

once. :)) Let's wait until my plate is clean, and then I will ask you to send your material. I am pleased with your interest. Best regards... Tony

My next correspondence from Tony came the following week. QT had mentioned to him that I preferred not to have the mistress be part of the story, and he wanted to voice his opinion on the subject.

6/9/10

Lynda,

I visited with QT about Sasha, the mistress. I told him I agreed with you that she was not a necessary ingredient to your project. Loretta and Sasha are good friends, so it wouldn't have been a problem with her, but as you, I failed to see what this "aside" as I see it, could bring to this most unusual story.

So, stick to your guns and just write away. You know Frank better than any of us, so who are we to wonder.

Sasha, to her credit, has been a very loyal friend to the entire group... She is not chasing after money or fame. She just loves Frank and wants to be in his life.

More later... Tony

Having now been told by QT to "just write" and by Tony that he would ask me to send my manuscript once he had time, I started pushing hard to finish my first draft. I was now picturing a book to write and how it would be interpreted by Quentin in a documentary format film. He had already taken steps toward its creation. I felt the need to work as quickly as possible, especially since Frank was slowly but steadily deteriorating, and I wanted him to be able to read the finished product before he left us. The school year had ended, and I had been told by Loretta and Frank, as well as QT, that plans were being made for me to come and finally visit them later in the summer. Loretta had even told me which bedroom I would have, and Sean had humorously added that they would be working on finding me a "real man" while I was there with them in Malibu. What an exciting time that was for me! I had a renewed sense of purpose, which vastly increased my ability to focus. It was time to push hard to the finish line.

12

Enter Micheline

After the untimely demise of Pastor Marco, Loretta and Frank remained in the DC area until 1980. Frank had become a highly regarded choir director and singer, and he was in demand. He was also busy with his high school teaching. Loretta was doing volunteer work of various sorts through their church, and she was busy raising their family. Their son was born in 1970 when their daughter was six years old. Life was good once again, and their love was strong.

In 1980, they decided it was getting too expensive to live on the East Coast, so they moved to Cozad, Nebraska. Frank continued his career there, teaching, directing, and singing, including performing in such musicals as *Fiddler on the Roof.* In 1986, they moved to Minden, Nebraska, where Frank finished his teaching career ten years later. He and Loretta were married for over fifty years, and their love for each other never stopped growing. Their relationship may qualify as a bit unusual to many, but it was solid as a rock. Frank and Loretta moved to Lincoln, Nebraska, in 1996 after Frank retired, and he then began substitute teaching in October of 1997. He was with Lincoln Public Schools for over thirteen years.

While Frank and Loretta had been busy building their life together in Washington, DC, Sean had been busy building his film career and trying to make his relationship with Diane, now the mother of their son, Jason, work out for the best. In the long run, that was not to be. Their marriage at times seemed to be more of a business deal than a loving, committed relationship. Certainly, it was complicated. Diane was also trying to build a career in film on her own terms, and this was often made more difficult in the shadow of her husband, James Bond, 007.

Adding to the difficulty of understanding just what kind of relationship they had was that, for some reason, throughout Diane's marriage to Sean, she seemed to accept his love and continuing relationship with Loretta. In fact, she and Loretta were themselves very close and remained in contact for many years after she and Sean divorced. Diane always knew, it would seem, that the love that Loretta and Sean had was immeasurable, and she accepted it, much as Frank had accepted it, almost as a fact of life. Loretta and Sean were intimate even when he was dating Diane and she was dating Frank. They went to bed when Loretta visited him and Diane at their home in California, with her knowledge and consent. The chemistry between them was not to be denied, and Diane, strange as it may seem, gave them her blessing, as had Frank.

Loretta and Diane's friendship had always been strong, but after 1965, after Loretta's "Year," when she visited the Connerys in their home, they found themselves especially drawn to each other. Sean didn't know about Loretta's horrendous year yet. He didn't know that Pastor Marco had tried to humiliate Loretta by forcing her to have sex with women. He didn't know that, as noted earlier, Marco's plan had backfired and that Loretta had instead come to realize that she enjoyed being with women as well as men. What Sean remembered was that Loretta had, on several occasions when they were dating, expressed her distaste for lesbian activities. So he thought it was very strange indeed when he came home one evening and found Diane and Loretta in bed together, giggling like schoolgirls. They greeted him together with, "Hi, darling! Welcome home! Come on in, the water's fine!" followed by Loretta adding, as Sean crawled into bed with them, "You forgot your trunks!"

By 1970, Sean and Diane were on their way to divorce, and they were no longer sleeping together. Sean says that during that period, he would have casual sex with women such as his secretary or women in his films, that sort of thing, but never anything that could be deemed an affair to his way of thinking. It was just a matter of sexual release. By 1971, their marriage was nearly over, though she and Sean still lived together. Sean was introduced to Micheline (Mickey) Roquebrune, a French painter specializing in portraiture, by none other than Diane herself. She had commissioned Micheline to paint her and Sean in loving poses.

Mickey recalled that Diane had wanted the paintings for posterity as a sort of history of what she once thought was a great love story. Sean had agreed to go along with the idea since he had promised her he would, in return for a favor she had granted him a few years before. So the paintings were commissioned, Mickey accepted the work, and that is how Micheline Roquebrune entered into Sean Connery's world, not on the golf course as some have conjectured in the past. They ultimately spent a great deal of time golfing together, but that is not how they first met.

Now it so happened that Loretta was visiting Sean and Diane the week that the portraiture work started. Mickey told me that Loretta would sit off to the side and watch Sean and Diane in beautiful poses. Then she began to comment about style and positions and lighting, and Mickey said she got some excellent ideas from her. By the third day, Loretta and Mickey had become close friends, Mickey was feeling a strong and tangible attraction to Sean, and Loretta had a good seat for noticing that Sean and Mickey were checking each other out. Complicated goings-on, to be sure. Loretta leaned over to Mickey at one point and said, "He's incredible in bed." Mickey replied, "Shush! I need to concentrate. He is so gorgeous!" Then the fourth day, Loretta leaned over and said, "I think it's time we put a plan into operation. It will be easy to get you into his bed. She has her own boyfriend, and I've met him. I'll get her into town to shop, and since her new love lives near where we will be..."

So Loretta came up with a plan for allowing Mickey and Sean to go to bed together if they so desired, and she, at least, was sure they did, but it didn't work out exactly that way. Mickey described her first romantic encounter with Sean like this: "As just noted, I first met Sean when I came to their house to paint Diane and him. Loretta was married to Frank, but she would come to California occasionally to spend time with those two. Loretta's visits would give Diane a chance to slip away to see her boyfriend more discretely. (What a life!)

One day, Sean and Diane overheard me saying my back was bothering me from painting for so long. Diane seized the moment to suggest that they take a break and told Sean that he should give me a full body massage. Then she just hopped up and left! This same scenario occurred more than once. Each time, Sean would have me lay on the massage table and give me the most incredible body work-over. Now, I was always utterly naked under the towel, but even so, the first two times, he never made any sexual advances... Damn!

The third time, however, it all changed. As I lay on my tummy and Sean was working on the backs of my legs under the towel, I felt his hands moving higher up the back of my body, and before I knew it, I was on my back, and his mouth was on me! Then we moved to several different positions for intercourse, but there was no orgasm on his part yet. This was followed by more oral sex for me. After that, it was my turn to go down on him, then back to him on me, etc. In total, that first time together, he had three orgasms, and I lost count. That first 'experience' with Sean lasted three hours. It was incredible, and here we are!

Many stories have been told about how Sean and Mickey first met, and they all center around their mutual love for the game of golf. That they both loved the game and played it often together is undoubtedly true, but that they first met and fell in love while playing golf is not. Their first encounters were of a far more intimate nature. Time passed, and the relationship continued. Once Sean and Mickey realized they were very much in love, they also realized that they needed to discuss his and Loretta's relationship. As explained earlier, Loretta and Frank had had, long before their marriage, a similar conversation that they liked to call the "800 lb. gorilla" talk. They had come to terms with the fact that Sean and Loretta would not, at that point, be good marriage partners. Yet, their love for each other was so strong and passionate that they also felt the need to see each other and continue their intimate relationship at times. This arrangement had been just fine with and even expected and encouraged by Frank and Sean's first wife, Diane. But how would Mickey feel about the whole thing? She and Loretta had also become very close, but would she feel comfortable sharing her husband with Loretta? As their relationship headed for marriage, Mickey and Sean both thought it was time to talk openly about this significant issue.

Mickey shared this story with me.

I remember that night before Sean and I were married when we had our version of the "800 lb. gorilla" talk concerning Loretta. Loretta, Sean, Frank, and I were really making a friendship of our group. Yet you only had to watch Sean and Loretta at our get-togethers to see the truth. It was so obvious they were in love. Then one night, when we were out on the town, Sean and Loretta were talking to each other, and I caught Frank smiling at me and then nodding me out to the dance floor. I can still remember much of what he said to me. It went something like this: "Don't be bothered by those two. We are loved completely by them. I believe you can love two people at the same time and that love is different from person to person. I am actually comforted by watching their love. And I am comfortable watching and experiencing the love between Loretta and me and Sean and you. They are both just different events."

I answered quickly that I agreed. I admitted to Frank that it had taken me a while to accept this lifestyle until I really knew Sean loved me deeply and truly wanted me as his wife. I went on to say that I was looking forward to the years and friendships ahead. Then I said what now stands as a very funny line! I said, "What if you and I also fell in love down the road?" Frank answered quickly, "I'm not going to rule that out. I find you so amazing. I'm not sure I'm not already in love with you. I think our not seeing each other often stays those emotions. Let's see how it plays out."

Mickey concluded, smiling, "Well, it's played out!"

Later that same evening, when Sean and Mickey got back to his apartment, Mickey told Sean about the discussion she and Frank had had on the dance floor. She started by telling him that she had heard about the "800 lb. gorilla story" as Frank had so aptly named it and thought they should have one also. Mickey told him it was evident that he and Loretta were deeply in love but that it wasn't a problem for her as long as she was a part of his emotional playing field.

Sean's answer went something like this:

Loretta and I have been in love since 1959. [It was now 1975.] Mitchell knows it and even invited me into his life. I was given carte blanche to love Loretta, make love to Loretta, write or call her, whatever. Since my first marriage and divorce, I've called her at least once a week. I flew her to our home in California to spend some time with us, and Diane was pleased with this arrangement. There were five visits from Loretta while I was married to Diane. Her visits included sex of all combinations. You can't imagine how amazed, pleased, and excited I am to see that you have taken Mitchell and Loretta into your heart as well. But if it's your wish, I will break off that arrangement and not continue my relationship with Loretta. Loretta and I enjoy being together but would never make a good married couple. It's just not in the cards. We know it. We accept it.

I love you, and I'm in love with you. I want to spend the rest of my life with you. My love for you is different from my love for Loretta. It's hard to explain, but in no way are you playing second fiddle. I await your thoughts.

Mickey responded, "Thank you for that, and I believe it and accept it, and it actually excites me. The truth is, I think that, as much and deeply as I love you, I could fall in love with Frank also, and I think that just for the hell of it, I'm going to try and get him to love me so that we can be a real foursome. So, we do not have a problem. On the contrary, I think we have an incredible setup for a very exciting marriage! We shall say no more."

Sean was delighted. They made love and went to sleep. Mickey later told Frank about that conversation, and Sean told Loretta, and everyone was thrilled. I must add here that the four of them sure made it sound simple! They are the only ones I have ever known who could make such an arrangement work, with all four of them happy and no one jealous or feeling left out. I do believe that it is possible to love more than one person simultaneously and that there are varying degrees of love. There is also a clear distinction between loving someone and being *in love* with someone, as we all know. So, I agree with Frank and the others that each love is different somehow—that they are "separate events" that sort of parallel each other. But to experience those separate events simultaneously is not something most people can do. We seem to be programmed to be monogamous. It can be serial monogamy, of course. Still, most of us have trouble tolerating our partner sleeping with someone else, let alone being perfectly happy with and even encouraging the situation. The bottom line, though, is that it worked out splendidly for the four of them.

The years passed. Sean and Mickey were married, and Sean Connery continued to climb the ladder to fame and fortune, quickly becoming the international star that he remains to this day, but now it was with Mickey happily by his side. Frank and Loretta continued building their life together also. They were all quite busy with careers and family and had little time to get together as they had in the past. Their friendship continued uninterrupted but was relatively quiet from 1980 till 1990. The primary contact was between Sean and Loretta, who would visit each other and talk on the phone regularly. In the early '90s, the four began to see each other quite often once again, and by 1996 they were back to a very dynamic relationship. By the year 2000, their friendship was at full steam once more, and they didn't look back. For eight years, from 2000 until November of 2008, Loretta traveled back and forth to California several times per year for one- to three-week vacations with Sean and Mickey, and at least three times per year, Sean and Mickey came to visit Frank and Loretta in their home in Lincoln, Nebraska. It was, from beginning to end, a pact of unbreakable bonds.

13

Secrets

We return now to our point of departure, Thanksgiving weekend, November of 2008. Frank and Mickey, with great sadness but with determination and peace in their hearts, had just told Sean and Loretta about "The Plan." When they were both gone, they wanted Sean and Loretta to honor their wishes and be together—finally, and to be married.

Laughter about their poorly hidden relationships was interspersed with quite a few tears that night, tears of sadness as they realized that too soon, two of the four would be gone. For now, though, they were all four together, and the bond they had always shared grew even stronger. Never have I known four people who seemed to share such a powerful love for each other.

Shortly after the four discussed "The Plan," they decided that Loretta would move to California to be with Sean and Mickey right away rather than waiting for Frank in Lincoln while he finished the school year. Nebraska winters are often harsh, and Loretta was having serious breathing problems from the cold, dry air. Also, she was finding day-to-day life in California to be much more enjoyable than in Nebraska. Not a big surprise there. Even if there are, of course, many beautiful things about Nebraska, it pales, at least in my mind, to life in Malibu, California. Frank would visit them often, but he did not want to give up substitute teaching until he had to do so, or so he told me at that point in the story. I would soon discover that wanting to continue his teaching was not the only reason he didn't want to leave. Before I continue their story, I feel compelled to explain and clarify what I mean by the four of them being so close and sharing so much love, as I would not want to mislead anyone. Mickey and Sean obviously had an intimate relationship, as did Frank and Loretta. Sean and Loretta had been intimate since they first met in 1958. In addition, however, Loretta and Mickey, both of whom enjoyed sex with other women as well as men, were also intimate. Mickey told me that during the first real conversation between herself and Loretta, the two of them had begun to talk about sex almost at once. She asked Loretta if it was difficult to be around her since she was with Sean, and she knew that Loretta also loved him intensely and had such a history with him. She said she found Loretta's answer to be "marvelous." Loretta said, "I get excited to be with you, and the fact that you have had sex with 'James' drives me wild. I may even want to watch the two of you in bed—without his knowledge, of course, as both these guys are kind of straight, as you know." Mickey said she laughed so hard and told Loretta that she would arrange that scene, and no, they wouldn't tell him. Then Loretta told Mickey to feel free to have sex with Frank if it should "be there." She also told Mickey that she wanted to have sex with *her*. Mickey said she was blown away because she thought each request was a terrific idea. She and Loretta were in bed later that week, and they were inseparable from then on.

Both women realized that they differed significantly from the norm. Not many women have these kinds of conversations, that is certain. When Loretta and Frank kept Mickey company when Sean was on location, Loretta would leave the door to their bedroom unlatched, and Mickey said she would sneak in and watch them make love. Loretta would wave at her when Frank was down on her. Once, she even motioned for Mickey to get her something to drink. So, Mickey got some tea and put it beside her bed. Frank was too busy down there to even notice. Mickey also knew that those two had had threesomes with Dianne, and she and Loretta talked about this happening with them. But Mickey also recalled that at that time, Sean was getting quite busy with his career, and the early years passed so quickly that it never materialized until the very recent past. Mickey added that she and Loretta just always thought about life the same way.

Mickey continued her discussion with me about her feelings concerning sex, saying,

Loretta and I have no jealousy concerning with whom our men are in bed, as long as we like the person. For example, when I was on location with Sean for the film "Entrapment," it was I who told Sean and Catherine that their intercourse scene looked phony, and why not just do it and let the film editors chop it up. The film editors were delighted beyond belief. So, the next time they filmed that scene, I directed it. I sat almost on top of them and instructed them to do this or do that and when and where. It took several days of those two screwing each other to get it right, and there is a copy of a beginning, middle, and end to them making love. It didn't make the theaters that way, of course, but we have the film as a gift from the film editors.

They asked me about my lack of jealousy, and I said, "I love Catherine. She's my friend. I don't care if Sean has sex with someone I like." They were just shocked, even for Hollywood types. Frank would have the same response if Loretta were to make love to a friend of his or Sean's. He would think nothing of it. We all have the same philosophy on love and lovemaking.

For example—a night with two great friends, good wine, and good conversation. The fact that such moments can end up in bed is just a part of it. Frank feels the same way. The other man or the other woman has nothing to do with the spouse. It simply doesn't matter. Very few people can live this way. Their egos won't let them. I've had some one-night stands since I married Sean, and he doesn't care. I would come home from an all-night 'affair' (I had called him the evening before and said something like, "Tom and I are having great wine, great conversation, and I think we'll end up in bed.") Sean would just say, "Well, drive carefully home tomorrow." When I get in the next morning, he'll ask how the bedtime was, and I'll either say terrific or boring, or whatever, and that's all he'll ask. Loretta does the same with Frank.

Mickey concluded by explaining to me that her sex life in France was never very satisfactory. She said that the French men she was with had no idea at all how a vagina worked. She smiled and added, "I guess you can't blame them. After all, they don't have one! Most of the time, I would have to tell them to do it, and they would kiss it or stick their tongue in it for a minute and then want me back down on them. So, when I landed in bed with Sean and his way of making love, well, that was amazing! Then to have Frank do it so incredibly well also (actually, he is much better at that than Sean) was simply fantastic!"

All of this leads to the fairly obvious question—in what different combinations had these four found themselves recently? Did the two women go to bed with one of the men? Were all four of them ever in bed together? Well, up until they discussed "The Plan" on that Thanksgiving weekend of 2008, at which time Frank and Mickey confessed that they too had been having an intimate relationship for quite a few years, though nowhere near as long as Sean and Loretta, the answer was "no." There were different combinations of partners, but with only two at a time, and never were Sean and Frank even remotely interested in being together. Their bond was strong, but their love for each other was of a brotherly, platonic nature.

Not long after the November heart-to-heart talk and their true confessions, Frank and Sean started wondering how long it would be before the ladies brought up the subject of a threesome or even a foursome. One day, the two of them were sitting on the beach talking and relaxing, and Sean said, "You know, Mitchell, this new lifestyle might now open other doors concerning our two women. You and I know that those two have spent time together in bed, and now that you and Mickey have opened the final door, I thought right away that they might bring up other options with us." Frank told him he had had the very same feeling that morning as he lay there thinking of what had been happening in their lives recently. Sure enough, shortly after that, the men were summoned back to the patio for a conversation with the ladies.

Loretta began by saying, "Mickey and I want one of you to join us when it works out right." Sean replied, "As long as the odd man out isn't in the house or sent off to a movie!" Then Frank added, "That's just fine with me too, but I want to make it clear that Sean and I are selfish people and no way are we going to be in the same room together at any point and share you!" The ladies agreed, and then Sean reminded them that he had to leave for San Francisco on business the next day. Sean looked at Frank and said, "This isn't going to be fair, Mitchell, but then after you leave to go back to Lincoln the day after tomorrow, I'll have them both to myself for a couple of weeks!" Frank reached over and took some Kleenex and began dabbing at his eyes in feigned distress and sadness.

Later that night, just before they all went to sleep, Loretta asked if it was written in stone that Sean and Frank would not be interested in a *ménage à trois,* the two of them with one of the women, or a foursome. Frank recalled that he and Sean looked at each other and said they had to talk. They ran outside to the beach to discuss that one. Sean asked what Frank thought, and Frank asked what Sean thought, and then Sean asked again what Frank thought, and Frank asked again what Sean thought (kind of reminds me of my teenage years), and then Frank finally said, "I dunno—maybe if it was a really large area?" Sean replied, "Let's go ask them."

They went back in, and Frank said, "The fact that you asked about this indicates that, indeed, you think about that as well as our current 'formula.'" Mickey answered that most of the time, they want just one of them but that they had discussed having the two men with one of them or a foursome from time to time. Frank said it would have to be a really large area. He explained, "Sean and I do not want to come into contact with each other at all! And here's another problem with a foursome: There are certain events in lovemaking that I particularly enjoy. In fact, to me, intercourse is wonderful, but there are some other 'activities' which I enjoy even more. Here's the thing, ladies, I'm not going to want to venture into these activities if a man has preceded me, hmmm, in that area." Sean agreed. "So," Frank concluded with Sean's full concurrence, "I think what we have in mind if we ever do that is for us guys to alternate with you, enjoying our favorite pastimes but with no intercourse until all other 'adventures' have taken place!" They left it at that and went to sleep, thinking about what kind of an arena could be set up for such an Olympic event.

The next morning, Sean left around six a.m. The ladies were still asleep, but Frank had gotten up early to watch the sunrise.

He would have the entire day to himself with both Loretta and Mickey, and so he hummed joyfully to himself as he walked along the beach in great anticipation of what lay ahead for him later that day. At this point, I want to mention something about Frank and Sean both. They hated all and any form of pornography. They detested "girlie" magazines with a passion. They wanted no woman treated this way. Having said this, they did, as is expected, love to have sex (Yes, even at their ages. I think that is great.), and so Frank was excited about what the day might bring.

He talked about his first day with the two women he so dearly loved in this way.

Today was a wonderful time for me! I cherish the experience because I was with women I respect and love beyond measure. These are obvious things to say, to be sure, but I can't think of a better way of stating it. Now, trying to be tasteful here, I will describe our afternoon of passion. The bedroom we were in can be made to change from very bright to varying degrees of darkness. Add to that the sensual lighting and Chopin's music, and it was like a dream. I can say with dignity that we made love; we did not just have sex. The time that we took heightened the experience beyond whatever can be imagined. My medicine did not fail me. Whew! What was also special was to watch the two of them love each other and then being brought into the activity with them, always two on one in various positions. Three and a half hours later, we just lay there listening to the soft music. I was trying to be funny and said, "I can die now," but they scolded me on that one.

Later in the day, as they were sitting around talking, Loretta and Mickey told Frank that he should never worry about his medicine or performing; that it still would have been just as exciting and loving even if he had not been "up to it." Men have such egos on this subject, they explained. They have it instilled in them from a young age that manhood is dependent on performances in bed when that is far from being the most important thing. Frank told me he thought that's why men can be such lousy lovers. So often, they are focused on the wrong thing.

Later that afternoon, the ladies sent Frank off to take a nap. They wanted to continue the lovemaking through the evening and most of the night with naps in between. Frank commented, "This is how they explained it to me. Since I'm leaving tomorrow, they want to use the time wisely. I thought that was funny, but they were serious, so I stopped giggling. I hope you will appreciate that my story here is just a beautiful thing that happened to me and that you would want that for me."

That evening, Sean called to inquire as to how the day had been. At his request, Mickey was to text him when it would be a good time to call. He and Frank talked privately for about a half hour, and then Mickey and Loretta spoke with him on speakerphone. Frank and Sean talked about how relieved they were that everything was now entirely in the open and that they were looking forward to what Sean called "our best years ahead of us." Frank added here, "I'm of the same mind as the other three. I don't believe I only have eighteen months, and I plan to keep on living. I mean, look at this life I'm leading now! Why in the hell would I go and die?" He and Sean also agreed that they definitely did not want a foursome. Sean said, "I think the cognac during Saturday's conversation got our minds into some kind of overdrive. You tell 'em, Mitchell, I'm afraid to." Frank responded, "Gee, thanks."

As for the late evening and overnight, Frank put it this way, "Well, you know what goes where, so what's to say. But I do want

140

to repeat the main thing, which is that our eighteen hours were defined by acts of love and not a porno film." Frank told them of his and Sean's decision firmly against the foursome, or even a threesome with the two of them and one of the women, and he said the women laughed and said that was fine, but they kind of looked at each other and winked. He said, "Hey, no fair winking! Why are you winking?" Mickey replied, "Oh, nothing. Loretta and I certainly respect and admire you guys for standing up to your feelings." Then Loretta jumped in with, "You guys are so strong. Not many men could ignore our mouths."

The next day Sean returned, and Frank headed back to Lincoln for a while. He wanted to spend some time with his family and to continue his substitute teaching. Frank explained that they were a very close family and that the time they spent together was quite precious to them all. He added that Sean and Mickey were also close with Frank and Loretta's children. Sean was trying to plan for a family reunion of sorts in the Bahamas in March, including his son Jason, Frank and Loretta's children, their spouses, and Frank and Loretta's grandchildren. Frank said that Sean and Mickey had always wanted things to be as in a family and keep them all close. He added, "Sean and Mickey are so wonderful to my family. Gestures such as this reunion I cannot talk about without tears. There is nothing I could do to thank them, and I know they would not be pleased if I ever let them know I felt indebted."

When Frank got back to Lincoln, he let me know what had happened with Mickey and Loretta the day and night before, but then he started wondering what they might be up to with Sean. He wrote me the following humorous account of his attempt to find out. It began like this, "I called the landline. No answer. So I left the following message: 'Everyone in the room who can walk outside without being arrested, please stand up.' Okay, no response. 'Anyone in the room who can stand up ... stand up.' Still no response. And finally, 'Sean, don't forget the caution about the four-hour time limit from Cialis!' Nothing. Fine. 'Nice talking with you folks. Don't worry about me. I'll just finish off my peanut butter and jelly sandwich and warm milk, say my prayers, and go to bed—by myself. Your resident husband and friend, Frank."

He had yet to hear anything back from them when he wrote me, so I jokingly told him that perhaps they had simply all gone out to dinner. His response was, "Yeah, that's it. Dinner. Yeah, dinner. Possible. Maybe. I mean, they have to eat, don't they? Food for thought..." Frank told me later that when they did call back, finally, he said to them, "So, you guys go out for dinner?" Sean answered, "Ok, I like the sound of that—we were out to dinner." Then he turned to the girls and said, "Mitchell says we were out for dinner." Of course, they picked up on his lead, "Oh, yes, dinner—that's where we were." Then Loretta got on the line, and they said their goodnights, and once again Mickey yelled, "Wish you were here, Franky," and Frank came back with, "Nice try, Micheline, but Sean and I are committed to our position on this." Loretta and Mickey called out in chorus, "Which position is that again?" Then Frank said, "Tell them, Sean—tell them our position." By then, it was just laughter all around, so he said good night to them all. His conclusion to the story was, "Great; I can't even carry on a straight conversation with them now!"

14

The Fab Four

Thus, Sean, Mickey, Frank, and Loretta became "The Fab Four," four fabulous people all very much in love and leading an amazing existence, despite the shadow of death lurking in the background. As the months passed, they took me on an emotional rollercoaster ride, and it never stopped. Some days I would be treated with stories of their times together so funny that I laughed until I cried. Others, I would receive short notes telling me that either Mickey or Frank or both at the same time were "down." The reality of how much pain they were both enduring, of just how little time they both had left and what they would yet have to endure, left me in tears, deep sadness, a heavy weight on my shoulders. During the first few months after "The Plan" took shape, the stories were more often lighthearted and funny, with an occasional reminder that all was not the perfect paradise that it might appear to be. But slowly, the tides turned, and the illnesses and impending death took over the spotlight, in spite of tremendous effort on all their parts to look on the bright side.

Reality first started to take hold for me in the spring of 2009, when Mickey was working on painting some portraits of all of them, which I will describe in greater detail later. She told me that she hoped she would be able to finish them. Her hands were starting to shake more and more, and soon painting would no longer be possible. She then explained that she thought of the two of us as having been "distorted," referring to our surgeries and various debilitating treatments for cancer. Still, Frank often used this quote from DaVinci that helped her feel better. "Nothing has beauty until it has been distorted." She then managed some humor and told me, "You and I have both been distorted to a point, and to have men still want us is Gold ... Finger (a little joke if I may)." During that same period, Sean also wrote to me about the portraits and said he feared they would be her last.

Late that spring, Frank seemed to be holding up better than Mickey, at least to me. Still, he started getting report after report from the doctor that his white cell count was climbing unchecked, despite the massive doses of chemo pills and other medications he was taking. He explained a little of what was going on with him physically. "Blood count at 53,500—not too much of a raise this week. The doctor says that if it goes into the 60's, then my lifestyle will change somewhat. As to how I feel? Well, OK. As usual, the day is my best time, but now the nights are getting more difficult to negotiate. I get what I describe as full-body nausea—almost a tired flu-like feeling that comes on me around 7 PM and goes through the night. It actually helps for me to get up early and go substitute teach somewhere—the physical activity keeps me feeling better." It was rare for Frank to even give me a glimpse into his world of illness and pain, so this vision of him so ill every night hit me hard. Yet, as was always the case with him, he would not dwell on the subject. He ended this time by saying, "Enough of that! How are YOU?"

Despite Frank's explanation, the seriousness of his illness was still somewhat unreal to me. How could he be that sick when he was always, unfailingly, in good spirits and far more concerned about others than himself? That is until one day at school when he was substitute teaching for one of my colleagues. I peeked my head into his classroom to see why he wasn't joining us for lunch. He would never really eat much as so many foods at that point were difficult for him to digest and would simply make him sick, but it was always a time of fascinating conversations, and we all looked forward to them. He was sitting in the dark at his desk, his back turned to me, and he was very still. I asked if he was doing all right and told him we were missing him at lunch. He turned to me and managed to answer, "I'll be OK. I just took some medicine. But I need a few minutes. I'll see you in a bit."

When sometime later he finally emerged from the room, his face was the brightest red I have ever seen on anyone, enough so that it truly scared me. He managed to finish his teaching day (he was a very courageous man) but left without saying goodbye, something he had never done before, so I knew he was having a tough time. I was frightened and genuinely concerned for the first time that day. Facing the truth of the situation was not easy, and in spite of Frank's unfailing sense of humor about the whole thing, I found myself thinking more and more about how much pain they were both in constantly and how the end might be drawing near.

In the fall of 2008, the doctors had told both Mickey and Frank that they had about eighteen more months to live. By spring of 2009, they had both taken their turns for the worse and been told they had significantly less time than that. Sean said the doctors were now saying that Mickey, at best, would make it another year. Frank's doctor, strangely, gave his honest gut feeling as being about the same. Frank added, "The doctors say my heart is taking a beating. I have had one heart attack, a stent put in, and a blood pressure problem that keeps me at marginal numbers. Their thinking is that my heart may kill me before the leukemia does, although it is a combination of the two, of course. I don't mean to sound so morbid, but Mickey and I talk freely about our futures.

It is only difficult for our spouses, families, and close friends, like you." Thankfully for both of them, it turned out that they far outlived those doctors' estimates, but both were nonetheless often in much pain.

Summer came around, and "The Four" had big plans for doing some traveling, their last as a foursome, they guessed. They tried to leave. They had the trips all planned. But Mickey would get sick as soon as she started to travel, so the plans were canceled. Frank, however, seemed to be feeling better again, and in the fall, he decided that he even wanted to continue with some substitute teaching, though for just a few chosen teachers and not too often. I was surprised but delighted, of course, and when I needed to be gone for a half day in September of 2009, I asked him to cover my classes. He was happy, I was delighted, and my students were thrilled to know that Mr. Mitchell was coming back. I checked with him the day before my absence. He said his latest blood work showed not such good news—his red cells were now starting to disintegrate as well as the white ones, yet he said he felt good and was looking very much forward to being at school the next morning for me.

That was not to be, however. By that same afternoon, Frank was quite ill. He managed to text me that his body was "letting him down a little" and that he was sorry, but he would not be able to substitute for me. He was headed for the hospital for some outpatient treatments. The outpatient visit turned into an overnight stay. He told me his red and white cells were now "attacking" each other and that the doctors said his health would begin to deteriorate markedly over the next few months. He added, "So… so be it. It was a great run I had in life! I have very few regrets. We just need to sit and talk again soon. Love you."

By the next evening, however, he phoned me and said he was feeling better and that he and Loretta, who had flown into Lincoln to be with him as soon as she had been told what was happening, would be flying back to California the next day. He wanted to get some rest surrounded by his loved ones and aided by the sounds and smell of the ocean, which he so much enjoyed. I told him I had been terrified, and he said, "I told Him I'm not ready yet. I still have a lot to do." For both Frank and Mickey, the pattern seemed to be that they would feel pretty well for a while, then they would be "down" for a time, and then they would bounce back to a certain extent.

This must have happened a half dozen times for each of them between the time we began our friendship and the fall of 2009. However, I noticed that slowly there were more and more down times that lasted longer and fewer and fewer of the good times. Reality was rearing its ugly head more and more, and I was helpless to change that for them. Watching, even from a distance, was so very difficult for me. For Sean and Loretta, it was an unfathomable nightmare. Nonetheless, they continued to try and steal as much happiness out of each day as possible. They were alive, and every moment was precious to all four of them.

Late in March of 2010, Mickey wrote to me concerning Frank's health. She explained it to me this way, "Frank will lie to you. He is not fine. He hurts continuously. As I understand it from the doctors, leukemia patients endure severe tiredness, nausea, and, because the blood is so thin, joint pain. He has medication, but it doesn't do enough. He sees cancer patients like you and me all the time at the oncology lab. He sees or hears of the invasive treatments we undergo, and he always talks about not having to go through all of that as we did. He says he is lucky. But he hurts. He bleeds so easily now. Food attacks his spleen. All of it together makes every day difficult. So, I'm warning you, when you ask him how he's doing, he will automatically say 'super,' and it's not true. But, ask anyway. We do."

What was remarkable, fascinating, and not at all depressing to watch during those difficult months was how Mickey and Frank lived their lives, however much time they had left. They consistently and unfailingly lived each day to its fullest, fighting through the physical pain and fatigue and seeing the beauty of each moment. It is how I want to be living my life, and I do try, but they were succeeding in living each day, each moment as if it were their last because they realized that it might be. Along with Sean and Loretta, they continued to love and make love, laugh, and joke as best they could, and I found this to be the embodiment of how life should be lived. I had the highest admiration and respect for all four of them, and I came to love them as part of my family. Many of the stories to follow will bear witness to their persistent and consistent "joie de vivre."

I begin with the amusing story of Loretta's confessions as to when she and Sean resumed their intimate relationship after their respective marriages to Mickey and Frank.

Loretta recalled,

Sean and I saw each other very little between 1962 and 1985, and we missed each other tremendously. In January of 1985, I wanted to go to Las Vegas, as did Sean. We were all four in California at the time. We sat around and talked about it for some time. Frank and Mickey didn't want to go because we stayed so long. Sean and I loved it there. He liked playing poker, and I enjoyed watching. Frank and Mickey enjoyed it for a couple of days, but then they would be washed out. I think Mickey said, "Well, why don't the two of you just go for as long as you want?" Frank would be busy with a musical when the two wanted to go, so no way could he have gone even if he had wanted to do so. He joined in with Mickey and agreed, Of course! You two go." They looked at us and then each other, and we went through the usual "are you sure that's OK with you" routines, and by that time, Mickey and Frank were insisting.

So, off we went. We flew down. We stayed four days, each in our own room. We really had a good time, but we could tell we were going out of our way to keep out of trouble, like not going together into one of our rooms or having too much to drink under soft lights, all of that. We just forced ourselves to stay with the bright lights. We made it through the four days, but we later discussed how difficult it was to do so and that we'd better not do that again. We both professed our love for our spouses. Sean adores Mickey, and I adore Frank. It was never a matter of needing to fill a need. Nothing was missing in our marriages. We were as happy as you can be. We resolved to never go to Vegas alone again.

But July came, and we were back there again! Mickey and Frank had insisted that we take advantage of a great Vegas offer. Mickey saw it in the paper, and Frank agreed that it was too good to pass up. So, we went. This time Sean picked me up in his car. We talked very little from Lincoln to Vegas. We knew very well what was going to happen. I stood behind him at check-in, and he got one room. I didn't protest or say anything. We went to the room, unpacked our bags, showered together just like old times, and within no time, the ritual of 1959 was once again performed. We talked about our love for two people. At the same time, we were hoping that Frank, who had now flown to California to stay with Mickey, was doing the same thing with her.

We know now they weren't—not yet anyway. Our first morning back was hell on earth. We felt so guilty! Sean and I could hardly speak. (We also know now that they both felt sorry for us all that time and that they could tell immediately that we had been together and didn't care, but they said nothing). For the next twenty-plus years, we repeated this scene from time to time, and it was wonderful. Sean and I had a life with both of the people we loved. Of course, the guilt was there, but we rationalized the hell out of it by saying it wasn't really cheating because we loved them as much as we loved each other. So last Thanksgiving, Sean and I learned the truth. Frank and Mickey had been laughing at us for years and had also started to make love. We had a real crying and apology scene, but those two wanted nothing to do with the apologies from us. Indeed! They were apologizing to us for not telling us that they had known all the time! Holy crap! They were apologizing to us! Now it's all on together. Mickey and I make love with Frank. Mickey and I make love with Sean, and of course, each of us with just our spouses. It's heaven on earth! All is open and forgiven, or whatever you call it.

A little later, Sean and Loretta found out that Frank and Mickey had not exactly been truthful about when their relationship started either. Loretta exploded,

Frank and I are having our first argument in the past 45 years! I say I'm going to hurt him, and Sean says he is going to hurt him! It seems our "boy scout" and his little partner were not entirely accurate in disclosing when they actually made it hand over hand to the bed! The new date places that event in early 1996, not this past January of 2009, as we were led to believe!! (I'm running out of exclamation marks.) Okay, Mickey gets somewhat of a reprieve as she thought Frank gave us the correct time frame when she went to the bathroom during the big Thanksgiving sit-down. After she learned that he had not been "forthcoming," she hung back not to make him look bad. Of course, in reality, thank God for us. We don't look quite so bad now. So actually, Sean and I are relieved. We've decided not to hurt Frank after all!

After Mickey and Frank finally confessed to their intimacy, we were all curious, naturally, to know about their first time together, so Mickey kindly gave us this account. Sean and Loretta were in Las Vegas on their third trip together. It was early in 1996. Frank and Mickey were having a drink on the patio. Up until that point, they had only given each other little kisses, hello and goodbye. Mickey said she was sitting there thinking about Sean and Loretta rolling around the bed in Vegas, and she was getting pretty worked up, not because the two of them were in bed together, but because she wasn't doing the same thing with Frank.

She told Frank that that just didn't seem fair. He agreed, but he was so shy in reality that he still didn't make a move over to Mickey. So, she waited until he was coming out of the bathroom, and she stood there, completely naked. He came out, and she simply said, "Take off your clothes!" Of course, he did, and then they stood there holding each other, naked as can be. Mickey slid down him to her knees and began using her talented mouth on him. Then he put her on her back and began a tour of her body with his hands and tongue. Almost an hour later and four or five orgasms in the "ten" range, as Mickey called them, Frank decided it was time to go in, literally. Mickey said he had the neatest way of putting his hands under you and pulling you up into him. She added, "Now here's the thing; it's exactly how Sean does it! What, did they read the same book or something?"

She continued, "In 1996, Frank's energy and stamina were noteworthy. He and Sean were both such powerful men, and that keeps the woman from needing to work very hard if that makes sense. Now both of these guys, when given a private home with room to roam, will spend as much as seven or eight hours off and on making love, resting, then another position or 'event,' rest again, etc. It is so refreshing not to have a guy get rid of his fluid supply and then roll over and go to sleep, not to wake up the rest of the night, or get up and eat or leave. These two both keep it going and going until I, and the same for Loretta, wave a white flag, something I thought no man could make me do!"

Mickey told me they could still do that even then, although they both liked to use some pills to help out sometimes, but neither Mickey nor Loretta cared about that at all. Over the next several years after this first encounter of theirs, Mickey said she and Frank had sex on the beach, in the water, in the kitchen, the living room, the bathroom, in a car, in an elevator in downtown Los Angeles, in a vacant room in the US courthouse where she, Frank, and Loretta had gone to get some papers filed. Frank even took them both into a quiet room and "serviced" both of them. She said he was dangerous in elevators; that the idea fascinated him. He also had sex with her in the back of an auditorium at Warner Brothers film studio, the backstage of a theater on the United Artists lot, and she and Loretta both went down on Frank in those places and many, many others too numerous to mention. Mickey ended by saying that they were never caught in the act—anywhere.

15

California cottage and Sasha

Sometime in February of 2009, just a few months after that life-changing Thanksgiving 2008 weekend conversation about "The Plan," Loretta called Frank from California. She had some great news to share. She said that the dinner conversation the night before had had to do with a beachfront cottage about a half a mile down the sand, as they call it, from Sean and Mickey's home in Malibu. Sean had decided to buy it. It would be Frank and Loretta's residence for now, and Loretta's alone when the time came if she wanted. Sean and Mickey said they would prefer that Loretta just lived with them when Frank was in Nebraska, but they also wanted her to have her own little place for some independence if she needed that. And whenever Frank was in California, it would give the two of them the option for some private time away from Sean and Mickey, if they so chose.

Frank was quite excited and said, "It's the best of all worlds, really." When Loretta finished explaining, they went to speakerphone so Frank could thank them, and then he said, in a little attempt at humor, "You know, with all of this fun we're having because I'm sick, I would have to just go out and GET cancer if I didn't have it already." All he got was silence on the other end, as you can imagine. So he said, "Let's lighten up here, gang!" and he gave off a silly laugh. Then Sean told him they were tired of hearing "thank-yous" and that they only do what they want to do.

Amazing friends! As an aside, I do need to admit, however, and perhaps somewhat selfishly, that as happy as I was for Frank and Loretta, part of me kept thinking how much *I* would also appreciate a little cottage on the beach in Malibu. Frankly, any kind of compensation for the writing I had been doing for well over a year at this point would be welcomed. But of course, I kept quiet, as saying as much to Sean would have come across as extremely rude.

The next time I spoke with Frank, he continued the story about the cottage. He said,

> Sean paid for it today. Loretta and I will sign for it when I get there. It will be in our names. It's unreal, but it's happening. We will look for furniture this weekend also. Sean has placed a certain amount of money in a new bank account for us. You could say he's adopted us. [Again, I wanted to say, "And how about adopting *me* too!"] So we have a home there now! When I'm in Lincoln, Loretta will stay with them most of the time. Loretta is a considerable help to Mickey. Sean feels so much more comfortable leaving for business if Loretta is in the house with her. She gets sick from time to time. I'll finish out my subbing in Lincoln through the end of the school year. I'll teach a few days here a week and then go there for extended weekends, and our new cottage will be available whenever we want it.
>
> My doctors are in Lincoln, but I'll pick up new ones there. This is all so wonderful!

Then, as was his style, Frank threw in a bit of humor concerning the beachfront cottage. He told me,

> Loretta is in heaven! She's ecstatic, of course. The beach in front of the "cabin" leads to a deserted beach. They don't even

wear swimming suits unless they're going for a walk along the shoreline. That's not my style! I think 72-year-old men should be arrested if they do that! I also hate it when old guys go to the mall wearing beige shorts, sandals with white socks, and a floral shirt. I always worry that everyone looks at me and says, "I bet that old fart has a pair of beige shorts, sandals, white socks, and a floral shirt on his dresser right now!" These old dudes are taking me down with them!

Frank was on break from subbing for a choir director at a high school when he wrote me about the cottage. He knew that everyone, myself included, would wonder why he didn't just move permanently to California with Loretta and the others. This was his response:

I love directing. This last sentence is a clue as to why I hang around Lincoln and subbing. When I leave this "gig," my days of directing will probably be over. I've been directing music since I was fifteen when I got my first church choir directorship. If my math is holding up, that was 57 years ago. Now, I only direct a school choir as a sub about once a week, but it's something, and I love it. Lincoln is my home. My daughter lives here, etc., etc. The point I'm trying to make is that I'm having trouble just pulling up and leaving for good. I'm going to have to do it, but I'm going to drag that out until this summer.

The main question from my children and friends is, "Yes, but how do you stay away from Loretta for so long?" And, that's the problem. Of course, I'm going to move to California entirely in June. I need to enjoy the cottage life with Loretta and our two dear friends for as long as I can. But for now, since the others understand my feelings about this and Sean is willing and wanting to provide me his personal aircraft to go back and forth, I am happier this way. Yes, I tell people, my wife does miss me. But she also sees my happiness at her happiness. The climate has cured her throat and breathing problems, and now with the cottage and Sean and Mickey at hand, it's all a dream for us. If I see her three full days per week, well, that's more than I saw her when I was working full time. So we pack those three days with the magic made available to us. Talk about quality time—wow! I'm having the best of both worlds!"

Mickey and Frank asked Sean and Loretta to be married when they are all alone, and as strange as it all seemed, that was their intention. Frank believed that death sentences affect everyone differently. In his case, his number one drive was to see Loretta comfortable, happy, laughing. In Lincoln, she and Frank had great times, but she was also coughing, her body felt miserable, cold, missing friends, and so on. Frank's Tuesday through Friday morning work "week" gave him the joy of teaching, along with the pleasure of just imagining Loretta's lifestyle out in California.

He explained,

It makes for one happy husband. In case you're wondering, jealousy and hurt feelings are not a part of the equation. People will say I'm covering it up or fooling myself, but no, I'm not. I've had people suggest I couldn't truly love Loretta to let her have her two worlds. That's so far off the truth. Mickey and I have private conversations every week. The other night she told me what a wonderful glowing feeling she got by watching Sean and Loretta make love. She said Loretta said the same thing to her later; that she, Loretta, just loved watching Sean and Mickey make love. My response was that I get those feelings even long distance.

This is so far left to our world, I know, but it's our truth. Last night about 3 AM, Mickey woke me up and motioned me to their door, and we watched Sean and Loretta love each other. It was priceless, as MasterCard would say. The real world does not accept this kind of thinking. No way is a spouse supposed to have these kinds of reactions watching their mate with someone else. Let me say here, though, that if it had been another man, and Mickey saw Sean with another woman, then—then it would be hell on earth.

Mickey and I slept together last night. Loretta and I had had our reunions earlier and would again later, but it just worked out that way. Mickey and I get tired before the others do because of our bodies, so we just left them and went into bed. It wasn't even a plan or anything. I've been thinking about things recently, and I'm thinking about things with a smile on my face and a warm heart. As Mad magazine used to parody years ago in the "Believe it or Not" section of the paper, "Believe it, or don't." Our story is too much to compute. It has been an incredible few months since the Thanksgiving meeting, at which time 'The Plan' was ratified by 'The Four,' and I'm loving every minute of it!

The amazing, loving devotion of the four to one another never seemed to waver no matter how nebulous their definitions of fidelity were, and I was able, quickly enough, to comprehend how this love could exist regardless of how most people would react. But then came a day when Frank and the others tested my ability to understand. I had been writing this story of the incredible love the four had for each other, about how within their foursome there existed no jealousy, how as Frank just stated, they were able to comfortably, with enjoyment even, watch their spouses making love with another man or woman from the four, but that they drew the line at an outsider coming into the picture.

One day in May of 2009, however, Frank explained that he had not been entirely candid with me concerning why he wanted to spend so much time in Lincoln when the other three were in Malibu. He said he hadn't lied exactly since he was very much enjoying subbing for as long as he could, and he was spending time with his family, but he had left out an important piece of information. Frank had told me he was having the best of both worlds, and I would say that was putting it mildly. Yes, there were Loretta, Sean, and Mickey in Malibu whenever he chose to spend time there, and yes, there were his subbing and family in Lincoln when he chose to be there. But there was more than that keeping Frank in Lincoln, and when he finally spilled the beans, I was in shock. Her name was Sasha. His first revelation of her existence came cryptically. Frank sent me the following email:

5/9/2009

I read from a book of Russian poetry the other day. I have a dear friend who is from the old Soviet Union. She translated a passage I'll use, but not many will accept..." There is no cheating. Sex is another event with another person. The two events are not related." Interesting though. Not many people would like it, but I only accept philosophies that give credence to my lifestyle.:)))

Later that same month, he would become more specific.

158

5/24/09

I, uh, oh, mmm, eh, ee. I feel sheepish. Perhaps I overplayed the poor lost boy thing a little tooooo far?? Mmm, sorry. Her name is Sasha. She is an accompanist for the Lincoln Public Schools. She is 34 and from the old Soviet Union. She graduated from the conservatory of St. Petersburg in Moscow in music!!! Her musical prowess is beyond any music teacher in Nebraska that I've ever met. Her father is a grandmaster chess expert who played first chair violin with the Moscow Symphony. We are talking world-class. But LPS and UNL wouldn't recognize real talent if it walked up and bit them on the ass. Due to L's insistence, we started going to bed in January. I, of course, was very excited but realistic. I thought for sure that once she spent a few agonizing hours in bed with a 72-year-old man, any feeling along those lines would fizzle. But, apparently, she has very little taste in men, and so we still exist as lovers. L is very pleased with this as it frees her up to chase S all over the place.:))). Ok, fine with me. So yesterday we fulfilled the fantasies of those two and spent the time in bed ... oh, ok, I enjoyed it also... I'm trying to look classy in an obviously unclassy situation. But I lost my class years ago, so I have nothing to lose. If you have any questions about our affair, I will tell you truthfully anything you want to know. I've not covered it all, thinking you would have questions anyway. So, fire away. Hope you are having a great weekend. More later. I was going to tell you so many times but thought I would look sillier than I do now.:)))

And no, I'm not in love. I kinda know who I am and where I am in life. She is wonderful and beautiful and so, of course, has all those qualities that make someone fall in love... But no... I'm just enjoying the companionship ... if that's what we call it these days ... and eventually we will part company. I'll get back to you tomorrow. I really do apologize, although I really couldn't talk about it now, could I ... or yes, I guess I could. I talked about everything else. 004

As a quick aside, by this time, Sean had taken to signing some of his emails to me "007." Sean and Frank were like brothers, but they would never say such a thing out loud. Instead, they were always teasing each other and poking fun. Once, Frank opened a story to me by saying, "Hi. It's me, or as Sean calls me, No. 4." I smiled at that and pictured the look on Sean's face as he would say it. Then I said to Frank, "So, you are 004?" Well, Frank thought that sounded fabulous, responding, "I like that—004! I just told Sean what you called me and said to him, 'Doesn't that make me higher than you, James? He actually grinned!" From that moment on, all of us called Frank 004, and he loved every minute of it.

Now back to Sasha. I had now discovered that they were five. Though I still wholly believed in the unconditional love of the four, I was experiencing great difficulty with reconciling the existence of Sasha in Frank's life. Soon after these first emails, I was told that Sasha had now begun flying back and forth between Lincoln and Malibu with Frank rather often. In addition, she was also having sex with both Mickey and Loretta as well as Frank, and finally with Sean. He tried to joke about their keeping Sasha's existence a secret from me, then explained how she had ended up in their world and in his bed.

5/27/09
Oh, did we neglect to mention that little piece of news? How clumsy of us. His "friend" was here for the weekend. She is very charming and beautiful. They are quite the love birds. Loretta thinks they look cute together?? I've never thought of Mitchell

being cute. She's cute, but he's not. Never has been. In fact, he is a has-been. (little joke) I thought it was up to the women to tell you, which they finally did. Mitchell is indifferent to this as news of any kind. Hope you are well, and it's wonderful that you are off to France. Have a great trip. S.

Sean continued:

Her beauty is haunting, again that word. She and Loretta became friends; I'm not sure how. Sasha apparently went to a concert that Mitchell directed about four years ago, and she was smitten with him from the start. Loretta and Sasha began a lesbian relationship. Mitchell got to know her when he came home from school, and the two women would be in bed. So Mitchell would sit and talk with them during their lovemaking??? (I guess they invited him to watch.) During one such liaison, Sasha turned to Loretta and asked if it would be ok if Mitchell joined in?? He did, and Loretta took Mitchell's chair, and Mitchell took Loretta's place. (this is the same story from both of them.) She is very blunt in her speaking. After several love sessions with Frank, she announced to Loretta that she was in love with both of them and could she be their mistress. Loretta gave her that permission with great enthusiasm, and they've been partners ever since. Her love for Mitchell, according to her, grows. She really is in love with him.

I just met her this past visit. I can see why Mitchell is so attached to her. Her intellect is overwhelming. She is not a gum-chewing cheerleading type at all. She speaks several languages fluently. Like her father, a chess grandmaster, she beat all of us again and again ... at the same time ... four chess boards... victory after victory. M and L insisted from the start that I also be her lover, and I did not hesitate. Mitchell gave me his blessing too. I'm not going to fall in love with her. I've more than I can handle with L and M. Frank isn't what I'd call in love. They are great companions, and the sex is terrific, but he still is a magnet to M and L in his mind. S knows this and appreciates it. She seems quite satisfied with these arrangements.

I hope this unwinds that question. You should never hesitate to ask anyone of us a question that we should not share with each other. We have no problem with that. If you have more, ask them ... to any of us.

Let me know if you have other questions, even super private. You have me at a unique time in my life. I can now answer questions that, up till now, I would not do so.

Later... Be well, Frenchie... Love from us all, and thank you for what you do. S.

Months later, I finally heard from Sasha herself. She had become more than his mistress by then, as Frank had had the ring finger of one hand amputated, and it had become even more difficult for him to type. He had shown me that finger at school one day—it was black and caused him great pain. The surgery took a severe toll on him since he was already so ill, and there was a point where he almost didn't make it through. So, Sasha became his secretary of sorts, and he would dictate stories for her to type and send me. These stories mostly concerned the assassinations, which have already been related. What follows here are emails I received from Sasha.

10/21/09
Hi Lynda, I am Sasha, the 34 yr old that loves him to death for the past several years. Young men today bore me to death. There

162

is no comparison between my guy and the idiot men. The men at the club go nuts cause he can outdo them in every department. (To clarify, the club refers to a sex club that Frank had told me existed in Lincoln, one with many safety and privacy-related rules, but one in which he described the occurrence of varied sexual encounters including, among other pairings, orgies and competitions of sorts. I found it difficult to believe such a thing existed in Lincoln, but then again, who knows?). The women there all ask for him first, and the young bucks can't deal:))) He is Superman, and then on the side, I get Sean Connery and Loretta and Mickey. I love my life. Now, I take dictation. Please note, this part I wrote and not his words:))))))

As Frank dictated to her, Sasha told me the stories of several of his contract killings; then, she returned to writing me for herself.

I don't know if he told you about our trip to the club last week. I enjoy the variety very much. It satisfies my needs to date idiot men... I can just fulfill my sexual fantasies and then walk away from them. On the other hand, Frank does not enjoy it as much, especially as his illness grows. I mention all of this to bring out certain aspects of his personality. He has several of them, as you may have surmised by now. He is several different people. Sean and Loretta will tell you many stories about the "several Frank Mitchell's." Sean and Loretta are enjoying their life together. This may seem harsh because Frank comes and goes in their world, but if someone is interested in Frank as a person, they need to know his solitude and private life without being alone. They all love each other intensely, but Frank comes and goes by choice ... one moment, he is in CA, and the next he's here and the next I don't know where he is??? We are all used to him. His life as an assassin has brought him to this world, and there's no way to change him. He is a great classroom teacher on the one hand, and then within moments, he becomes a terrifying predator. I talked with some of the shrinks in CA who love to study him, and they say he is a man of many worlds, but we are never to fear him. In fact, we control him... he loves us all so much and would never allow any harm to befall any of us.

They talk of your patience ... so much writing ... so many stories ...but your time is coming when you will join their world... Mickey's health has kept you all at a distance, but that will change soon. Your bedroom is being prepared!!! Sooo, hang on a little longer ... and the most important ... your money will make its long-awaited entrance soon.

Of course, these words were exciting news for me, as it renewed my faith that I would, eventually, meet them and be financially rewarded for my work. She continued:

Tonight, I'll send you a terrific story, as I mentioned in my early letter. Why do I love him?? He is a Ghost to me. To try and figure him ... to understand what he may be thinking ... his gentleness, his softness and yet in a moment you can sense the predator... not many men meet those traits and qualities. The women at the club sense these characteristics and are drawn to him. The men can feel his inner strength and are cautious of him... more soon... Sasha

Later she added:

Lynda... Sasha again... I told him this [story] was too boring... my favorite one will come tonight when I tell you about the time Frank gave the battered wife a chance to participate in her husband's demise ... and does so. That one will really grab you.

I also have such neat anecdotes about Frank that you will enjoy. Anyway, this is something boring as all get out, but something. Sean gave me many stories about Frank and his work, and I'm going to have him dictate those to me, so get ready... I love doing this... He is an exciting man ... you cannot believe his past life... looking forward to our meeting. Sasha

Once the secret of Sasha's existence had been revealed to me, it became a given that she was involved in much of what the four were doing. When Mickey would have moments of illness and weakness, Sasha would also help Sean and Loretta care for her. She had become a part of their world and was entirely accepted. On the other hand, I was still on the outside, being promised entrance onto that stage. She *had* given me renewed hope that my needs and desires had not been forgotten, and she seemed to be all the things I had been told she was: brilliant, talented, kind, loving, and gorgeous. Frank showed me a photo of her once when we met for coffee. They were not exaggerating her beauty. But my jealousy still existed. She was with them and flying back and forth on the private jet as I had been so often promised I would do, and I was still working and waiting to reap the rewards of my labor.

16

Clowning around

Not long after The Plan had been discussed by the four, Frank had talked with the others more specifically about his hopes for the two who would remain after he and Mickey had left us. He explained:

Some thoughts about Sean and Loretta's eventual marriage. This is just one more unbelievable ingredient to this story. I asked my kids if this was going to be awkward for them. Both said no way. Like Loretta and me, they believe in sort of a parallel universe. Even before all of this came into focus, at different times in their lives, they had talked about having the exact same feelings for two different people. So the time will come when Mickey and I are gone, and my children want life to go right on for their mother and Sean, just as Mickey and I do. So, Mickey and I tell them we will both be at the wedding. Again, we would really get strange looks from people on that one if we talked about it openly. Most would be against discussing Sean and Loretta's marriage until we are both gone. Then I ask, 'Why?'

Sean brought it up at our Thanksgiving meeting. When all was decided about "The Plan," he said, "Well, Mitchell, I've never said this line in all the movies I've made, but may I have your wife's hand in marriage?" We all got a great laugh.

I had not thought about it that way, but Mickey and I loved it. I said I wouldn't be able to give her away. I asked who would be the best man? He told me my son would do that and that my daughter would be bridesmaid. He then turned to Loretta and proposed, and she accepted. Let me tell you; it was a weird moment. We all teared up as we thought about the scene. Sean has since asked both of my children, and they were wild about the idea. My grandchildren will be in the group somehow also. Wish I could be there? Hmmm...

In December of 2008, Frank started routinely going back and forth between Malibu and Lincoln, thus alternating between substitute teaching, about which he was quite passionate, and being with the other three, about *whom* he was quite passionate. As he said, it was the best of both worlds for him, despite his illness. Typically, when Frank arrived in California, their time would be divided between the beach, dinners out, shopping, or just relaxing, and of course making love with each other. Often, the others would get him at the airport, and they would go out to dinner. Mickey and Loretta did not like to cook much anymore, and Sean and Frank didn't think they should have to do so unless they felt like it.

One can imagine the restaurant choices there in Malibu. Upon Frank's arrival just after Sean had purchased the cottage, they went to dinner and then to the cottage to look around. Frank said he just couldn't believe this was happening. "Life just doesn't work like this," he explained. "In all of the 50 years I've been friends with Sean, I never ever thought about receiving any special treatment from him, but I did. Taking me/us to dinners, flying back and forth, some lavish gifts, you know, the usual, right?" he said to tease me, adding, "Try not to throw up!" just to make me laugh.

"But this," he concluded, "this is above my crazy mind." Little did Frank know that by this point, the teasing had ceased being funny to me, as there were times when yes, the seeming injustice of the situation frankly made me ill. I never told him, of course, as it would have completely spoiled the moment.

When the four were simply at Sean and Mickey's home relaxing instead of out on the town, journalists and photographers would sometimes still come by and try to sneak onto the property looking for a good story. The story had been right under their noses for more than fifty years. Still, they had never taken any notice of it, and even at that point, with Loretta and Frank practically living in the same house with them much of the time, they couldn't seem to see the proverbial forest for the trees. To Sean, these intrusions into their privacy were just that, and he often went downstairs where he couldn't be seen and read until they gave up and went away. But Frank, well, Frank thought these unsolicited visits were the occasion for some fun and games, so if he was there when reporters showed up, he would go out to play, with some rather comical results. These games served to show the humorous, playful side of Frank, in stark contrast to the darkness lying just beneath the surface.

One of the first times Mickey was writing to me, she was interrupted by two photographers trying to get some interesting shots of them. When she returned to her computer, she told me this story:

Lynda, excuse my sudden departure from the last e-mail. We seem to have two would be photographers lurking around the house. You need to know that Frank loves to go out there to visit with them. He tells them things like, "I'm Sean's father. He can't come out to play today until he cleans his room. Kids!"

They ask who he is and why he's been staying at the house and who that other woman is. Now, Loretta just told me that now he just handed them a note to call the police, that he's been kidnapped. She watched him write it when Sean was writing to you, and he was watching them sneak around the house. Of course, they ignore him and keep trying to find us standing near a window.

We do have to keep an eye on Sean during these intrusions. He would never abuse a woman, contrary to the news reports, but with men... I don't want a scene. I'll sign off now to keep my husband away from them, as Frank has apparently changed his story and is now telling them that he would like them to listen to some poetry that he's just written. I'll let you know how this turns out.

I laughed until I cried when I first read this story. Another time, several months later, Frank was at it again, but with much greater flair this time. First, I must explain that Sean had a collection of strange memorabilia from movie lots. In an old storage bin, he had stashed all kinds of props from different movies, some that he'd been in and some not—he just found the articles interesting sometimes. So, one Saturday afternoon in the middle of March 2009, they noticed a group of photographers and reporters parking and walking up to their place. Mickey remembered Frank noticing them and getting up and going out the back door, but she didn't give it much thought.

This time they knew it was going to be a real pain in the rear for them. The reporters were knocking on their door and ringing the bell, but they wouldn't answer if Sean just went downstairs to read and ignore them. If Sean ignored them, they all ignored them. Sean went downstairs, so no one answered the door. The reporters soon realized that they would not get an answer, yet they knew someone was home. So, as a group, they all started around the house to the back. About five minutes later, they heard people screaming and saw the whole crew running around in disarray. Sean came running up the stairs, and he, Loretta, and Mickey ran to the back window.

There, apparently hanging from their large elm tree, was Frank. It looked just like he had put a rope around his neck and jumped off of a box that was tipped over underneath him. His head was slanted to the side, making it look like his neck was broken. His arms were just dangling by his sides. Sean took one look at him and said, "Oh, Mitchell has found that old harness that you put under your shirt, and then the main rope is hooked to that and not to the one around your neck, but you can't see that, so it looks real. The reporters think that a man has hung himself in our backyard!" Some of the reporters called 911, but the police never responded. It seems Frank had called them and told them they were practicing a movie scene in the back of the house, and some people might think it was real.

The three let the reporters take pictures and stand around in a morbid deathwatch, waiting for the police for a while. Then, Sean sauntered out with a drink in his hand, sat down, and started reading the paper. Loretta and Mickey followed and also sat down with books and started reading. They acted like nothing was happening. Finally, after the men began trying to get Frank down, Sean looked up and said, "Mitchell! Get down from there!" Frank then looked up and worked the latch loose allowing the rope to slide him to the ground. The reporters were obviously, shall I say, stunned? Sean felt sorry for them, so he gave them an interview. Meanwhile, Frank cleaned up his mess and took it back to the storage without saying a word to the reporters or photographers.

They just stared at him and then started asking Sean questions. When they asked Sean who that man was and who Loretta was, he just said, "Friends." And they let it go at that.

Loretta told me she really needed to watch over Frank when he would decide to start playing with the reporters, and after that story, I understood why. She said he loved those encounters, and he loved to drive the reporters crazy with his antics. She recalled how she left him alone outside with them another time. Frank was telling them that he was composing two-part harmony for barbershop. The guy with the camera then told Frank that the point of barbershop was to perform four- to six-part close harmony (if only he had known Frank's background!). Frank had then looked at the photographer and just said, "Damn!"

So the reporters kept trying to walk away from him, but he kept following along behind them, telling them one story after another. Loretta added, "At this very moment, he is tap dancing around them, and just for the record, no, he can't tap dance!" At times, Sean enjoyed watching Frank "perform," and this was one of them. He took up a position at an open window where he could watch and hear the different things Frank came up with. Most often, the reporters just got tired of Frank's games and would leave, but this time, Loretta abandoned her writing to me, saying, "I hear the reporters yelling at Frank, so I will close for now!"

The fun for Sean and the others didn't end with snooping reporters at the house, however. Even at eighty years old, Sean was still swooned over and pursued by women, pretty much wherever he went. He was still amazing to look at and continued to command quite a presence. One afternoon, Sean and Frank went to a small shopping mall, and they went into a little flower shop to get something for the women. The shop had one clerk, a young woman about thirty years old, who clearly wanted to be a starlet.

She recognized Sean right away and was falling all over him. She told them she would bring out several different displays for them to consider. As she did so, it became apparent that she was wearing less clothing on top each time she came out from the back. She had been wearing layers of coverings, but as each new trip from the back room took place, something seemed to go.

Frank left them alone and went to the other side, and Sean looked at him like, "Where the hell are you going?" Finally, the woman had no bra on, just a sheer silk large scarf of sorts. She kept leaning over the counter to Sean, coming closer and closer until finally, Sean said, "My dear young lady, I can't even handle the women in my household! How in the world could I tango with a whirlwind such as you? We'll take that one and that one. OK with you, Mitchell?" She laughed and said, oh well, it had been fun to do anyway. They bought the flowers and left.

17

"The Man"

What was Sean really like, one might ask. Was he arrogant or condescending? Was he anything like James Bond, 007? Not in the least would best sum it all up. On occasion, Frank overheard women talk about Sean after meeting him for the first time. They, in essence, all said they were surprised to find him so non-Bondish. They all thought they would be meeting a genuine chauvinist pig. Not true. He was conscientious not to offend, bluster, act like he knew a lot, or patronize. That was Frank's favorite characteristic about him. All who met Sean were quickly comfortable with him sitting next to them. Frank explained:

I don't need to build up such a known person, but I thought back in 1959 I would be meeting a real stuffed shirt. Then on top of that, a stuffed shirt that was my love's ex-boyfriend! I was prepared and planning to dislike him and distance myself from him as soon as I got Loretta out of California. But Loretta reminded me that it was he and I who sat for hours, sipping on our excellent wine, laughing, and talking till early in the morning. Loretta would often say, 'I thought you were going to distance yourself from him.' After Sean and Diane divorced, we were sure our time with him would come to a close. Then the next thing I knew, Loretta and Micheline were sitting in the corner for hours and into the night discussing art, and it was Sean who answered back, 'Maybe we should leave them alone.' It will be 50 years this February (2009) that we met!"

The first time Sean wrote to me, I was stunned that he took the time to do so, and then in stitches reading his note. It read:

This is Mickey's husband, Sean. We hear so much about your friendship with Frank. I can only assume that you are some kind of volunteer to assist people who are socially inept and personality challenged! Thank you for your fine work and sacrifice.

Then Mickey added, "That was my husband. Just ignore him!"

As Sean and I got to know each other, I was struck by his ability to make me feel at ease talking to him. He was often very complimentary—genuinely so. His sense of humor, when he decided to allow it to surface, was subtle yet uncanny, as demonstrated in his introduction to me. His honesty and sincerity were noteworthy, though, in the final analysis, I suppose I should say that became debatable. The others had warned me that Sean would not write to me. They told me he never wrote to anyone, so I felt truly honored when he answered my letters and initiated the exchanges at times. The others were astounded by this behavior, so unlike him. They were equally astonished that he created a nickname for me— Frenchie—and by the way, he often signed off in his letters to me. "Lovingly, 007" and then, "I only sign that to my friends." I was touched.

I had read some of Sean's biographies, naturally, by this point. One of the stories that had surfaced several times in separate works concerned his supposed violence against women. According to sources, I read how he was known to have hit women from time to time and how in an interview with Barbara Walters, he had even said that that was true—that at times he felt it was necessary. I asked him about that one day after seeing a broadcast that in part recounted that same interview with Barbara. He told me what had happened that led him to fabricate an answer when she was interviewing him that day. He recalled:

> She kept asking me again and again whether or not I hit women. I could see what she wanted, I was tired, and I didn't like her, so I gave her what I thought would be a harmless anecdotal prank. It was not taken that way at all, as you know. Actually, it turned out that it helped my career! It was never a drawback. And again, for the record, I have never hit a woman, nor would I put myself in a position to do so! I would simply leave the room. Thank you for clearing the air for me.

Though, as stated, I never met Sean in person, I did get a sense from all of our conversations that he was a good, kindhearted man with a wonderful sense of humor. He did me an injustice by dropping the book and film project without explanation and especially without compensation, to be sure. Still, I sense that, all in all, he was a very likable human being.

I next wanted to get a sense of what Mickey thought of Frank. Mickey spoke about her relationship with him. They were close from the beginning, she said, but as already stated, it was many years into their friendship before it evolved into more. She recalled, "Frank was the kindest man I ever knew." Mickey always spoke so highly of Frank, and she wanted me to make it clear just how wonderful, kind, warm, and giving he could be. She recalled an afternoon when she and Frank were alone for a few days, just the two of them. It was the summer of 2002, so Frank and Mickey had also secretly been lovers for a few years at this point. Sean and Loretta had gone to—you guessed it—Las Vegas for a few days of gambling, so Frank had flown out to spend the weekend with Mickey. The two of them decided to drive up the coastal highway as it was a gorgeous day. They stopped for gas and noticed a Hispanic mother of four crying and talking to the mechanic. It turned out that her car had blown the radiator and the alternator all at once and that the replacement cost would be around eight hundred dollars. Mickey explained:

> They had very little money. The kids were crying, the mother was crying, the whole scene was terrible! I walked past them to use the restroom. When I left the restroom, I saw Frank at the cash register with the mechanic. I stopped to watch, and then I saw through the window that his credit card was being swiped. He always paid cash, and I had already seen him pay for our gas, so I knew it couldn't be for that. The mechanic thanked him, and Frank headed to the car to wait for me. I went into the office and asked the guy, "Did he just pay for the work to be done to their car?" He grinned and said, "Not only did he pay for the repair, but he swiped $1,000 above the cost, and I'm taking the money to her now with the news that someone has paid for the car's repairs."
>
> I stayed back to watch the scene, and it was right out of the movies. You can imagine the joy and happiness with that family! I watched Frank, who stayed out of sight as the mother looked around for her savior. She couldn't see Frank

from where she was. I came out of the office and went over to the car, and hopped in. I asked Frank if everything was okay, and he said, "No problem," and off we drove and had a great weekend. Frank never mentioned it, and I never said a word about it either until about a year ago. We were watching some movie on TV, and there was a scene where a mother and two kids were stranded along a highway. During the lull, I said quietly, "Don't worry. They'll be okay. I just saw YOU drive by." I was so tickled by my quick thinking. Frank didn't say anything for a minute, and I could see him blush. He turned to me and said, "Hell with this show! Let's make love." Then he turned off the set and the lights... It was a fun evening!

Mickey continued telling me about her feelings for Frank. "I love him so much," she confessed, "but it took me over 30 years to get him into my bed. People would not believe how straight this man really is. Sean and Loretta are so frustrated by the fact that while they were enjoying each other, he and I were watching the late-night news for so many years. I didn't force myself on him because I simply thought he wasn't interested that way in me. Yet, since he wrote me ten e-mails every day, he must have been in love with me for at least the past ten years, don't you think?" At this comment, Sean piped in, "I told you he was slow!" And Loretta added, "He just has to be seduced. He won't be the aggressor. I had to maul him before he figured out what I wanted him to do!" Now that everything is out in the open, things are different. Sean and Loretta sneak around and watch Frank and Mickey make love. Frank knows that they watch from a distance, but Mickey thinks that sometimes

Frank doesn't realize that they are close by and chuckling; in a nice way."

When Mickey and Loretta compared Sean and Frank in the bedroom, they agreed that their lovemaking was almost identical. Loretta had expressed earlier her surprise that the first time she and Frank made love, it was almost like being in bed with Sean, the techniques were so similar. Mickey said she, too, had been shocked to be treated the same way in bed with Frank as she was with Sean. She joked, "I wondered if they both went to the same coach!"

She said that men can be so silly about the bed and that often they just don't get it, but these two sure did. She continued:

It's the affection, caring, and sincerity that matters to us, not the caveman approach. Although, to be a little honest, it doesn't hurt to see a hunk with brains lying next to you in bed. Anyway, while reading Loretta's letter to you this morning, I was reminded of MY first experience with Frank. I, too, could sense his nervousness. He got me laughing with the line, "Great, now I am following Sean Connery into bed with another of his women!" But wow! To tell the truth, Frank is a master. He knows where and when and what and how to maneuver around a woman's body. To be even more direct, those two should both have their tongues bronzed—not yet, but someday! Sometimes, in the middle of intercourse, Frank will just pause and almost stop, and I'll ask him what's the matter, and he'll say there's no hurry. Well, Holy Christ, man! He likes to get us to a certain point and then back off and kind of wander around our bodies and then bam!—he's back up to full speed. Those two are the only men I've ever known who can do that.

Mickey concluded by saying, "Loretta and I are, for history's sake, making sure that the world knows that Frank Mitchell can compete with Sean Connery in the bedroom anytime, so he can stop taking a back seat."

When Sean read what his ladies had written to me about Frank being his equal in the bedroom, he had quite a reaction. He wrote:

Mr. Connery here. So I read this description of my lovemaking, only to find that Mitchell stole my work ethic in the bedroom. He shall hear from my attorney! How kind of Loretta and Mickey to try and make him feel worthy. Like you, they seem to have a need to protect the weak and clumsy. (When you know me better someday, you will notice that I adore this man. Snide remarks are my way of telling him I love him. I'm sure as hell not going to say THAT to him.) But, I will tell him that I cannot digest the thought of his equality with me as far as women are concerned. Thank God they didn't say he was better! I would probably have hyperventilated.

18

Portraits

A few months after all four started writing to me, and it had been decided there would be a book, Mickey said she wanted to do some paintings to commemorate their love and add to their published story. As previously noted, she and Sean had first met when he and Diane had commissioned her to do some paintings of the same nature. Now she wanted to forever preserve images of their love on canvas and in photos. Sean explained that he and Loretta also wanted these paintings for their own comfort and memory. The paintings were to be of Loretta and Frank making love and Mickey and Sean, then some of Sean with Mickey and Loretta and some of Frank also with Mickey and Loretta. Mickey explained she had also commissioned photographers to capture the moments and paint the scenes she was in using the photographs as her guide. Mickey then added her reasons for wanting the paintings she did. She explained:

The paintings represent my wanting to visually remember my intimacy with men and women that I love. I want to be able to look over and see a huge photo of Sean and me in each other's arms, or Sean and Loretta, or the three of us. It is as heartwarming for me as it is for Loretta. One other thought about the paintings and photos—I want people interested in us to see our love. Sex is a huge part of that, and why not show it to them?

Mickey described the first of several days of photoshoots and painting for us. She said:

I started the first painting yesterday. I had them naked on a beautiful huge blue blanket. I didn't want them, or any of the subjects for this project, on a bed. I wanted a mysterious background where it's not discernible as to where they are or what they're making love on. I did three preliminary sketches, three different poses; two on the blanket and one outdoors.

She explained to me that they have a very private fenced-in side area. The nearest neighbor is a block away. The outside shot was Loretta lying back on cushions spread around, and Sean had his arms under her legs and bottom, lifting them to his face. She commented that she thought the sketch had come out perfectly. Sean wasn't able to hold that pose for long, so she captured the basic positioning and went back to it from time to time.

As for the indoor blanket scenes, the first was full intercourse in the missionary position. Sean, and Frank when it was his turn later, was to pull Loretta, and later Mickey, up into him with arms under them. Mickey sketched wildly so as not to create realism. She worked them for over three hours. She needed to get Sean's body movements during orgasm, so they "had to" go through that several times. The third canvas was of Loretta and Sean. Mickey said it was beautifully staged. She added, "I'm going to have a similar scene with the photos where, for example, Loretta's or my mouth gets closer and closer to them and then completely..." She said the sketching would be done in the same fashion for the oral sex as it was for the intercourse. She explained, "I want the body reaction obvious though not clear from both subjects. It's very hard to capture. I'm going to start by taking pictures so I can catch those moments and then add them to my sketch."

Later that day, Loretta wrote me this note about the afternoon's activities, in which she and Sean had been the subjects. I had to smile when I read how she opened. She said, "Lynda, I am exhausted!! I kept reminding Mickey that I'm 70 years old, and I kept asking her when is break time? Sean can't move. The sketches are beautiful. When Mickey adds the colors, it should be astounding! It shows what is happening, but you can't make out specific parts except for my breasts. I think this project is going to be beautiful. I'm so spoiled. I'll be reminded of my love with my two men until my last breath. Sean will have the same treat, if that's the word. But sadness rears its ugly head as Mickey and Frank will obviously have a different perspective on the whole thing, I imagine. Yet, they will love it."

Then Loretta continued on a very moving, sad tone. She confided:

I had to stop writing for a moment ... got kind of choked up about the paintings. Sean and I cannot believe that Mickey and Frank will be gone soon. We just can't compute this. The two of them act like nothing is wrong. They never appear down or moody around us. Sean and I don't get a feeling of false bravado with them or over-the-top play-acting as to feign happiness and the "isn't this fun" kind of thing. They are just as they've always been. Frank and Mickey now say they want their ashes sprinkled about the side yard where we spend so much time. Sean and I will bury some of the ashes to hold on to them longer. Maybe we'll spread some and bury the urn with the other half. Well, let's move to other things.

I could feel her pain as I read her words—such a constant dichotomy of emotions. Not long after Loretta wrote to me, Mickey said, "I must hurry with the paintings. My hands and arms are becoming difficult to control. I'm beginning to shake a little. It hasn't kept me out of the studio yet, but it will. Like Frank, we are sad about leaving our loves and our lifelong work." But as always, they regained their composure, and the following day, Sean and Loretta resumed the posing. Loretta commented that at least Sean would not be required to produce that much "fluid" that day.

Next, it was Frank's turn to pose. Mickey commented, "I think Frank's nervous about the posing, but he'll relax." Frank, however, described the scene this way: "I'm getting nervous. I see several cameras being mounted on different shapes of stands all over their home and yard. There are not two but four female photographers in bathing suits unloading their equipment. Mickey and Loretta are excitedly showing them the different background scenes, and the four women are offering their suggestions.

"Now, hiding behind the large tree in the back of the cottage, you can see two old men peering around their side of the tree look-ing scared to death! Sean thinks we should make a run for it. My gosh! They are serious about all of this. We asked meekly one of the women why so many different cameras and angles. She looked at us and said something like, 'We are going to capture you two in so many poses to superimpose over each other, making some of it like it was one continuous movement. Other prints will be two or three photos slightly ajar from each other to show just some motion.' Well, us two old geezers had no idea really what the hell she was talking about, so we didn't even answer."

As they called Frank to the scene, he was writing to me, so he said, "I gotta go now... It's time. As Daffy Duck, when in dire straights, would turn to the camera and say, 'Mother...'"

Mickey also commissioned another painter to help with the scenes in which she would be posing. The other painter would be there Saturday and Sunday to paint her and Frank. She was an art instructor at UCLA, and Mickey loved her work. She had painted many such poses before. She was a master at catching the subjects at the height of the "event." Mickey added that Frank knew her well, too, so he wouldn't worry so much about another woman painting him as such. Then she added, "Lynda, Sean said to tell you he's in better shape than Frank. I doubt it."

The schedule was hectic. To get the photos done, the two female photographers would be there for a five-hour shoot over two days. The photoshoots would be done by having one photographer with Sean and Loretta and one with Frank and Mickey on the first day. Then they would shoot Sean with Mickey and Frank with Loretta. They would take hundreds of shots of them at different angles, in various events, and with different backdrops. The one woman, who was uncommonly expert at capturing the "moment or moments," as Frank called them, was to capture each pair when it got that serious.

Mickey summed up the shoot in this way:

It was a wonderful day. We saw the first printouts, and they are breathtaking. The men, and they are men, held up (pun intended) very well for over 4 hours; well, not continuously, but when needed. Not bad for a couple of 70 yr. olds! It took the guys a little while to be undressed around four strange young women, but eventually, they relaxed and followed their directions perfectly.

Mickey continued:

I told you about the one gal who has the knack for filming the "end" of the event. (I'm searching for softer words). She took unbelievable sequences. She was amazing. You can follow the "event," and it's conclusion and it looks real, except you don't really, really see it at pinpoint vision. Even the other women were amazed at her talent for that. There are also some beautiful pictures of each couple standing in an embrace, and as you study it, you see more and more their excitement, but again, with no pinpoint visual. Amazingly done.

The final day of posing in LA was centered around *ménages à trois,* and all went as planned, but Frank made this amusing comment at the prospect of "performing" in threesomes in front of so many others, "Well isn't that special, as the church lady would say!" Mickey said that she thought the scenes were put together with such grace by the photographers. She couldn't stop talking about them. She thought they might just have the usual scenes in mind, but they had really thought it through, and the blocking was terrific and original. She also commented on the stamina of the men saying, "Again, the men 'held up' very well, although I'm thinking that Loretta and I will not be having any more sex for several days!"

When they had finished the *ménages à trois* scenes, they packed up and headed for Sean and Mickey's home in the Bahamas. There, they completed the work during the following week.

Mickey's plan was for her and the other woman painter to finish the paintings over a four-day work period, and that is what they did. Mickey worked fast, and so did the other painter. The paintings and photographs were intended to be a wonderful part of Sean and Loretta's life together. Frank and Mickey added that they would enjoy them also, but sadly for a shorter period. The pictures were also in a series of photos in a smaller version that could be kept in a drawer to look at. Sean and the others all agreed that I should have a set as well, saying that I should have most of the artifacts from this adventure in my life as the author of this tale.

Frank mused:

"While I would prefer you remember me in my blue jeans, vest, and tennis shoes, and not pretending to be some Greek idol of love, this will be important." He continued, "I've been trying to imagine the expressions on faces when this book comes out, and people get to the photo section; faces like those of former colleagues at school, of my kids and grandchildren (even though they are aware), former students of mine both in my career and subbing, and so on. It's probably a good thing I won't see those moments. This might be a good place to say that I've always known what I wanted written on my epitaph: 'ONLY REMEMBER THE GOOD THINGS ABOUT ME.' Hopefully, they will do just that!"

Of course, and sad to say, I was never sent the photo album nor any other artifacts.

19

The book

By early December of 2008, all four of them had started writing to me regularly, as they had decided to create this book. At that point, all of them were writing to me from Frank's email address, simply stating at the beginning who was writing. This was getting confusing for me, and I wanted each of them to have a place where they could tell me, privately and individually, what they were thinking, and perhaps share some secrets they had kept from the others all these years. To my surprise and delight, they agreed. Sean's opening line to me made me smile. He said, "Frenchie, this is my secret place. Haven't had one since I was a boy!"

I thought that was a great start to our future communications. They said the private addresses would be a good way for them to have a place to "unload life-long thoughts and secrets from each other"—not everything, as people should be able to have certain secrets, but quite a few. They added that it would be like "an emotional Christmas to be able to see in some depth into each others' lives," since eventually, they would all be able to read what was sent to me in private. Frank explained further:

I feel very confident that now we can all say things that will really interest the reading public, which of course is our purpose, and to surprise each other with conversations that we thought in the past should be left unsaid. I suspect every family member keeps things from their fellow loved ones to maybe not hurt them. In reality, if the family really loved one another, the "revelations" would not be hurtful or embarrassing or whatever. So when the day comes when the private venues are "unsealed," so to speak, it will only serve to bring us closer together. I think we are all in store for a terrific round table of confessions that will only serve to strengthen our already incredible bond!

The first private letter I received was from Loretta, and it caught me completely off guard at the time, leaving me in a state of shock. It was the letter in which she first told me the story about Pastor Marco and being raped. If I'd been asked to guess the topic, never could I have done so. She opened like this, "Here's the story to be told. I was repeatedly raped starting in April of 1964. I was 25 years old. I was raped by the associate pastor of my church. The assaults on my body continued for a year! This letter explains why I didn't report the abuse and what happened to everyone involved." After this attention-getting opener, she went on to tell the story related earlier.

Sometime later, I asked Loretta how she had managed to continue a happy, healthy sex life after being abused for so long. She had an interesting response. First of all, she acknowledged that, even though she was without any doubt a victim of rape, she was never tortured or literally kidnapped. She was not forced to the ground by some terrifying and disgusting stranger, nor was she ever beaten or restrained. The emotional toll was there and remained there until the end, but she was, in a sense, far less traumatized than many other victims. That being said, she told me that she got upset when she heard of women who were assaulted many years earlier but who hadn't yet been able to negotiate life.

She told me she was not trying to diminish the horror, for it is just that, but that women should find a way to work through their emotions and move on positively whenever possible. Yet, Loretta also agreed that many factors play into a woman's ability to recover and live a normal, healthy life. For example, it helped tremendously in her case that she had already had extremely positive sexual experiences with Sean and Frank. If a woman's first sexual experience is rape, recovery would seem to be a tremendously difficult process. Regardless of the circumstances, there was no disagreement about how devastating any kind of rape truly is.

Case in point: After Loretta wrote me her story of rape, she waited for the right moment to tell Frank what her letter had been about, and in fact, she needed several days to get up the courage and strength to do so. Frank knew the story, of course, but it had happened so very long ago, and they had never really discussed the details in any depth, nor had they ever sat down and worked through the emotional aspects of it all. After the pastor's death, they had simply pulled themselves back together, "forgotten" about it, and moved on without further analysis or comment. So now, almost forty-five years later, she went digging into her subconscious only to find that some ghosts were still there haunting her after all.

Several days after writing to me, Loretta found the right moment to talk to Frank. She had told him that she had written me about something "huge," so he had already spent the past few days wondering what it might be. Loretta wrote:

I can see him thinking. He always has the same posture and eye contact when his thoughts are in overdrive. I believe he has attached himself to one particular part of our past, the one that I just wrote about. I've been wondering why he wouldn't go there almost immediately when he knew yesterday that I'd written a very powerful letter to you. There is nothing in our past that would remotely come close to this drama. He watches me out of the corner of his eye and studies me. It has to be that. If I know him well, and I do, he will have to talk about it, and soon.

March 1, 2009, it was time. Loretta took a deep breath and asked Frank to come and take a walk on the beach with her. It was walk and talk time. It was a beautiful day in California, but around there, that is redundant. After saying "beautiful day, eh?" a dozen times to Frank, Loretta said, "I want to talk to you about my letter to Lynda" (Loretta was shaking at this point). But that is all she got to say. Frank came right back with, "You mean about the pastor? I figured that's what it was. I told Sean the other day that I figured that was it." At that same moment, Sean came walking up from behind and put his arm around the other side of her. They both started to swing Loretta back and forth off of the ground.

Then she broke down. The three sat on the beach and cried and cried, and they just kept hugging Loretta. Frank would bring Loretta's head over to his shoulder for a while, and then Sean would bring it over to his shoulder and so on. Loretta said it took several minutes before she could speak. She told me that she thought having that on her mind for close to forty-five years was just too much. Then Frank apologized for not talking to her about it sooner but said he hadn't known how to handle it, and Sean apologized for not having asked her what was wrong so long ago, for having been so unaware.

Both told Loretta how sad they were for her, and Frank told her how sorry he was not to have figured out earlier that something was very wrong, that he should have been more suspicious and saved her from further attacks. Frank and Sean both picked her up, and they hugged and said it was all over with and that now they could put it to rest, and at that point, they really thought they could. Loretta recalled that the rest of the evening was spent in great friendship. She said, "I can't tell you enough how special it is to have two men like that being in love with me, and I with them—and I have them both! I'm the luckiest woman in the world!"

20

Ghosts

Putting it all behind her was not, as it turned out, possible for Loretta at that point. She had dug up ghosts of the past, so long buried, and now they would not let her rest. A few days after the "walk and talk," Sean noticed that Loretta just couldn't seem to stop talking about "The Year," and Frank agreed that it seemed to have become a concerning issue. Sean told Frank that the Sunday after he left for Lincoln, Loretta had started talking nonstop about her "year," with more and more specific details. When he and Mickey tried to change the subject and get her to talk about something else, she quickly returned to the same topic. He was worried, and so were the others, so he called a psychiatrist friend of his, Marsha, for advice. Sean spent two hours with her on the phone explaining, giving her the skeleton of the book I was writing, the emails from all of them, and then quickly went through Loretta's revelation about the pastor. Sean told Marsha that he thought Loretta needed to talk with a professional. Marsha agreed, saying that it would not be enough for Loretta to spill her guts to the three of them because she knew they would be sympathetic; she needed an objective voice.

The doctor was especially concerned that Loretta seemed to need the others to know that she had at times enjoyed the sex with Marco and even had orgasms. She said that this was a sign of underlying guilt that must be curtailed. The doctor explained that it is a normal response in cases such as this for the victim to brain-wash themselves into thinking that they are in love with their captor and believe that they enjoy the captivity and look forward to it. It is a survival mechanism that allows the victim to cope. Marsha then said that from what little Sean had been able to tell her on the phone, Loretta was being torn apart because it appeared like one minute she hated the pastor and the visits, and the next, she enjoyed them. For example, Loretta had told Frank that she had insulted the pastor's technique with oral sex on her and that he was so humiliated he never performed it again on her. But after Frank left for Lincoln, Loretta broke down and said she had lied about some of that. She said that after she had insulted Marco, he had asked her to teach him how to do it. What that did, said the doctor, was to switch the power from him to her. She was now in charge at times, and most likely for a few months, Loretta was in charge of the sex, including positions, style, different events, whatever.

Marsha continued with her preliminary theory that Loretta became his teacher, as he knew he was a poor lover. That would explain his ramming himself into her in the beginning. He wasn't trying to control her or hurt her; he was simply trying to impress her. It sounded to the doctor as if Loretta began to use her power over the pastor and started to pick some of the times, even initiating some of the visits herself, which would help account for the vast number of "sessions" they ultimately had. Loretta was then effectively in charge. What a great move on her part, the doctor added, even though neither she nor Marco knew it. It may very well have saved her from further psychological downslides. Marsha also believes that the pastor fell in love with Loretta at some point and that if we could see their sessions, it would be clear that she had become the teacher and he the student. The doctor

198

thought the pastor sounded like a little boy who needed to be spanked, and when Loretta, in effect, started to rule him, well, everything changed.

When he heard this, Frank's reaction was not anger toward Loretta but rather a significant concern for her current mental health. He went on to say that he thought Loretta must have "fallen in love" with the pastor and fooled herself into believing she looked forward to the sex. He said that was the only thing that made sense to him. But he knew that he could never convince Loretta that that information would *not* be devastating to him. On the contrary, it was the only logical explanation when he and the others watched her talk about it. The problem was that, after all these years, Loretta had fully regained her hatred of the pastor, and though she realized what he had done to her, she still felt guilt-ridden for having, as she believed at that point, enjoyed part of it. Sean and Frank were not jealous, nor hurt or devastated as Loretta feared, but they were now scared to death for her mental health. She was quite confused as to what the truth was about her and Marco, rambling on and on and out of control. She needed professional help to sort it all out and truly put it all behind her this time.

Marsha arrived at the Connery home that same afternoon, just in time for them to all have lunch together—Loretta, Sean, and Mickey. Frank had returned to Lincoln at that point and was kept up-to-date through frequent phone conversations. He said he was frankly relieved to know that Loretta was in such good hands. The doctor began her analysis of Loretta even as they ate. She wanted Sean and Mickey there since they had been with Loretta from the beginning of this project. She believed that Loretta would relax more with them there. She gave Loretta a preliminary analysis and told her that she wanted to take time over the next weeks and maybe months to help Loretta sort things out. Loretta not only agreed that this would be a good idea, she wanted it. She told everyone right away that she knew that her recent reactions had been "off the charts," a favorite expression of hers. She also said that she wanted to go back to the stories she had already told and "throw in the truth." Very well put. She was reassured by Sean and Mickey, as well as by Frank, that they were not going to be devastated, or shocked, or "any of that heavy stuff," as Frank called it. On the contrary, they just wanted her to have peace, and she would have their blessing whatever the outcome.

Later that same day, Marsha gave Loretta a mild relaxant drug with a small dose of truth serum. By the time the doctor had finished her first session with Loretta, she was aware of many things concerning "The Year." She also conferred with two of her colleagues for confirmation of her opinion. They all agreed that, had the pastor not met his untimely death, he would most likely have killed Loretta before too long. They think he had been fantasizing about the abduction but probably didn't plan on actually doing it. They also felt that the night of the "kidnap," Loretta was perhaps close by after choir practice, and he jumped at his chance. No one would have thought a thing about it. The doctors all felt that the first night went so well that the pastor was then off and running with it. Had Loretta turned and run, he would most likely have killed her. As the months rolled by, he probably became more aware of his surroundings, so to speak, and wondered, as Loretta did, "What the hell have I done?"

At a later point in time and out of curiosity more than anything, the four spoke to Sean's lawyer friend about what had happened to Loretta back in 1964. Even the lawyer said that, in reality, the pastor would have received much more news coverage than Loretta had the rapes been made public. Marco was well known, and

200

the newspapers would have wanted to bring him down. Loretta might have just been regarded as a kept woman or mistress, but he would have been big news. Probably after covering her story for a few days, it would have all been focused on him. The doctors and the lawyer all think he would never have let that happen, and he would have killed her at some point. He was probably planning on how to dispose of her body when he met his demise.

A few days after the initial consultation with Marsha, when Frank was back with the others, the analyses continued and deepened. One of the many things that Marsha and her colleagues discovered was that the last six months of abuse were, for Loretta, like a job; sometimes she didn't mind going, sometimes she was excited to go, sometimes she hated to go, etc.—all of what we feel when the alarm goes off, except that her job was mainly at night or when Frank was out of town. Frank thought that was an interesting way of looking at it. The doctor told Loretta to correct her if she was wrong but said she bet that Loretta would, during those last six months, just walk into the pastor's office, take off all of her clothes, and do everything he told her to do.

Loretta was surprised by the doctor's insightfulness and said that was precisely how the sessions went. The doctors continued to conjecture that Loretta would initiate all conversations at that stage, that even up to the end, there were times he didn't know if he was her leader or the follower. So he let her control many aspects of the sessions. Then, when he was done, she would shower and go home. Sometimes, during the last months, she would even give him a goodbye peck on the cheek. The doctor, amazingly, told Loretta that she was guessing that at no time was there ever a "Hollywood Kiss" or embrace—never. Loretta said, "How did you know that?" She said he never, never tried to kiss her, ever, and she could not stand to think about kissing him. The doctors also told Loretta that she probably talked incessantly as he performed oral sex on her—again—correct. This was to block out her enjoyment of what she was doing behind Frank's back. Finally, Marsha told Loretta, "I'm guessing that sometimes when he wasn't looking, you would spit semen into whatever he was drinking!" Again, right on the nose! This would give Loretta an even greater feeling of power and one-upmanship over him in her mind. She asked Loretta, "Did you ever get him into a sexual act right underneath a picture of Jesus or a cross in his office?" She thought for a minute and said yes, that she had intentionally done that but had forgotten until they asked.

As the days went by and Loretta's story began to unfold in more and more detail, Marsha and her associates shifted their technique for analysis to hypnosis, and this time they had precise questions they wanted her to answer while she was hypnotized. They began with generalities during the time right before the "abduction" and then started bringing her through "The Year." Frank, Sean, and Mickey were all in the room at first. As they sat around listening to her unfold the story, they could hardly breathe. Mickey said, "Even tough guy Sean sat there frozen." Frank was motionless in his chair as well. Loretta told her story so well, calm and matter-of-factly. There were descriptions of the pastor's early attacks that were so excessive for sexual encounters—no pain or torture, but a very methodical use of her body. He didn't miss much. The first six months, she had had to bend to his will completely, and so she did. As the analysis continued, the three could tell the questions were becoming more specific and detail-oriented. The doctor was probing in a step-by-step fashion, trying to get deeper and deeper into the story. At one point, the doctor asked Frank and Sean if they would mind leaving for a while; they would be told everything later, but they would prefer the men were not there for the actual asking and answering. Besides, everything was being taped. So Sean and Frank went out to the beach.

What follows here is a brief account of what was discovered during Loretta's lengthy analysis. It may serve as a good look into the mind of a psychotic and a good look into the mind of a victim before and after they tip over the edge of reality. The way Loretta reacted the first six months is so like her—true to her personality—but the last six months, she became someone that the others did not know, or for that matter, that she did not know. Even her speech patterns would change from the church to home and back. Under hypnosis, Loretta was able to bring back her actual voice sounds, and it was scary for the others to hear. As they waited for Loretta to go into a deep trance, Marsha told them that she suspected Loretta had felt the need to modify the sounds her voice usually made as a means for self-protection. They would hear the change take place almost immediately after she began talking about her October "takeover" of Marco.

Mickey said, "One minute we thought we had covered everything in the analysis, and the next minute Marsha was telling us the most interesting was yet to come, and boy was she right! No wonder she is considered one of the world's foremost hypnotists in psychiatry!" Mickey continued, saying that it was quite unnerving to watch Loretta go through the transformation into October of 1964. She asked Marsha if Marco wouldn't have wondered about it, and she could not believe the answer. Marsha said, "He would not even have noticed it because he too was now becoming a different person, and HE probably talked differently as well!" She added that he was also becoming a more dangerous man, as he was thinking more clearly about the outcome and knew it would be bad for him no matter which way it ended. Probably by March 1965, Loretta was in mortal danger. Marsha thought that Marco's change of attitude is in part what may have prompted Loretta to seek out a psychiatrist.

Mickey recalled:

It was all so strange today. As I said, we all thought the questions were coming to an end, and then we learned that we were just beginning! I'm still not dealing with it. Now, as to Loretta's stories under hypnosis, her new voice, and their ways of having sex, the session lasted about three hours and was incredible. Some of it embarrassed Loretta a great deal, but the doctor would wipe out the guilt as she went along in the storyline under hypnosis. I didn't change my opinion of her at all, of course, and listening to the voice that came out of Loretta; it wasn't her anyway. When we played the tape back for her later, she was really helped, not hurt or embarrassed. She kept saying, "I wouldn't do that... wouldn't do that!" But she knew she had. Some of it she'd put so far back in her mind that it was brand new to her. She just kept staring at the tape machine and saying, "I don't / didn't remember that—until now—but now I can see it vividly!" Oh my God! I remember now! OH NO! I was so awful," and so on.

Mickey spoke in private with the doctor after this four-hour session had ended to inquire about Loretta's level of stress and her ability to cope with the resurfacing of all this nightmarish detail. At this point in the interviews, the doctor was quite concerned as well. Loretta had not been given any drugs for the hypnosis sessions, but she had been hooked up to blood pressure monitors. Marsha told Mickey that Loretta was exhibiting the same stress that soldiers do when returning from combat. As their questioning moved to specific events, she had noted that the blood pressure

204

readings would move up and become dangerously high. This can be normal, but what bothered her was that the typical reaction is an increase, for say, a minute or two, and then the blood pressure surge begins to subside. Loretta's would remain "sky high" for as much as ten minutes—until they would ask a silly question to get her off of that subject. But then it would go back up after answering the silly question. In other words, her mind was not dismissing it and still hadn't.

Marsha said it might just take care of itself, but there was a chance Loretta could have a real "meltdown." The doctor, who worked almost exclusively with post-war soldiers usually, was quite concerned. She said, "I don't like this one bit." So at that point, Mickey, Sean, and Frank made a pact that Loretta would not be left alone until they could be sure she was stable once again. Of course, she would be given her privacy, but she would not be alone in the house. Marsha did reassure them, however, by saying that Loretta's sex drive was above average, which is unusual for someone who was sexually assaulted. Many women lose interest or are afraid to be in intimate situations after being raped or abused, but not Loretta. She loved it all and often. Marsha said this was an excellent sign that Loretta would be all right.

Returning to Loretta's interview under hypnosis, Marsha now began to talk to Loretta about relating the October transformation. Frank and Sean were at this point still on the beach, but for a moment, Marsha and Mickey thought that Sean had suddenly come into the room. Then they realized that Loretta was talking with his accent. She was now using a Scottish brogue almost identical to Sean's. Mickey just sat there, practically unable to breathe. After the session was finished, Marsha asked Mickey, "Has Loretta ever, in kidding, used Sean's accent?" Mickey replied, "She does it all the time! We think it's really good!" So Loretta, using Sean's accent, began to relate the threesomes the pastor had ordered. She talked about Marco hiring the high-class prostitutes and male escorts. The sexual episodes now consisted of her having sex with both women and men.

She went on and on about how a woman would be there when she came into the pastor's office, and they would have sex. Then he started to have a male escort there—same thing. Loretta loved it all. She talked slowly and in the Scottish accent about what they would do together as Marco watched. Marco's plan had become evident at this point. If it all came out in the open, he could produce men and women prostitutes who could testify that she was a willing participant. They would be able to testify in court that she did not at any time protest. Marco was still going to kill her. It was just that now he knew he had a backup defense should it be necessary. The prostitutes would not even have associated the disappearance of a housewife with the woman they had seen in Marco's office. In a large city, these kinds of news stories, missing spouses, whatever, were not as unusual then. He could have walked out clean.

As Loretta was relating the sexual episodes, she would stop and say things in her own voice such as, "NO, PLEASE, I DON'T WANT TO DO THIS!" and then she would return to the Scottish accent and gleeful participation. These personality shifts would move in and out, back and forth; one minute, she was Loretta, and the next minute she was someone else. Mickey said, "It was incredible!" After the escorts and prostitutes went home, Loretta would relax, and her real voice would return, and she would just be Loretta as she headed out the door to go back home. As she continued her story, some other interesting questions were answered, and they all began to see things more clearly.

For example, Marsha asked Loretta, "When was your first *ménage à trois* with Diane?" Loretta's answer—1973. Marsha: "Had you ever done that before at any time in your life?" Loretta: "NO." Marsha: "Had you fantasized about doing that?" Loretta: "NEVER." Marsha: "Does it bother you now?" Loretta: "No, I love it."

Marsha explained the connection between Loretta's "Year" and her enjoyment ever since then of sex with both male and female partners in this way. She said that Marco set up encounters with multiple partners of both sexes to humiliate and debase Loretta further. But since he never participated in those groupings, she came to look forward to them because they kept Marco off of her. Loretta said Marco always watched and never participated in the group sex he ordered for her; his fantasy was to look on, not be actively involved. Therefore, sex with other women and with several partners at the same time became, for Loretta, a positive psychological event, and this, Marsha said, would stay with her for the rest of her life.

At this juncture in the analysis under hypnosis, Loretta was asked to continue with specific descriptions of some of the threesomes she had had and a foursome a couple of times. Since the details of some of these sessions when I spoke of Loretta's "Year" earlier have already been recounted, I will not repeat them here. Still, two of the escorts hired by Marco on many occasions, Kelly and Samuel, were noteworthy and were credited with having been instrumental in saving Loretta's life. Samuel is the escort who first asked Loretta what was wrong, the one to whom she first confided that she had been abducted and threatened with exposure, but then she had begged him not to go to the police. He is also the one who told Loretta he could see two personalities in her and who told her that she should see a psychiatrist as soon as possible.

He had then been able to tell his friend Kelly, who was also one of Marco's frequent escort hires, what was happening. Together over the next few months, they had watched over Loretta and let her know she was no longer alone. She had two good friends and both of their phone numbers. She was told to call immediately if she ever felt in danger, and because of their help, she had felt hope that things might end in her favor. Just ten days after creating this bond, Loretta had found the strength to go to a psychiatrist for the help she so badly needed.

When Loretta's "Year" had ended, she had met Kelly and Samuel for dinner, and she thanked them so much for literally saving her life. They also met several times after that just to visit. Later, she learned that they had both left their work as escorts and had finished college. Working for the escort service had been their way of making money for school. The last time Loretta had heard from them at the point when Marsha was analyzing her was two years prior, so essentially, Loretta had stayed pretty close to them all these years, though she hadn't seen them for quite some time.

After Frank heard Loretta talking about them with Marsha, he asked Loretta to arrange a meeting with Kelly, Samuel, and the four of them. Sean added that he would fly them to California in his private jet if they would agree to come, and they would have a great reunion. I must add here that, though I understood the vital role Kelly and Samuel had played in likely saving Loretta's life, and I also thought this reunion was a great idea, I was once again feeling left out. It seemed that everyone but me was being taken to California on Sean's private jet to visit them. Yet, once again, I said nothing, as it would have come across as petty and childish—what about me? In hindsight, though, I should probably have addressed my concerns each time someone, but not me, was flying off to

Malibu. Loretta thought inviting them was an excellent idea too, but she said she needed to add "one more little tidbit" to the story of Kelly and Samuel. Mickey told me later, "We all knew what she was going to tell us, and we started to giggle." Sean kept her from having to tell. He said to Loretta, "Your visit with those two a couple of years ago, tell us. Did you all climb into bed together for old times' sake?" Loretta answered immediately with laughter, "You're damn right we did, and it was at my request."

In effect, I loved those two for what they meant to me. Think about what it all entailed! Those two saved me as far I'm concerned, and I thought it was important for the three of us to love each other without Marco directing, or me being so afraid, or whatever. So, hell yes, we went to bed, and I'm glad we did! I out and out said to them, "Guys, for old times' sake and without the fear and oppression, could I make love to the both of you at the same time?" They thought that would be great. So we went to bed and had a wonderful "reunion," and we don't think it was wrong, even though they now have families of their own, and I, of course, have you three. It wasn't a betrayal or an affair. It was a great, great loving "tribute" to a most incredible piece of our life history.

All of them, Sean, Frank, and Mickey, agreed wholeheartedly that it had been the perfect thing to do. Frank said it would have been a terrible waste of a chance for her to "appropriately" thank the two of them *not* to have done it in that fashion, in the vein of what happened. Then he added with a smile, "I like the way we all explain away everything to fit our philosophy! You gotta admit, we have a firm grasp on the art of rationalization!" Here I must agree with him. Their ability to claim fidelity, all the while rationalizing any number of infidelities by usual social standards, was almost comical.

21

Saviors

As desired by the four, in the middle of March 2009, Kelly and Samuel were invited to spend a few days in the Connery home, along with Marsha and two of her associates to keep an eye on Loretta. Loretta called both Kelly and Samuel the same evening the four discussed inviting them. She also wanted to fill them in on how her life had worked out. She naturally wanted to hear about them as well. First, Loretta gave Kelly a summary of what had been going on the past few days with the psychoanalyses. Kelly was overwhelmed. Then Frank got on the phone and, almost in tears, thanked her repeatedly for what she had done for Loretta. This was followed by Sean getting on the phone to thank her. One can imagine Kelly's excitement to find herself speaking to "the man" himself. Next, Loretta called Samuel and had virtually the same conversation with him as she had had with Kelly. When she told him about the last five days of analyses, he said it "blew his mind." Then Sean got on the line, and Samuel was elated to be speaking with him as well. Both Sean and Frank kept thanking him profusely for saving Loretta. Sean told both of them he was sending his private jet to get them for the weekend. They were as thrilled by the invitation as the others had been in extending it, and they accepted without hesitation, though obviously, they were in a state of shock when they received the phone calls. It was to be a jam-packed weekend.

Both of their lives had significantly changed since Kelly and Samuel had first met Loretta as escorts hired by Marco. They had both managed to complete their doctoral work and had become university professors. Dr. Kelly, PhD, age sixty-six, was only twenty-one years old when she had first met Loretta and was now a retired professor of mathematics at the University of Maryland. She had been married to the same man for thirty-six years and was now widowed. After his death, Kelly had sadly discovered that he ahd been involved in some secret, unscrupulous financial dealings that now haunted her. They had chosen not to have any children. Dr. Samuel, PhD, age sixty-seven, was twenty-two years old during "The Year" and had gone on to become a professor of English literature at Colombia University, New York. He was married once, for thirteen years. His only child, Michael, had been killed in a car crash at age nine. Samuel and his wife divorced two years later, and he had never wanted to remarry.

Marsha and her associates were anxious to see Loretta's reaction to the reunion and also, mostly out of curiosity, anxious to speak to Kelly and Samuel in general. The doctors wanted everyone to be aware of the obvious. They said that just because Loretta recovered nicely from the first trauma didn't mean she would be able to mentally reproduce the same positive outcome this time. She had recalled her terrible year several times at this point, and she had reached deep into her subconscious to do so.

Marsha cautioned that this could cause Loretta post-traumatic stress, much like what soldiers experience at times, though obviously for very different reasons. For example, after Steven Spielberg's *Saving Private Ryan*, which supposedly was the most accurate visual of what the landing at Normandy had been like, the veterans' hospitals had been inundated with vets from that era with severe post-war syndromes. After all those years, seeing that

212

film so accurately displaying the terrible event had been too much for them, even so many years later. For that reason, the doctors, as well as Sean, Frank, and Mickey, believed that Loretta should be watched over for the next few months. "If two or three years go by and she remains strong, fine," all three doctors agreed.

Over the next few days, during Kelly and Samuel's visit, Frank made the following observations concerning Loretta's behavior, "She seems fine, but is less likely to enter conversations. She's not sullen and says she's not depressed, but there are some peculiar changes to her daily responses. Sean and Mickey noticed as well." Kelly and Samuel both saw symptoms from the past. While they were not familiar with her habits over the past forty-four years, they said she was exhibiting some of the same quirks she had had during "The Year," not obvious ones, but subtle. For example, they noted Loretta had some of the same nervous tics she had had then; twitching of fingers and hands, things like that. Frank said she hadn't done that in years. It had just started up.

They all also noted that Loretta was holding on to Kelly and Samuel constantly since they had arrived. She went into their bedrooms at two a.m. to visit, for example. She had asked Sean and Frank if that was OK. They said, of course, it was. Frank later wrote to me, saying, "She cries easily today." I was worried, too, at that point. But, there was nothing to be done for now other than to go on with life and keep Loretta in view. The doctors agreed. She did not qualify for hospitalization.

On a lighter note, Loretta's desire to keep Kelly and Samuel close was literal as well as figurative. The doctors had all agreed that her sex drive might be quite strong for a while, and they were correct. They had added that Loretta should have no reason to seek "comfort" outside of the four, but since Kelly and Samuel had arrived, it was evident to Frank and the others that she had "wandered off course a tweak" as they put it. Frank said they didn't give a damn about it, that that kind of contact was different and accepted by them all, another example of their uncanny ability to rationalize practically any infidelity. Samuel and Kelly came to Sean at one point and said they were worried about how they should handle Loretta's advances. He replied, "Just don't interrupt me when I'm watching the History Channel specials." Then he added, "Mitchell is old and feeble, but he's not paying any attention either." Of course, this meant neither of them was bothered by whatever Loretta and the two visitors decided to do, as long as the two of them weren't interrupted. Sean was joking, of course. They all realized the contact brought her much comfort and love, and they were happy about that. Loretta spent both Friday and Saturday nights with Kelly and Samuel.

As their busy weekend with Kelly and Samuel drew to a close, the others could tell that Sean was planning a surprise for the two who had played such a significant role in saving Loretta's life so long ago. He had numerous business meetings, and the others knew better than to ask. Sean loved to surprise the people he cared about (I honestly kept waiting for him to surprise *me*). Loretta said, "Sean is going to do something really, really nice for Kelly and Samuel, and they deserve it!" When the time came, Sean had a private meeting with each of them separately. He told them of his and Frank's overwhelming gratitude for having helped bring Loretta back to them, that there was no price tag to be put on that one.

To Kelly, Sean said that he would be paying off her one-hundred-thousand-dollar delinquent income tax bill, which was left over from her late husband's questionable dealings. To Samuel, Sean explained that he would finish paying off his home mortgage of over forty thousand dollars and be handing him a cash gift of

214

sixty thousand so that the sums would be equal. It may have taken a while, but the adage "what goes around comes around" certainly seemed to fit here. Loretta added, "Think about those two for a minute. In society's eyes, they were considered scum, tramps; the lowest society has to offer. Yet look at what they did for me and what they've done with their lives. Forty-three years later, they are still friends and helping each other out, including giving each other the emotional support they need from time to time. Does this sound like rotten people? Society needs to know more than it does before drawing conclusions!"

I would certainly agree with Loretta on that issue, and I was thrilled for the two that they would be so generously compensated for having taken care of Loretta so long ago. Yet, you guessed it; I couldn't stop myself from once again thinking how much one hundred thousand dollars would help *me* as well. I had been writing for them for close to two years at this point. I kept waiting for *my* surprise—"oh yes, and Lynda, we are sending you that contract and retainer we've been promising you now too since you've been working so hard!" Clearly, that would not be the case.

As the reunion drew to a close and the four were conversing with the psychiatrists about this horrendous year in Loretta's life, someone asked what had happened to the tapes that the pastor had made. He had filmed every encounter the entire year of Loretta's abuse, and Frank had taken them on the night he had gone to kill Marco. Where were they? How amazing it would be if Frank had not destroyed the tapes, they said. Imagine the impact such films could have, they continued. Loretta and Frank looked at each other, and she said, "Tell them!" Frank then divulged that they had not destroyed the tapes for many reasons: They were in their possession and safely hidden away. Emmett had told them he felt the recordings should be kept—that "you never know," and

Loretta and Frank had concurred. Loretta had gone so far as to say to Emmett, "There is no way those films or pictures are to be destroyed—never ever! I don't even care what reasons you have."

Sometime after Kelly and Samuel had returned home and things were settling back into a more normal routine, Loretta seemed to be returning to her old self. So, I felt the need to ask what is probably an obvious question to most concerning Loretta's "Year." I was picturing myself in her shoes with the pastor, and I could not imagine myself allowing his abuse to have occurred, let alone to have continued for a year. Not wanting to cause Loretta any more pain or guilt, I spoke with the other three to ask their opinions on the matter. I learned that the others all thought she should either have run away in the first place or, more likely, have let him rape her that first night but then told Frank what was going on.

However, the truth is that we are all analyzing the situation using hindsight, which, as they say, of course, is 20/20. So much was different during those times, especially when it came to convicting a well-known, highly respected, and on top of that very handsome pastor of raping some unknown member of his congregation, with the only evidence being her word against his. Plus, Loretta knew that if Frank's connection to the Mafia, although it had been as a civilian, had become known, his career and their lives would have been ruined. She was young and terrified, and as time went on, it would have been more and more difficult for her to prove that she was a victim. Though the situation might at first be difficult to comprehend, upon further analysis, Loretta's decision was perhaps not as incomprehensible as it appears.

But what of the end to this story? Did Marco deserve to be killed? He was a despicable pig, for sure, but was his assassination warranted? Loretta told us she was certainly thrilled that he was gone, yet she also added that she would have much preferred to see him go to jail for a very long time and to have seen him stripped of his power in his church, humiliated as he had done to her, etc. The truth is, however, that no court would ever have convicted him. So I asked, what about just scaring him—threatening him with torture and assassination if he said a word to anyone or laid a hand on Loretta ever again? Frank said, quite honestly and without hesitation, that once he had heard Loretta's story, "At no time did I consider anything but that he would die. My level of anger, deep, deep sadness for Loretta, and all of the other obvious emotions were so in control of my thoughts. I'll be the first to admit that I was not rational. I'm not a psychiatrist, but I would think that I was at some level of insanity. Since I called my father almost immediately after hearing Mary Sue's story, that was out of the question anyway. He did not just scare people, and I knew that. I knew that the phone call had sealed his doom.

"Now, after I've excused myself so neatly, let's look at the situation for the sake of argument—scare him? How? He would not know I had someone like my father waiting in the wings, so I think it would come off as big talk. I don't know, of course, but I think so. I don't think he would have tried to see her anymore since I then knew about it. I think that would have ended it, but in my selfish state of mind, and I think Loretta's, that would never have brought us even near any closure. You mean we would just say, 'You'd better not do that anymore, Pastor!' and walk away? No way. So after that, what is there? Bringing it out in the open, a major scandal? And he still possibly wins as the congregation might forgive him? And we would have to leave the area? Why should we have to have our lives ruined, and he keeps on ticking? All of these thoughts came into play. But this is all digression. My decision was final—right or wrong—it was final. And I have never regretted it for a moment, ever." Well, that was clear. Frank was never one to mince his words.

Sean further explained the dilemma. "Mitchell and Loretta had many conversations with Frank's father Emmett after the fact. The very question of scaring Marco as an option was discussed. Here's what Emmett said, 'There is no way that Silvano Vitale, the Mafia Godfather who had been in the photos Marco used as a blackmail technique against Loretta, would have done anything to help her. He might have told Marco not to talk about him to the public in general, but he would probably have enjoyed a so-called man of God kidnapping and multiple raping an upstanding member of the community.'" Sean continued, "The Mafia was under terrific attack by government and the general populace during this time. Not only would Frank have lost his job, but he also would never have taught again. What Emmett did say Loretta should have done was to oblige Marco that first evening, go home, and call him (Emmett). That would have ended the siege.

"Mitchell and I placed the question to the psychiatrists as to why Loretta did not seek help from Frank or Emmett almost immediately. Their answer was so simple. I remember them saying, just a month ago, when we all talked about this when Loretta was not around (we were not scolding her in any way, just discussing ways she might have altered the situation), the doctors said, 'You're thinking like men. Loretta was devastated, embarrassed, and humiliated. There is no way she could easily go home that night and tell Frank what had happened. In those days, women blamed themselves for being raped; even society blamed women for being raped.'" Good point. Things have changed now, of course, to a certain extent, but in those days, Loretta would have been considered the guilty party in all probability. Returning to Sean's analysis:

"We discussed this so much this past month because the doctors were saying that Loretta was feeling so guilty that the abuse went on for so long. Now we could see that her main deterrent from telling someone right away had had merit. Marco was so loved by his congregation, especially the women who were probably all in love with him anyway, that the whole thing could have crashed back down on her. Loretta has said many times that if it had been a different man, she would have run out of the room or at the least have gone home and told Mitchell. But she was being assaulted by one of the most revered men on the east coast!"

Next came Mickey's opinion on the matter. "Your question—do I think killing Marco was justified? Probably not. Loretta was still alive. However, I do agree with much of Frank's analogy as to what would have happened. I think the Pastor would have 'walked.' I think Frank and Loretta would have had to move, which is not the end of the world. Personally, I might have wanted to start a new life. But I also would have wanted the man destroyed. I have a philosophy that, now and then, justice comes at a price. Frank made a fascinating statement at the end of his explanation. He said the most curious thing, almost as a tagline, a pause after his quote mentioned earlier. Frank said, 'Sometimes the answer changes.' Interesting line." Mickey continued, "This was revenge. Revenge rarely works, if ever. Loretta says she's fine, but that's probably not true. She's so strong that she does better than most people. She was dragged through twelve months of the most unspeakable terror, not at the level of war, but an incredible horror nonetheless. I'm going to cut Frank some slack on the 'right thing to do' question. But as Loretta says, 'Marco being dead is no satisfaction. He felt no embarrassment or humiliation and did no prison time, which is what he deserved.' Yet, the bottom line is he needed to be removed from the pulpit one way or another. It sure beats the hell out of him standing at the alter preaching to his flock and, maybe, who knows, abusing some other woman or women!"

As to what Loretta would have wanted, when I finally felt the time would be appropriate to ask her, this is how she responded. After years of consideration on the question, her thoughts were that she would rather he had been exposed and her story told to an open forum. Her thoughts, then and now, were to embarrass him publicly, to disgrace him, to try him in a court of law, all that good stuff that revenge should, though seldom does, carry with it. But the bottom line was always there. It was the belief then and remains so now that this man would have emerged unscathed. He would have been seen no more or no less as a pastor who was sexually attacked by a parishioner. It would have all fallen back on Loretta. She would have been the antagonist until the end, and as Mickey said, "Wouldn't that just have been another ton of woe piled on top of her already humiliated body and mind? Logic and rationale will never have a comfortable place to sit while this story is being told, but what if Frank's right? Sometimes, the answer changes."

22

The shadow

As the story of Loretta's "Year" and all that went with it slowly returned to a less conscious level for the four, their attention turned to Mickey, as her illness had now taken a turn for the worse. Loretta became her nurse of sorts, I was told, tending to her regularly and giving her massages as needed to help ease her pain. The others were apprehensive. Sean was quiet and depressed. Their writing all but stopped. The trip to Lincoln that the four had planned for the end of May to meet with me and my colleagues and our families was canceled. The reality of Mickey and Frank's illnesses was hitting home. Frank was doing reasonably well, but his lab results showed a steady decline. The doctor told him that in the not too distant future, the *bad times* would begin. As always, his reaction was to say to me he had no intention of going "gentle into that good night" but instead kicking and screaming and fighting for every last minute.

At this point, Sean told me that Mickey was to undergo yet another round of grueling radiation, which would leave her exhausted and feeling even more ill. He summarized it this way, "More radiation treatments are in store for her, and they are vicious!" But it was all that could be done for her at this point. Then he added, "You won't hear from me or Mickey, and probably Loretta, for some time now. We need to take care of our girl." Then he added, "If only Mitchell and Mickey were well, our lives would be complete happiness. I just can't believe this is happening. Mitchell is getting sicker, and I'm sure you notice how quiet he has become these days. His pain is increasing, and the doctors can help him a little bit but not enough. He and Mickey are both beginning what the doctors refer to as 'the bad times.' Loretta and I just feel sick and so helpless as we watch them suffer in silence. They won't ever tell you they are in pain, never."

A couple of weeks later, I received the following message from Sean. Frank had been spending less time in California and more in Lincoln, and all of us saw this as a way of not allowing the other three to see how much pain he was in. He seemed to want seclusion, but the others wanted him with them so they could give him their love and support. Loretta told me that Frank was the only one of the four who could enjoy days off from their group living. She said, "He is so private, and his downtime is important to him. Even when he is in California, he goes off by himself. He even goes to movies by himself. We never ask. We just let him go wherever and whenever he wants. He lives in his own world. You never know what he is thinking. I find him so interesting—well, all of us do!"

Everything Loretta said was true, of course, and I could see perfectly well Frank wanting his alone time. When Sean and the other two had first lamented about Frank secluding himself in Lincoln, I had felt quite sad and sorry for him. I would think of him alone in his Lincoln house, writhing in pain perhaps, and refusing to ask for help. There was even an instance when I wrote him and begged him to get back to Malibu, as the others had told me they were missing him terribly and were quite worried. Later, of course, I would learn that he was perhaps in great pain, but he was not alone. Sasha was there to ease his pain.

Sean's next message gave me a glimpse into how Frank's desire for time away from them affected others. Sean wrote:

"Frenchie, not a good week here. Both Frank and Mickey were down. Frank's fine now, and Mickey is getting better, so it's a good movie ending for now." But the next day, Frank headed back to Lincoln, against the wishes of the others, and Sean wrote, "He's back in Lincoln. It's sad here. We can't talk him out of his hideout. We have to honor it, though as you suggested, should he not also honor our feelings? I used that one on him, but he said, 'You guys know that I wouldn't insult you or hurt you. Please allow me to spend my last times with you—and without you.' At that, we were all crying."

Frank gave me the following explanation for his constant desire to go back and forth between Lincoln and Malibu, saying, "Mickey is very ill. Loretta is her sort of live-in nurse. Sean needs her for both of them but didn't ask for her in that way. It was my command that they concentrate on the three of them and let me be the wild card. It seems to make my life more enjoyable to fly about the skies from California to Nebraska, staying in both places, subbing, seeing my friends" (and Sasha) "in Nebraska, and then a flight back to California for a while, etc. I want those three to enjoy the lifestyle they love, and I want to enjoy mine. So don't go thinking that they have abandoned me and all that stuff. It's my call entirely. I'll have it all this way.

"'So this is how I envision our set up for this school year—" (August 2009) "I am not now, nor will I ever be wanting to retire. I will sign up for subbing again. I won't do it very much, but if I should be in town and I like the assignment, I'll take it. Don't worry. I'll never embarrass myself. I would never go into a classroom if I were too sick or could not function very well. I always know where I am on that scale. So, for as long as I am able, I want to be back and forth to Lincoln. My health is holding well, and I want to stay active. To tell the truth, even though it sounds so wonderful to sit on a beach all the time, it bores me to death. I get bored out here. Loretta loves it, and her life is going very well with all the activity. I know. It's a strange world we live in. I can never be under the sun anyway, so it feels foolish to sit under an awning while everyone else is frolicking about the beach. Heck with them! I'd rather be lurking in the halls of Lincoln High School!"

Shortly after my conversation with Frank about his plans to continue substitute teaching even into the fall of 2009, Loretta and I talked about her deep love for both Sean and Frank and about Frank and Mickey's illnesses. Her love for Sean started first, of course, and continued to grow through the years, but what of her love for Frank? How did it compare? Did she love one more than the other? Loretta spoke of Frank in these terms, "My love for Frank has grown from the minute I first met him. From a 'Gee, he's a nice guy,' to 'Gee he's a sexy guy' and so on up my emotional ladder. As of today's writing, I am unable to put into words the depth of my attraction, caring, and the deep, deep love that I have for this man.

"I love Sean in a rage of a way if that makes sense. I am obsessed with the man. The energy behind my love for him is immeasurable. And—but, so is my love for Frank. It is immeasurable as well, but not at the fervor level as it is for Sean. Frank knows of my passion for Sean, but he also knows that I love him to death also and in all ways. Trying to measure the quantity of love I have for each of them is of no interest to him—or to Sean for that matter. Sean said to me on one of our trips to Vegas in the late '90s, 'I don't mind being in 2nd place.' I was startled at what he said and asked him to explain, so he went on to say, 'I know you don't realize that you talk about your husband all of the time when we're together, and I love it. You seem to glow as you speak of him. Of course, you love me too, but now Mitchell has the main room in your heart, and I couldn't be more pleased and comforted. You've always loved him, but now it's off the charts. Your love for him can't be measured! I'm going to tell him this when we get back.' And, he did."

Loretta continued, "When we got the terrible news" (about Frank's cancer) "as we sat in Dr. Green's office that October of 2004, I almost passed out. They had to bring me a sedative. At no time in my life can I remember hearing such terrible news save for my Mother's death, with whom I was so very close. He's always been there—here. It never occurred to me that he would leave before me, never. I just took him for granted. But now he's dying. He never complains. If you ask him how he's doing, he'll say, 'Super.' The past four years, I've actually come to love him so deeply in my heart and soul that I throw up now and then when I stop to think of what's happening to him. I cannot compute this event. I will have a terrible reaction to Mickey's death as well. We are all so close. These three are my life, but this man, in particular, is beyond my ability to tell the world. I don't know what I'll do."

As the months passed, I began to see more clearly how tremendous a toll Frank and Mickey's illnesses were taking on Sean and Loretta. Frank and Mickey were in constant pain and often nauseous, they said, yet somehow, they continued to live their lives to the fullest extent possible, their positive outlooks rarely waning. Frank would tell me many times how wonderful and amazing of a life he had lived, that he had few regrets, and that though he would put up one hell of a fight to stay alive as long as possible, he was at peace with the knowledge that his time was near. Mickey's feelings paralleled his. They both told me they believed it was far more difficult for Sean and Loretta to cope with their illnesses and impending death than it was for them. The two of them had come to terms with their deaths, had accepted their fates. Sean and Loretta had not. Sean became very sullen and reclusive. Loretta followed suit. The *bad times* were in full swing even more for them than for Mickey and Frank, and all they could do was make their beloved mates and friends as comfortable as possible and help-lessly watch their conditions deteriorate. I was on the outside looking in at this point, it seemed to me. There were few if any calls from Frank, few if any letters. When I did receive news, it was often a message from Loretta telling me how very ill Frank and Mickey were and how devastated she and Sean were. I could feel their pain and sense of helplessness.

I have no firsthand knowledge of Mickey and Frank's physi-cal and emotional condition during this period. My updates were most often from Loretta now, though at times I would hear from Sean, and Quentin had also described Frank's condition to me—it wasn't good. The last time I saw Frank was shortly before his fin-ger was amputated. I can state that he was quite ill and suffering even then, and I am relatively sure that the pain and decline for both of them were real. That being said, both would live far lon-ger than I was led to believe. I was happy for them that they were given more time on this earth, but I remain confused and skeptical about how that came to pass. The medications they were taking were possibly doing their job and helping them in their fight to stay alive. Perhaps by now, I was intentionally being misled so that they might significantly reduce their communications with me. I did not know it until much later, but I had entered a period in which their truths were rapidly transforming into lies.

23

Ménages à trois

Returning now to happier times, soon after discussing "The Plan" in November of 2008, the ladies, Mickey and Loretta, had started pondering the similarities and differences when making love with Sean or Frank, and those conversations led to some rather humorous exchanges, with Loretta in particular. She was telling me that she figured the number one question that people would probably want to ask her was, "How can your excitement and pleasure, your sexual gratification, your body's reactions and orgasms, be the same with both Sean and Frank?" She said the answer was that they were not the same—their techniques in bed, as explained earlier, were almost identical, but her reactions to them were not. Loretta described the differences in this fashion:

When Sean takes me, it's a lightning bolt throughout my body and mind. I almost think I'll pass out, but I know I won't. The pleasure is immeasurable. That same moment with Frank is an incredible force of power and control over my body and mind. It's as though his sex was the most comforting, the most protective, the most 'I am safe from the world now' kind of feeling. It has taken me years to come up with these thoughts in such a specific way. Of course, sex feels good with both of them, it's always all of that, but with these two, the mental and physical feelings are entirely different.

Frank asked Loretta bluntly after she told him this last November, "I would need to know which of us gives you the most sexual relief and release." Without hesitation and with great anguish in her heart, Loretta told him, "Sean." Frank sat for a moment and then gave her his *always honest* answer. He said, "Well, I would have preferred first place. But second isn't bad. I will have some sad feelings about this, maybe even jealousy. These are new emotions for me as far as Sean is concerned, and it will be the only area that causes me pain. But it's just from a man's ego that I speak. Other than that, it has no effect, and in every other aspect, this is wonderful. I'm not okay now, but I will be."

What Loretta didn't realize at that point was that Frank was playing with her. He wasn't jealous or hurt. He just wanted to tease her, he told me. That was in November of 2008. Months later, they returned to that conversation. Frank said to Loretta one morning in January of 2009, as they went over it again, "I'm okay with that now, at least as well as a man can be—what with our immense ego—but any down feelings I have are so overridden with the joy of what the four of us do have—so, it is no longer an issue, at least not on the surface." What a joker! Loretta, still not having realized that he was playing with her, attempted to smooth things over a bit by saying, "But what does it matter? I don't wish for one of you over the other, and isn't that the most important point?" Frank didn't let on and simply smiled at Loretta. She told me, "He smiles, but what else can he do? I tell you one minute he seems to feel no jealousy, and the next that perhaps he is, in fact, a little jealous. It makes you wonder what the truth is!"

A few days later, Frank let her know what the truth was. Loretta wrote me saying:

Lynda, I'm feeling a little foolish. I think I didn't read Frank right last November when I answered his question about whom I enjoyed sex with more. You know yourself; it is so hard to read him, to know when he's serious and when he isn't. Last night he explained it all to me, saying, 'Let's go back to that conversation last November when I'm wearing that puppy-like look on my face, and I inquire as to whom you enjoy sex with the most, and you tell me it's Sean, and then I answer that I'm not okay now, but I will be. Well, this is going to sound weak. This is going to sound like I'm just trying to make you feel better, but this is what my actual response to your telling me it's Sean in bed that does the most for you really is.

[The all capital letters were Frank's] ARE YOU TELLING ME THAT AFTER 45 YEARS YOU CAN'T TELL WHEN I'M GOING THROUGH ONE OF MY 'FEEL SORRY FOR ME' LITTLE ROUTINES? WHY WOULD I CARE WHICH ONE OF US YOU LIKE SEX THE BEST WITH? WE'VE HAD A GREAT SEX LIFE! WHY WOULD I CARE IF YOU LOVE HIM THE MOST? IT'S NOT A MATTER OF THOSE KINDS OF QUES-TIONS. IT JUST DOESN'T MATTER. I KNOW YOU LOVE ME TO DEATH. I KNOW THIS. I NEVER DOUBT IT. I KNOW OUR SEX LIFE HAS BEEN TERRIFIC. WHAT DO I CARE IF SOME BALD, OLD, CREEPY MOVIE STAR TURNS YOU ON A LITTLE MORE THAN I DO (uh, scratch the bald, old creepy movie star line)? THIS REALLY SOUNDS LAME NOW, AND IT WILL SOUND LIKE I'M JUST TRYING TO COVER MY LIT-TLE MINI TANTRUM, BUT I WAS GIGGLING TO MYSELF THEN AND AM DOING SO NOW!! SEAN IS MY BROTHER.

229

I WANT YOU TO LOVE HIM. I WANT HIM TO EXCITE YOU IN BED. I WANT ALL OF THIS KIND OF THING. AND SO WHAT? I'M GETTING THE SAME WORLD WITH YOU THAT HE IS. AND BY THE WAY, HE WOULDN'T CARE IF YOU'D PICKED ME. SEAN AND I USED TO TALK ABOUT THESE VERY QUESTIONS OVER SOME VERY GOOD SINGLE MALT SCOTCH AND WE ENJOYED EVERY MINUTE OF THE CONVERSATIONS! So there, my Dear!

Loretta concluded, "Well, now that I think back, I can see the smirk on his face. I think I was so emotional about the conversation that I expected him to be hurt." Ah, Frank! Never a dull moment!

In keeping with the subject of comparing Sean and Frank in bed, one day, Loretta and Mickey got in the mood to tell me how they compare when the two women are with one of them. Loretta began by saying that Frank is better at the threesomes than Sean. She said they keep telling Sean to be more patient, to slow down, and enjoy both of them for as long as he can. Loretta's theory is that perhaps it embarrasses Sean to be in a threesome more than it does Frank and that that is why he hurries just a little bit. She added, "But hey, don't get me wrong! It's still beyond terrific! These guys are incredible! Any way you slice it, bedtime with either of these two is out of this world. There are no criticisms whatsoever! You don't have to color us silly or spoiled. We know what we have!"

What follows is a rather graphic description of bedtime with Sean *or* Frank, and it leaves little to the imagination. Loretta and Mickey told me that few men understand the vagina like these two did. They described here a typical *ménage à trois* for them involving Loretta and Mickey with Sean, though they said it would be much the same with Frank. Mickey began by explaining both Sean and

Frank's technique during oral sex, saying, "They suck the clitoris into their mouth gently, slowly and twirl their tongue around and around and blow warm air. Those two know that if you 'ha' your breath it is warm and if you blow your breath it is cool. Few men seem to know that. These guys move back and forth with both temperature changes, and it's so great I can't begin to explain. So, this is for the women to enjoy and for the men to learn!"

Loretta continued, "Their mouths come over the vagina so slowly, and you barely know they are there. Then, more pressure and the tongue goes in and out, and then the clitoris is sucked into their mouth and is sucked on slowly so as not to hurt, blowing and ha-ing, and the tongue moves along the side of the vagina where there are nerve endings for a few inches at least. On and on, faster and faster till you just go out of your mind! And that's only the beginning!" Those activities would be followed by sex in a variety of positions and in different combinations. Loretta added, "Sean's body is still magnificent, so to have this hunk of a man on top of you is electrifying! Frank has a nice body, and it doesn't matter, but he will be the first to tell you Sean was blessed with the most incredible structure to live in. I have no complaints about either of them in the physical sense, even though they are in their 70s and 80s!"

Mickey continued discussing what their threesomes were like but now focused on the two women with Frank. "Frank likes to have us lie face down, naked, of course," she says, "and he is between us massaging our backsides at the same time. Then he'll put a little lotion on his hands and rub it into us very carefully. Then we are turned over, and he does the same to our front side. His left hand on my breast and his right on Loretta's breast will stimulate our nipples. He is a master at rubbing our tummies in a slow circle-like motion. Following those activities, Frank basically

231

follows the same delicious pattern as Sean." Mickey added that it's not always the same person initiating the *ménages à trois*, but probably the ladies started it more often than the men.

The love-making generally took about two hours or more. Then the three of them would nap in each other's arms. Mickey concluded, "Now, we do have 'quickie' three's just for relief, but this is our favorite. Why in the world would we want any other men? Really—why would we even consider it?" On top of the mind-blowing technique both men used in bed, both Loretta and Mickey said that the sound of Sean's voice as he made love was enough to drive you insane as well. They told me that Frank used to have a beautiful deep bass voice, and it was so warm and sexy. He hated that it was gone (because of his illness). He told me he didn't miss the singing so much, but he missed his speaking voice. The ladies concluded by saying that none of this mattered, really. It was kind of a bonus. They loved them both so much and said they couldn't care less, even if they had a high-pitched female voice. They loved them, no matter what. Mickey humorously compared sex with these two to sex she had had with other men before they entered her life. She said that most men wanted her to give them extended oral sex, followed by intercourse, and then it was off to the café for wine and cheese. She summed up those days by saying, "Gee, thanks a lot!"

24

Turmoil

Returning for a moment to the somewhat comical and frivolous topic of who loved whom more, one afternoon at the end of April 2009, I received a flurry of emails from all four of them concerning the same story. It seemed Sean and Loretta were horribly embarrassed and ashamed, and Frank and Mickey were attempting to convince them that everything was fine. It all started one Saturday afternoon when Mickey asked Frank to take her shopping, and off they went, or so Sean and Loretta thought. It was not a problem that Sean and Loretta went straight to bed; that part was common for them even if the other two were there. But, as they made love, Loretta began talking to Sean at the same time, and this is what she said to him in a very loud voice (she said to keep in mind that she was crying out with joy and pleasure):

Sean, you are the only man I have ever loved. I love my husband to death, but nothing like this. My intestines are knotted every time you touch me, and that goes back fifty-plus years. When you are inside of me, I cannot think; my body screams out in pleasure like I've never known. Frank is a great lover, and in some ways my darling, better than you, but he cannot bring with it the animal lust and electricity and love that you combine into one event. I could not live without you. To be brutally honest, I have to live with you immediately after Mickey leaves us. Frank has ordered us to do so, and we will, and I'll love it. I'll always be at his side till the end, but though I try, I can't bring him into me past you. You are blocking his entry into my soul. Thank you, Sean.

Sean responded in kind: "Loretta, it is the same with me. I am in a heaven of some kind when I'm holding you in my arms. There has never been anyone but you. Of course, we love our spouses. But OUR love is for the books. For this reason, we were never able to stop seeing each other. We have been having our love nests since my marriage to Diane, your marriage, all of it up to this very day."

Good stuff, right? A scene for the film industry, one might think. One problem, though. Mickey had gotten carsick, and she and Frank had already returned. Loretta looked up, and Frank was just sitting in a chair in a dark corner watching—and listening to them. He had the nicest smile on his face as he slowly got up. He came to their side and sat down on the bed. He started to stroke Loretta's body, and he said:

I love the four of us so much. I'm going to miss us all so much. The joy I feel to know you are in Sean's hands and his soul and mind give me complete peace and freedom. I will not tolerate any show of guilt from either of you. It has nothing to do with me, remember? Remember, remember, remember my wishes for you at the restaurant so many years ago? I love your love, and I love the love we have for each other. I meant all of it. We will worry no more about the four. The four are bonded.

Later that day, Loretta and Sean talked some more with Frank. Loretta said he made them both feel better with his usual, "I've known this all along" and "I knew you were seeing each other, so what?" What a guy! Frank continued his commentary concerning the conversation he had overheard and his unnerving ability to witness Loretta's intense love for Sean without jealousy. He explained his ability to accept things as they were by reminding Loretta that he knew from the moment they met that her love for Sean and his for her were immeasurable. He said:

I knew your love for him was forever. I had to decide to marry you and remain number 2 or lose you altogether. I chose the latter and have never regretted it. I've never even thought about it one way or the other all these years. I knew you saw him almost every month when he wasn't away on location somewhere. Over the years, I actually saw the two of you going into a restaurant for lunch one day in DC when I went into the capital to buy some music! I giggled and felt happy for you. I've come across motel stationery, I've overheard phone calls. I came home early from an out-of-town music clinic once and saw him go into our house. I turned around and went up to Pittsburgh three hours away to visit my dad and stay with him all night and came back the next day when I was supposed to return. I didn't think about it. I had you, and it was a great life. I knew you were still getting together over the years, and it was making you happy to be with him and also making you happy to be with me. It was going just as I had imagined it would. So, forget about it. It is not an issue.

Loretta said she bought the story because she wanted to have it to lean on, but as Sean told her, "You know, Loretta, we're never going to know the inside of his mind. His face shows no expression. We just don't know what his true feelings are. We hope it's what he says, but how will we ever know for sure?"

Therefore, it became clear that Sean and Loretta were planning on fulfilling Frank and Mickey's wish for them to be together after they were gone. After all these years—decades—they would be married. But what about their notorious fighting in the old days? Would they be able to get along now, or would they still make each other crazy as they did back then? They were proclaiming their profound love for each other, but were they able to maintain the peace on a day-to-day basis at this point in their lives? The response I got from both of them was an unequivocal *yes*—telling me they had matured and changed over time in so many ways that they no longer found themselves bickering about this, that, and the other. Given this response from them both, I was surprised and amused when Mickey told me the following story in March of 2009 about a screaming match those two had had the night before. She wrote:

Lynda, a short story from last night. You remember being told that Sean and Loretta used to argue at a world-class level, but since then had matured somewhat—or so we thought? Well, it was about 11 last night, and Frank and I were walking from the beach to the house when we heard this yelling and screaming—such things as—'You haven't changed in 50 years!' 'You're still as blockheaded as you ever were!' 'I'm not going to discuss this; we're doing this my way!' and 'You do that again, and I'm going to burn all your hair.' and so on and so on. Frank and I sauntered into the living room, and Frank said, 'Aren't you two a little old for rough sex?" And I said, 'Should I call the police just for old times sake?' Well, those two were standing in the living room, Sean's hairpiece was out of place, and he was holding a towel over himself. Loretta was holding a towel over her otherwise naked body, and they were both flushed to the hilt! They turned to us, and Loretta said, 'Oh, hi guys! James and I were just discussing our trip course for tomorrow.' Frank then added, 'Oh, will you two be coming with us?' Then Sean and Loretta both glared at each other like old times, went in and got dressed, came back out, and we sat around the table having some cognac and fruit. At this point, there was very little talking, just those two glaring at each other. Looking at me, Frank broke the silence with, 'I think they're getting better at this.' Frank and I didn't say another word. We just sat in silence—me looking at Loretta and Frank looking at Sean with this innocent look on our faces, but we didn't say a word, which really added to their discomfort!

Finally, Loretta said, "He always insists on doing it on the back porch at night, and the bugs eat me alive! And I'm not going to put that stupid spray all over me and then make love! I mean, it really discourages using the tongue in any way when we taste like bug spray." Then Sean spoke up. "There isn't any taste to bug spray! And I never said we had to spray all over us!" Well, then Frank chimed in with, "How 'bout I stand there with a fly swatter?" Sean retorted to Frank, "This isn't humorous, Mitchell, and besides, I'm out of the mood." Loretta responded, "Oh gee, whatever will I do?" Frank then ended the stalemate with, "We could all play Scrabble, but there are not enough letters to keep spelling out 'you bastard!'" Well, that broke it, and everyone rolled over with laughter!

Sean and Loretta told me later that it had been a long time since they had gone at it, adding that it was great—just like the old times. Mickey said it was particularly funny because she knew they were not all that angry and that they would, in fact, give each other a little kiss between nasty remarks. Frank concluded the recounting of this story on a related but slightly different theme by telling me that he and Loretta never argued, that he and Mickey never argued. He and Sean just exchanged insults, which Sean maintained his way of telling Frank how much he loved him. The only ones prone to arguing seemed to be Sean and Loretta. In stark contrast with the others, the fiery nature of their love and passion appeared to be a double-edged sword, leading not only to intensity in the bedroom but to arguments at a sometimes explosive level as well. They were few and far between now that they had matured, but the cauldron was always simmering just beneath the surface.

25

Illness and enigma

Frank was still going back and forth between California and Lincoln during this period, and he was spending more time in Lincoln than the others liked. They knew his health was deteriorating further and that he was in ever-increasing pain, but they also knew that one of his ways of dealing with it was to be reclusive. He was spending more extended periods alone, it seemed, and the others were worried. Early in May of 2009, Loretta wrote me the following note, which frankly brought tears to my eyes.

I can hear the sadness in his voice when we talk on the phone. He doesn't want to come" (to California) "for a while. He is sitting alone 'thinking.' He acts like he's happy, but I can tell his body is beating him to a pulp. He does well in the daytime, but the night brings such pain to him. He doesn't want us to see him. He doesn't want us to wait on him. Sean told him that if he were not here by Friday night, he would fly there and bring him back, and so he will. Our daughter told me she found a piece of paper the other day in her Dad's handwriting by Edgar Allen Poe. It said, "The agony of my soul is answered by a long, loud scream of despair." I cry myself to sleep.

Frank explained to a certain extent how the emotions ran from his perspective. He said he thought that he and Mickey, and perhaps many others with their projected time frame, do not carry the same burden as do the relatives. He said that he and Mickey had spent many hours talking about this, and they both said that they wish it were as peaceful for their loved ones as it was for them. The only sadness was that they wouldn't all be together, and that fact carried a considerable impact, one of depression and heartache, but at the same time, he continued, their bodies, at times, were in so much pain that they just wanted it to stop. He said that it was kind of a double-edged sword. At that point in his illness, when I asked Frank how he was feeling, he answered, "As to how I feel— well—okay. The day continues to be my best time, with the nights becoming even more difficult to negotiate. Staying active during the day keeps me feeling better."

Shortly after another of his returns to Lincoln, I had asked Frank to reconsider and go back to California for a while. The others were so very sad and not dealing well with his absence. Two days after I received Loretta's letter, the following message from her arrived: "Sean is on his way to get Frank." Then, "We got him back … whew! He's here. He came quietly. When Sean Connery comes for you, then you will be going. Sean flew out, landed in Lincoln, drove his rented car to the house (he has keys to the house), went in and grabbed Frank's suitcase, had him pack it, and the rest is history, as they say. All Frank said was, 'If you'd just mentioned it, I would have done that myself!'" So Frank was back in California, and the four were together, but he didn't stay long—just long enough to reassure the others.

Things were not going well for anyone at that point. Sean and Loretta were anxious about the decline they saw in both Mickey and Frank. Loretta said, "It is not a happy valley around here.

240

Mickey requires our attention, and we are also concerned about Frank. He is looking worse. His blood is so bad that it causes major skin blemishes all over his head. His spleen is enlarging and functioning less and less. He is moving downward much faster than we had been led to believe. The enlarged spleen has moved down below his rib cage and is crowding other vital organs, causing great discomfort. We are distraught, and we feel so helpless! Sean is becoming more sullen and moody each day at the thought of losing his beloved wife and now Frank. He and Frank are truly like brothers. There is all kinds of sadness these days, and on top of that, guilt for Sean and me concerning how the relationships are playing out."

Loretta was talking here in part about her continuing remorse over the conversation she had had with Sean in bed when Frank was listening, but also in general about her growing love for Sean, which was noticeable to all—except Loretta herself. One day Mickey finally took her for a girl's night out so they could talk. It seemed that, quite unexpectedly, Loretta's already deep love for Sean had continued to intensify over the past six months. Mickey opened the conversation with:

You realize, Loretta, that your love for Sean has reached an incredible level and is climbing. The point is that it is moving Frank out of the position of being your husband. You don't mean this to happen, and no one blames you, but Frank is now more of a Father figure to you, and Sean is your true love interest—actually, in your mind, your husband! Frank knows this. I've watched him watch the two of you, so I got him into the same kind of conversation. He waved me off by saying, "Mickey, it's what I want for her in the final scene of this play. There is sadness for me, but there is no jealousy or anger. It is logical. For this reason, I find it easier to spend so much time in Lincoln. I want no confrontations. I want no sad discussions between us all about this. I want you to ignore it and don't tell Sean, as he will not know what to do with that kind of information. His love for Loretta has also reached the same level, and because of this, you and I have to let them go.

As Loretta listened to what Mickey had to say, she realized how right she was about her behavior the past few months. This revelation had quite an impact on her, and she knew she had some soul-searching to do. One would think that Mickey would perhaps be angry with Loretta or bitter or jealous, but Mickey, just like Frank, had long ago accepted this scenario and had had the same response as Frank. After giving the situation careful thought, Loretta concluded, "It is all so difficult, and it's my fault, but as Mickey said, it is what it is, and in no way shall our foursome be disbanded or end on a sour note. We will be solid to the end." As it turned out, the foursome might not have terminated on a sour note, but they would be ripped apart by circumstances unforeseen by any of them, and their lives certainly would not end according to "The Plan." When Loretta told me about the conversation she had had with Mickey, she concluded, "So that's why you see so much of Frank in Lincoln. I've told our daughter, and she understands. She watches over her father with so much love. This is difficult for her to be sure. She said to me last week, 'I've known of your intense love for Sean for several years now. Dad and I talked about it, and he really is happy for your pleasure and happiness. He doesn't feel cheated. He knows he's received so much of your pure love. He told me he knew the rules of the game when he suited up to play, and he said he'd won his part of the match.'"

After their talk, Loretta began a more in-depth evaluation of her feelings, thinking about what Mickey had told her during their evening out. She concluded that she disagreed that Frank had become a father figure for her, but trying to figure out exactly what *was* going on was not so simple. She said, "I have always been attracted to Frank sexually, and I still am, and I sure as hell don't want to make love to my father! Frank is still marvelous in bed!" She discussed this with Mickey for quite a while, and they returned to the original premise that it is possible to love more than one person at the same time—it was the only explanation that fit. So Loretta asked Mickey what was different at that point in her interactions with Sean and Frank, aside from the fact that she and Frank had overheard the conversation they had had that Saturday when the two thought they were alone in the house. What Mickey told her came as a shock to her. She said, "I can detect in you minor irritation if Frank's presence interferes with your and Sean's romance. Frank just laughed out loud at something that happened a few weeks ago. You almost pushed him out of the way and out the door with me so you could find Sean!"

Mickey went on to say that Loretta now sat next to Sean at all times, that she essentially only talked with him, that she only waited on him with any energy, and that it was apparently down to "Frank can get his own drink." Loretta responded, "I was completely denying this, I guess. As I started to think about what Mickey was telling me, I could see the truth in it. So, I've got to make an effort to change that. That sentence alone is awful, that I would have to make an effort—an effort to not be irritated at Frank's presence, an effort to talk with him or do things for him? How awful is that? And, what punishment for Frank, although Mickey says he just smiles and looks away. She says Frank tells her, 'it's the way the play ends in act three. I asked for it, and I got it. No regrets.'"

Mickey then pointed out that if Loretta suddenly began paying more attention to Frank, it would be so evident as to be insulting. So, she decided she would try changing her ways slowly but concluded that he would see it even then. Mickey told her that the only way to deal with Frank was with the truth, to come right out and say that Loretta had suddenly been made aware of her behavior. She said that would be the only way Frank would get into a serious conversation about it, and even then, he was going to conclude with the usual, "That's where we were headed in the first place. I'm fine with it. I've no regrets." He would just tough it out, as it were. Loretta summarized this entire episode by saying, "Well, this is indeed a minor Greek tragedy. I wouldn't hurt him for the world, but it's a little late. He's so damn strong emotionally that he just lets it bounce. Mickey says he really just goes for the humor of it all."

Honestly, I don't know of anyone else but Frank who could react so calmly and rationally to this kind of scene, but I'm reasonably sure his acceptance was sincere. He was without a doubt one of a kind, and I truly admired his ability to be so accepting and at peace with such a unique situation. Frank, true to his usual self, spoke with Loretta about all of her guilty feelings and extra attention towards Sean. Afterward, he told me:

I have Loretta understanding now that it would be insulting to me if she were sitting next to me wanting to be sitting next to Sean, that kind of thing. Her instructions from me were to respond to any of us at any particular moment the way she wants to at that particular moment. If she wants to walk over and kiss him, do so! Don't sit there in heat trying to be a proper spouse. That would get me laughing. And by all means, don't come over then and give me a kiss to even things out. I would laugh even harder. Mickey was there when we talked and backed up everything I was saying. She and I are starting to increase our affection so Loretta can relax. Sean, really, in general, has no idea what we're talking about! It's really a gas. He was not in on Loretta's latest concerns and so didn't read between the lines of our conversations, which we sort of hide from him for the fun of it!" Frank concluded his talk with me by saying, "I know that you have been briefed on Loretta's dilemma. It's really her problem, not mine. I've known the boundaries and guidelines since 1963. Of course, I would have preferred to be No. 1, but I knew that was never to be. Think about it; I could have walked away from her and ended up with someone far more problematic than she ever was. Toss in my morbid, sullen personality and being a recluse, and you have a man who can deal with this quite nicely, thank you.

Loretta also spoke of Frank's need for solitude and explained that he had always been a loner, socializing for a while and then retreating into his own world. This, in part, helped to explain his seemingly devil-may-care attitude to her relationship with Sean. It is difficult to explain unless you spent time with Frank, but Loretta gave it a try. She began:

Sean and I are not going to be looked upon favorably by our readers, but that's the cost of this kind of living. Sean and I have wondered for years about Frank's nonchalant attitude to all of this, not only to our love affair but other things in life as well. I don't know of anyone who thinks as he does.

It's very refreshing, really. If Frank had not married me knowing of my love for Sean, Sean and I would have made a mess of our life, having affairs throughout our relationships, still probably not getting along, and maybe ending up away from each other for good. If Frank had said that I had to choose, well, it would have been Sean because I would want to be honest with Frank from the beginning. As Frank says now, we all won. We all got the golden ring off the Merry-Go-Round of Life. We booed him on that analogy.

Loretta continued:

As the years passed, I began to realize that Frank was not unhappy with my love for Sean. In fact, he nurtured it. I was always on the lookout for little ways he could sabotage my relationship with Sean, and he could have. He could have used the kids against me; many things. But he never did. Now, he's enjoying his mysterious lifestyle. Have you noticed that he will only socialize with you so far? It's nothing against you. It's him. If he thinks someone is getting too close to him, he backs off. I don't think he's even aware of it. He would even do it to Sean and me. He does it now. Notice how he only stays a few days, and then he's out of here? We are not insulted. We take bets on when he's going to bolt the scene. We even make wagers on when. During the evening, he will have to run to the store or run an errand or something. He just has to get away. It's a kill. (I probably shouldn't use that word.) So, if you realize one of these days that he runs hot and cold, don't give it a thought. It's nothing personal. Just laugh at him when he's not looking. Try the game yourself. Sean's the best at predicting his exits. Then, when Frank is gone, we all sit around and giggle. Mickey scolds us for picking on his little social peculiarity, but I notice she laughs also. She even won the last bet!

26

Frank

While on the topic of Frank's unusual personality, it might be interesting to share what the psychiatrists who helped Loretta to deal with her rape had to say about him. They interviewed Frank extensively and on quite a few subjects and then gave him their analysis of his psychological make-up. The short version went something like this:

Mr. Mitchell, we have thousands of questions, but we don't have the time, so let's go after a few of them. The most mysterious to us is how you have so readily accepted your wife and Sean over the years. We know you're not lying. We know in this short time with you that you mean exactly what you say about this relationship. We believe your conversation with Sean and Loretta at that dinner where you gave him complete access to her then and forever, and still, you love her as a husband should love his wife or his true love.

But we don't meet many men who can do that. So we want to work on that one first. You seem to have inherited much of your father. We think your mother was afraid of you. She needn't have been, but she was. No one needs to fear you, at least under normal circumstances. Marco was not a normal situation. History will not condemn you for that one. But, men simply are not programmed to watch their wives love another man as well as themselves. It's just not our nature. For that reason, you, Mr. Mitchell, are abnormal in a sense. Nothing serious—you're just unusual. Here's what the three of us [the three psychiatrists] agree about. In a way, Sean and Diane, Sean and Micheline serve as your guardians, a parent-like attraction for you that you never had. You don't think of them as your parents, but the bond is there. You are also extremely, extremely antisocial, as was your father. People who know you would be shocked to learn this. They may not even believe it. You have excellent social skills. You are always on stage around them. You choose your words so carefully so you will not be discovered. This comes from your father. You like/love very few people, and you are always, always on guard.

Then they added:

You love Loretta as a husband should. She loves you as a wife should love her husband. Your marriage is almost perfect. Sean is no threat at all. You love him. He is your dearest male friend after your father. It gives you comfort and peace to see Loretta and Sean together because you, Mr. Mitchell, do not have all the ingredients to be a complete husband. You are animal at times, needing to get away from your habitat, go out and hunt, and live solitary for short periods. You are unable to take care of a house, fix things, to go to social events. (You do, but you don't like it.) You don't want a steady or predictable lifestyle. Sean is your out! Since he is in your heart completely, as is Loretta, it is only natural, and it is wanted by you, for them to be together in all ways. This has allowed you to come and go on the stage of life without anyone noticing you in an unusual way. You know that Loretta loves Sean more than she loves you, and that's just perfect for you. She does love you completely as well but loves him so intensely that you have the freedom you so seriously need. Sean and Loretta know all of this, but you give them no cause for concern, and they love you. So, it all works beautifully. Micheline just adds frosting to your cake. You do love her, but she's married to Sean, so once again, you do not have to commit entirely. You have been given an out, both with Loretta and with Micheline. It is perfect for you!

Now to the exception—your children and grandchildren. Those folks you love without exception, without a clause, fiercely, intensely, on and on. You like being their guardian and Papa and Grampa. Your love for them is the real kind. In your non-family life, you have hundreds of acquaintances but few close friends by your choice. Your attachment to the teachers [at Lincoln High] is heartwarming. You find them very interesting, enjoyable, and you respect them very much. For those and other reasons, you have turned your attention towards them in your last times. It is an extraordinary friendship to you. Normally, you would not attach yourself to a crowd of people in the outside world. It has been perfect for you.

A couple of months later, Loretta added to this analysis of Frank's personality. She explained:

Frank's air-tight personality is strengthening. He is becoming more reclusive in his sickness. He is not going to have to be watched over and cared for as Mickey will. Frank will go quietly. It sounds so heartless, and it sounds as though I've / we've just abandoned Frank. Not so. It's his insistence, his choice, and his desire. As you've noticed, he spends several days in Lincoln and then flies back here for a while, but then back home again. He loves the cottage when he's here. He wants to live there—alone. We are only six blocks away if you can count blocks in the sand. He wants to come and go on his own, visit or stay overnight on his own terms. There are no hard feelings among us. There has not been a breakdown in the foursome. He has just come around full circle into his personality. He is now a complete loner. He is just like his father. This is kind of funny to us because Frank's mother always said, "You're just like your father," only she didn't mean it in a nice way. He spends a lot of time in the cottage. Of course, we visit him and he us, but for the most part, he stays alone. In the early days of this discussion, I explained to him that this puts me in the role of the abandoning wife. I could picture the headlines, "Husband dying of cancer, wife moves out and moves in with her lover, Sean Connery." Great! I told him I know that has a selfish ring to it—me worrying about my reputation. But think about it; no matter how you put it down on paper, this is how it settles. He laughed and said people will say things anyway, and what do we care? We stay to ourselves here regardless.

So after months of arguing and pleading and discussing, I capitulated, as did Sean, and we agreed to his plan. Once we were out of Lincoln, we would, of course, move into the cottage, but he planned to spend the majority of his time alone there, while Sean and I and Mickey would live more in the main house. If Mickey were to go first, it would be Sean and me living there and Frank down the road, so to speak, on the beach. He and I would still behave as man and wife regardless, and I would continue my 'affair' with Sean. When Frank goes, we'll probably rent out the cottage and use it for an investment. So, there you have the details of his last year, and it probably is his final year. The world will think he lived sadly alone, but they didn't know this guy. To him, it was heaven. When I think back to the early dating days, Sean and I always wondered how he could be so comfortable with my loving Sean, even to the point of insisting that we remain a threesome and now a foursome. It gave him his freedom, which he cherished more than anything. That's it.

Knowing Frank, I could only agree with Loretta that that was the way he wanted their lives to be.

27

Sex, love, and seniors

While on the topic of their lifestyle, I inquired about their daily routine in California. I had heard quite a bit about all of their sexual escapades, but I wondered how else they spent their time, as I was sure—well, reasonably sure— that they were not continually making love, despite their apparent obsession with sex. In May of 2009, Loretta described their routine by saying that they usually got up around seven a.m. and would go to the beach for a swim and to watch the waves come in. Then they would go back to their separate homes to read or correspond with friends. She said they did not hang around all together the entire day. Sean was gone much of the time as he was still involved in many projects of one sort or another. Mickey slept a lot, and Loretta would either read or go out shopping. Frank rested a great deal during the day and read regularly. Loretta said that he was with them only a few hours each day. Then, in the evening, maybe they would go to a movie or shopping, or a concert. If none of those, they might retire to their own rooms for *private time*. She summed it up by saying, "We are fortunate lazy people, but people in their 70's, so—so what?"

The women also openly discussed the topic of their love for their two men. They had previously spoken concerning who gave them the most pleasure sexually, but I also asked them if they could quantify their love for Sean and Frank. Could they answer the question, "Do you love one of 'your husbands' more than the other?" I would like to clarify at this point that the four had recently come upon the theme of each of them having two spouses. Frank said they all just loved the idea. He said, "We really do think of the four of us in that way. Sean and I have two wives, and Loretta and Mickey have two husbands. The outside world will say that it goes against all definitions. We say we have never been more at peace with our love life, both physically and emotionally!"

Returning to the question, Mickey's response was in a sense for both her and Loretta. She said:

I think we love them almost the same, and the difference is of no importance, and the women out there will understand what we mean by that. But let's say that we had to choose; that we have to make the choice public. I think Frank already has the answer and would tell the world as much; that Loretta's love for Sean is more intense than her love for Frank, even though her love for Frank is profound and complete in its own right. But strangely, the answer to that one was not important to him at all anyway, no matter how it would go. He, Loretta, and I talked about this in the past in private, away from Sean. Sean's the one who will be pissed to know that we even bothered to mention or consider it. The question is silly, but it will be asked, so what the hell, let's answer it. Frank agreed. We had discussed it with him in advance. So, now I've answered the question before answering the question. Are you confused? [I was at this point.] Well then, bottom line, whom do I love the itty bitty bit most? Of course, it would be my husband, Sean.

256

This whole topic—who gives the women the most pleasure in bed and who do they love the most—took quite a few days and several conversations for the women to answer to their satisfaction. Then the ladies decided it was time for the men to answer the same questions, expecting the same kind of detailed self-reflection that they had given it. The two men, however, addressed the issue succinctly and without hesitation. Frank wrote me the following letter from Lincoln on behalf of both him and Sean. He wrote:

> I got a call from my main squeeze, Loretta, last night. You know what she required of me to put in the form of an email to you. So, I called Mr. Connery, and he had just been informed that he must do the same. Our conversation lasted two minutes. He told me just to write both of our answers to you and save the airwaves space. We've informed the ladies as to our answer, which is this: "AS A REPRESENTATIVE OF ONE SEAN CON-NERY, I, FRANK MITCHELL, WISH TO INFORM YOU TWO WOMEN THAT THOSE TWO QUESTIONS ARE SO RIDIC-ULOUS AND UNIMPORTANT IN OUR WORLD, THAT WE REFUSE EVEN TO CONSIDER THEM. So, go make Sean's breakfast and be still. (Oh, don't worry about MY breakfast, I'll just rummage around the fridge until I come across some tiny morsel to sustain me through the day.)" Signed, Frank Mitchell and Sean Connery.

I was always under the impression that as people aged, they became *less* interested in sex, not more, especially when discussing people in their seventies and eighties and beyond. In all honesty, I must reveal that when these four began relating their sexual episodes to me, I was frankly in shock, but in a very positive way. It was comforting to know that there was no particular age when sex was suddenly no longer important or enjoyable and that it could even be the opposite—that sex could become *more* important than in one's younger years. I was discussing this with Mickey one day, and this was her response:

It's not lost on you that we are showing the "old age over-interest in sex syndrome." [I had never heard of such a thing, so I was intrigued.] They say us old folks start getting turned on at an amusing pace in comparison to the lack of athletic ability we have. I'm sure it must be pathetic, but we don't care. Well, I don't know how to describe or explain older people when it comes to the sex drive. Your abilities are much less, of course, stamina as we knew it in our 20's and 30's is gone, but sex is such a powerful drive in us all, and maybe it's because each experience could be one of the last. Maybe we panic? I just don't know. And it isn't all seniors, and I haven't any statistics. I just know it's on our minds a great deal of the time, maybe even more than when we were younger. After all, years ago, we knew we could do it anytime, but now? [I thought that summed it up nicely.]

Along the same lines, I asked them about their views on sex and fidelity, or infidelity in general. Their opinions certainly did not reflect those of the general public, I must say, but they are worth consideration perhaps, as so many problems in relationships could be resolved if couples shared the attitudes of the four. As a matter of fact, Frank was asked by a pastor friend of his to speak on several occasions with couples in marriage counseling at a church in Omaha. His thoughts were a good synopsis of how these four view sex and relationships. Frank said that first of all, he did not condone infidelity as such and that he would tell the couples just that. The subject he addressed with them specifically was how to respond to their hurting when one of the partners had been unfaithful to the other.

He stressed the point that sex is rarely a form of revenge against one's spouse. It just happens sometimes. Couples say things like, "I can never touch my spouse again knowing that he/she has been with someone else," or "How could you do this to me /to us /to the family?" But those attitudes do not solve anything. He tried to get them to see that there is no cheating. Sex is another event with another person. The two things, one's relationship with their spouse and the sex with someone else, are not related. He continued with the idea that sex is just sex. When you love someone and perhaps even marry him or her, then the sex becomes something entirely different. When love is inserted into the activity, it does not matter if your partner is a good lover. It doesn't matter as to their physical beauty or lack thereof.

Frank did not believe that committing to spend the rest of your life with someone, the trust issue, if you will, needed to have the boundaries of physical fidelity attached to it. He used the example of him and Loretta, saying he knows Loretta loves him. She has always shown him that she loved him, and so Sean didn't matter between them. Plus, he truly wanted Loretta to be as happy as she possibly can, and if being with someone else made her happy, then he was also. Frank added that he had felt this way since he was in his twenties, and he had never looked back. He realized that this went against how almost every bound couple—man to woman, woman to woman, or man to man—defined being bound to one another. Most people think that you are bound and committed on a physical and emotional level from the moment the union has been decided. Frank said the four of them just didn't fit the mold. They were able to separate the physical from the emotional in the sense that, if someone involved in a committed relationship were to have, for example, a one-night stand, that physical act had nothing to do with their level of love for their partner.

The four of them gave me cause to analyze and ponder this way of thinking in great depth. My conclusions were not of a black-and-white nature, as many factors influence a conversation of this type. For example, I have always believed that if a couple were truly, deeply in love—a soul-mate kind of unconditional love—that neither individual would even feel the need or desire to be with someone else. I still, for the most part, adhere to that line of thinking. That being said, I also realize that in our world today, there are many unexpected temptations. Many situations exist in which it might be easy to lose control; situations in which physical desire might overwhelm—although be it temporarily—rational thinking. In such cases, sex truly is *just sex* and should not negatively impact the committed relationship. Frank and the others would agree with me that if the other relationship became what could be deemed an affair, there would most definitely be serious concerns for that relationship's future.

Specifically, looking at Sean and the others' relationships, it became clear that this was a unique situation. I never doubted for a second the level of love, the depth of commitment that Sean had for Mickey. She was his life, his soul mate, and he was hers. Yet, he was also very much in love with Loretta, and Loretta with him, and that had been the case for over fifty years—a love with a different temperament, to be sure; intense, an inferno. That intensity is what made it difficult, if not impossible, for the two to live together for any length of time in their younger years. Loretta and Frank's love mimicked or paralleled, in many ways, the kind of love that Sean and Mickey shared, and Frank and Mickey's love grew out of many years spent in each others' company—a profound yet somehow more sedated type of love perhaps.

In this case, I can comprehend the foursome. Add to that the impending death of two of the four, and the entire scenario takes on a very natural, though quite sad, feel—an "of course that is the way it should be" kind of reaction. And frankly, how wonderful is it that they all had each other and could express their love so openly. As the two got sicker, imagine the comfort they derived from all of the love surrounding them. Loretta and Sean could hold onto each other and help each other through the pain of their impending losses and the mourning period that was soon to be upon them. Mickey and Frank could have candid conversations about their illnesses and deaths that no one else could truly comprehend. They could also be at peace knowing that their loved ones would be well taken care of after they were gone. Loretta confided in me that the four of them had gradually evolved into Frank and Mickey more often together and her and Sean together. She said, "Frank and Mickey feel ill most of the time. They have had a horrendous six months [this was in the summer of 2009]. Our worlds find Frank and Mickey more as a couple, as are Sean and I. They spend many hours on the beach at night."

28

The decline

The four entertained me with story after fantastic story from November of 2008 until more than a year later, when the illnesses reached the point of being all-consuming, and their letters were few and far between. There was still news, but it became more sporadic and focused wholly on how ill Frank and Mickey were. The last anecdote I received from Frank himself concerned the amputation of the ring finger on his right hand. The topic was horrifying and grotesque to a certain extent, but he always managed to find humor in a most desperate situation.

September 2009: Circulation to Frank's right ring finger had nearly stopped for some unknown reason. It was causing him a tremendous amount of pain, added to his usual constant suffering. Still, the doctors wanted to wait another month or two before amputating in case circulation should unexpectedly return. Frank was still managing to do a little substitute teaching at Lincoln High at that point, which I found remarkable, and he came to talk with me after school—and to show me his finger, which was bandaged so that others could not see it. He pulled back the bandage, and I saw that the entire top half of his finger was black—gangrene had set in. He told me it was extremely painful, and for Frank to admit any pain at all was unusual, so I knew how bad this must be, but he was still joking about it. In fact, on September 30, Frank sent me a poem he had written on the topic of his finger and life after death that, in addition to making me laugh, frankly left me wondering how many pain killers he had taken that day. I have included it here for its entertainment value and because it gives some insight into Frank's thoughts concerning how he was picturing life eternal. He prefaced it by saying, "I am insane, you know. I am doing an up and down kind of living, but I'm enjoying it all. I will not go gently into that good night. Never fear about me. I have time to invent the light bulb, you'll see."

ODE TO A FINGER
By Frank Mitchell

I may hold the secret of life after...

What do we know for sure?

The ring finger on the right hand will be rudely omitted.

I myself will follow a similar course thereafter.

(My son wondered if there would be an urn for the finger. There is to be an urn for me, of course. Isn't there? Anyone?)

I hadn't thought that far ahead, but that idea is now on the table for discussion, and may I say, a brilliant addition to a growing collection of possibilities.

WHY? You ask. Think about it. As a philosopher might say,

"I hold." Meaning, I believe.

What don't we know for sure? And here enters the exciting possibility that I may hold the secret of life after...

Here it comes: The finger, and let's call him "Little Franky, or LF," is to go first and will be cremated, but what we don't know – Do the spirit vibes from LF remain, waiting for me to follow? And if they do, will my remaining body receive vibes and communications of some sort from the soon-to-be-released finger or LF? Think. What if Little Franky has been released with extreme

264

prejudice? What if I begin to receive messages, or images, from the said finger?

Let's say I'm awakened with the sight of LF wrapped in a little white robe, resting on the arm of a beautiful, "WHITE," Lazy Boy rocker waiting for – "Big Franky?"

Maybe even some music playing, a deck of cards, a fan blowing on the rocker? Of course, I'm guessing, but would some experience like that not prove that indeed there was an afterworld?

I hesitate to bring this out to the real world. There are "scoffers" out there, and who needs that?

Well, I can't take it any further than that but, but if a few weeks after LF has gone, and I begin to describe a beautiful cottage and only one of many houses in a semi-circle, and it's the compound that I've talked about for years, and my entire family has a final resting place, and we are all together just as I've always wanted?

Far out? You got that right!

At the end of October 2009, doctors decided to schedule the amputation, as there had been no sign of improvement. The surgery was scheduled for November 2. Frank's October 30 message informing me of this went as follows:

"The date of the execution is set—this Monday, November 2nd, at 6:45 AM. My flag salute will be lame, to be sure. I hope no one sees."

Then, on November 1 he wrote to me and some of his family members saying,

Dear Family and Friends,

My finger's last meal will be to tear apart a cinnamon roll. No chaplain will read Bible verses, and it wants no black hood placed over it. What a gutsy little fellow! Makes me proud…

The surgery took place in Lincoln, but Frank flew back to California later that same afternoon. All had gone well, or so they thought. On November 4, Frank wrote, "Doing well. 'Little Franky' is cute. The first two days sucked, but now I am beginning to get some energy. No need to worry about my slapping you! By next week I should be semi-wonderful. I've lost half an ounce. More later…"

Frank's recovery did not go as smoothly as he had hoped and anticipated, though, and Mickey was not doing well either. At the end of November 2009, Frank told me, "Mickey and I have not been doing well. We are both doing a little better now. Our world has shut down dramatically. I underestimated the amputation and its effect on my system. The anesthesia did not mix well with the chemo I take. It was a bad recovery. I have not felt like talking to anyone. Sean spends his time with Mickey and is not conversing with the outside world. Loretta goes back and forth between me and Mickey."

In December, Frank managed to phone me, saying, "I'm in California. I'm not doing very well, though I am not at the point of… yet. I'm having problems with my internal organs. My spleen has stopped working, and my liver is trying to work overtime to compensate for it. They're trying to figure out what to do. I'm going for a CAT scan in a few minutes; then, they don't know. They might need to do some exploratory surgery or something.

Someone will be in touch with you if I can't, and we'll keep you posted. You won't be seeing me for a while. Love you..."

After that phone call, I wondered if Frank would be able to pull out of this one, but he and Mickey both never ceased to astound me with their unwavering courage and resilience. I wrote Frank a letter telling him how much he meant to me and how grateful I was to have had him be a part of my life, and how I couldn't imagine this world without him in it. Then again, it felt selfish at times for me to keep hoping and praying for his pulling through. He and Mickey were both in such constant pain, always fighting it—nonstop. I imagined they must be tempted, at least at times, to give up the fight, let go, and finally have the pain stop, to finally be at peace.

Miraculously, Frank survived the crisis, and he and Mickey would continue their battles to stay alive. In January of 2010, Sean wrote one of the last emails I would receive from him merely telling me that they were overwhelmed and would be, for the most part, silent for the foreseeable future. He said that they would let me know when the unthinkable came to pass so that I might be a part of whatever arrangements they would make. They would send his private jet for me, and I would finally be with them, though it would obviously not be under desirable circumstances. This was a most difficult conversation for him—and me. I knew that this unfolding tragedy was destroying him and that he felt helpless to stop any of it. Frank managed to send me a few short messages during that same month. They generally said such things as, "I've been very sick," and they were signed "The Phantom." I would not hear from him again after that, nor would I hear anything from Mickey. I had saved a voice mail Frank had sent me at the end of November 2009, and I listened to it once in a while, simply so I could hear his voice, for quite some time. Loretta kindly sent me an occasional update on the two, but she was also having a tough time coping with the situation, and it was never good news when she wrote. Mickey had become skeletal, she said, and Frank, though mobile, was less aware of his surroundings.

On September 13, 2010, while on a lunch break at school, I received an email from Loretta. It was short and heart-wrenchingly simple. She told me Frank had passed away in his sleep during the night. They were in shock because he had seemed to be doing okay. She added, "He requested no service, so we will honor his wishes. Cremation tomorrow." She also said she feared Mickey would not be far behind. Naturally, I was quite upset that Frank had left us and devastated that, once again, I would not be flying out to be with them to say our final goodbyes together. I remember being surprised and a bit confused that Frank would be cremated two days after his passing. It seemed unusually fast, but I guessed arrangements had been made months before. I couldn't hold back my tears and went down the hall to tell my colleagues, who also knew Frank and cared deeply for him. They shared my shock and sadness at the reality and finality of it all. Later that day, I sent an all-staff email to those in my school, as I knew that he had subbed for many over the years, and they would want to be informed. The story, little did I know, was about to become quite bizarre.

The following day at school, I was in the copy room at the same time as our amazing theater teacher, Paula. Paula had long ago lived in one of the same small towns as Frank and had taught with him and been involved in musicals with him during that time. I knew that their children were acquainted as well. She pulled me aside and told me that I was mistaken, that Frank and Loretta were currently in Lincoln with their daughter, and that they were in the process of relocating to Utah to live with their son. The look on my face must have been priceless, a combination of shock and

268

outrage that she would invent such a thing. I insisted that she must be mistaken. She told me I was the one mistaken and that she didn't know why I would have been told such a horrendous lie. She had spoken with Frank and Loretta's daughter, who had confirmed that Frank was in town with her.

Stubbornly, I refused to believe her. I wrote to Loretta, who told me her daughter was having trouble accepting the truth of her father's passing and was therefore making up stories about them being there and all being well. I had absolutely no reason to doubt a woman with whom I had now been corresponding for over two years and whom I considered a close friend, as close as one can be not having met in person. Paula sensed my disbelief, frustration, and frank anger toward her and the situation, and we did not broach the topic any longer. I knew she felt sorry for me, but nothing she said could change my assessment of who was mistaken at that point, so she stopped trying. Over the next months, I mourned Frank's death as I would that of any close friend. I cried, read and reread emails; I held on to the one voice mail that I still had from Frank and played it many times over so I could still hear his voice—and I kept writing.

I started thinking once again about "The Plan" and how life was playing out for the three who were left. When Frank had first told me about it, I had thought, "How amazing!" and now it seemed to be slowly coming to fruition. I had been struck by the ability and outright desire of the two who were ill to so selflessly encourage the other two's relationship and love, even while they were still alive. It was a testament to the depth of the love they felt for their spouses—unconditional, and perhaps unfathomable to most—a level of love one hopes to find at least once in a lifetime. For the four, they had had the incredible good fortune of finding it not once but twice.

After Loretta's email informing me of Frank's passing, the writing stopped. I was not surprised by this. It seemed perfectly normal. I sent my condolences to Mickey and Sean, but they did not respond. Time passed. I continued to write. Given that I had no more information from the three concerning how "The Plan" was working with Frank gone, and that I had finished the manuscript excepting the conclusion, I decided to create a fairy-tale ending to the story as an epilogue, telling the reader as much. What follows is my original ending to this fantastic story of the four.

Epilogue

The story I have told is a true one, recounted to me by the fab four themselves, though I would agree with those who say it reads more like a fairy tale. Therefore, I thought it might be fitting to conclude this story with a cinematic happy ending—the one that Frank and Mickey imagined and described to me in rather minute detail—the story of Sean and Loretta's wedding.

Sometime after Frank and Mickey left Sean and Loretta to fend for themselves, they decided the time was right for them to be married—finally—as the other two had requested, even mandated, they do. The wedding took place at their beautiful beach-front home in Malibu, California, on a clear and warm spring day. Frank and Mickey's ashes had been scattered there, and all in attendance could feel their presence. Guests included Sean's son and his family, Loretta and Frank's children and grandchildren, and a few of their closest friends.

Loretta was wearing the wedding dress she had worn for her marriage to Frank—a symbol of her eternal love for him as well as for Sean. Sean was in a black tuxedo that Mickey had chosen for him to wear for the occasion, as she had wanted to be sure he would look his best. The music was soft and moving and included pieces written for the ceremony by Leonard Cohen, Frank's all-time favorite singer and composer. Loretta and Frank's son gave Loretta away, and the grandchildren served as flower girl and ring-bearer.

As Sean and Loretta exchanged vows, incredulous that they were finally being married, they looked into each others' eyes, wearing bittersweet smiles that said it all. The spirits of Frank and Mickey watched over the ceremony, Frank and his amputated finger reunited. They were happy and holding hands, exuberant that their wishes for the other two had come true. The ceremony was perfect, and Sean and Loretta lived happily ever after.

29

Betrayal

Once I had completed this invented conclusion to the story, I wrote to Sean, Loretta, and Mickey and a note to QT telling them that the long-awaited manuscript was ready for editing and publishing. I had been told Sean's publisher was anxiously awaiting its completion, and QT wanted to proceed with the film. It was now the beginning of April 2011. Sean's response to my excited message that the manuscript was finally complete shattered me. It was incomprehensible and devastating. It took me weeks, if not months, to fully absorb the enormity of this betrayal of trust, for that is what it was to me. The first email containing the bombshell was short and devoid of emotion. Sean wrote:

Friday, 8 April 2011 12:01 PM
From: "Thomas Connery" <*************>
To: Lynda Graham-Rowe <*************>
Lynda,
We all realize the time and effort you have put into your manuscript. It was a great idea.

However, due to reasons I cannot discuss, I will not grant permission to publish this book. Think in terms of people Frank worked for.

Mickey says Hi, and sorry, she is doing ok.

Best wishes, Sean.

I wrote back shortly after receiving this disastrous news, as soon as I could breathe and think reasonably straight, asking Sean to discuss the matter further with me. There could easily be compromises made. I could simply tell the love story and omit any reference to Frank's and his father's underworld connections. It would still be a best seller. I could also change all the names except for Sean and Mickey's, as I have done in this revised account of the story. I certainly didn't want to have Mafia members angry with me. The response I received a few days later was signed by both Sean and Loretta. It seemed to be their attempt at a further explanation without explaining:

Monday, 11 April 2011 4:45 PM
From: "Thomas Connery" <************************>
To: "Lynda Graham-Rowe" <************************>
For reasons we cannot disclose. I Sean Connery do not give permission for any publication about me or Loretta.

For reasons we cannot disclose, I Loretta Mitchell do not give permission for any publication about me or Frank.

Frank not only worked for public schools, but he also worked for very "unusual organizations." They would be most unhappy if such a manuscript were to appear in print. You do not want these people at your doorstep. Sean Connery and Loretta Mitchell

This would be the last correspondence I would receive from Sean, Loretta, or Mickey. My next attempt at reasoning was to ask Sean, at the very least, to compensate me financially in a lump sum for the work I had done the past two years plus. No response. I wrote to QT and asked if Sean was trying to scare me by claiming threats from the Mafia. I asked him if he had a better explanation of the sudden about-face on this project Sean had formerly deemed so important and whether he would be willing to find me a publisher if I changed the necessary names, Mafia names included, of course. Quentin responded:

Dear Lynda,

Sean meant no threat, just a caution. Frank worked for some very powerful people who are very "sensitive." If the book and movie had been made with consent, then they would go along. But since Loretta and Sean declined for the reasons you have, it could cause notoriety that would be unwelcomed by them. They will not send Mario and Anton to break your legs.:))))

As to your publisher or agent...give me some time to investigate, and I'll get back to you on that.

Frank's story should be told. He wanted it told. You are lucky to have talked with Mickey (One day at lunch at school, Frank had called Mickey and passed the phone to each of us in the department so we could all say hello). Usually, Frank is so cautious that he shares with no one. BTW, Mickey loved talking with all of you. Who knows????, maybe all will turn around.

Loretta and Sean felt terrible about your hours of work and then cut you off. There was no choice. The children rule.

Frank may be the world's greatest enigma. Imagine the impact of your story. A music teacher who, in fact, was a world-class Assassin...not a hitman...but an Assassin. That's all they do... A hitman is just a mobster who also works in gambling, drugs, prostitution, etc., and at times is assigned to kill. The Assassin has his own income. He is a "law-abiding citizen." :))) Very few are caught or killed. He lived in a dark and quiet world.

I remember November in 2008 when he told one of you he knew Sean Connery!!!!!

He had no idea it would go anywhere.

Question: do your fellow workers make fun of you for believing all of this?? How about friends and family. Are you now being criticized for listening to him? I've had it happen many times, and it is not easy to deal with.

Sasha will write soon as I've said. Soon to Sasha can mean a month.:)

Give me a while to get back to you. I assure you. Everything Frank told you was the truth.

Be well. QT. forgive my spelling or grammar... I hurry my email.

I expressed my sadness and frustration concerning the abrupt end to this dream project of mine, essentially venting to none other than *the* Quentin Tarantino. He was kind and thoughtful in his response.

Wednesday, 20 April 2011 6:43 PM
From: "Quentin Tarantino" <************************>
Lynda,

Of course, you can write a fictional account using other names. I know how you feel. I lost a ton of money.

When the kids learned that the storyline would contain her year in bondage... Frank's real profession with his dad...they balked... Said no way...

Sasha still plans to write you soon. She is still devastated by his death.

It would have made a great book and a movie.

Be well, QT.

276

Some time after being told of Frank's passing, I had written to Sasha to express my condolences to her and asked how she was coping. It took her quite some time to reply, as QT had predicted. Her first message was as follows:

Friday, 22 April 2011 2:18 PM
From: S, the Mystery woman
Lynda,

I was going to write sooner, but his loss has been overpowering to me. I heard from QT. He mentioned visiting with you. It is all a mess now.

What we thought would happen isn't. It would have been a great tribute.

He was my love. He cannot be replaced. I find younger men boring and childlike.

You and I might meet someday to talk about him but probably not a good idea right now. I am in California with Sean and L when I'm free.

Mickey grows weaker. We all care for her.

I thank you for your hours of labour (I am Russian and know the correct spelling. :))) I know this has been a blow to you and your family. Please know we did not take your work lightly.

The children did not want the world to know that he is considered one of the world's greatest Assassins. His targets were Pedophiles. (I do not spell that one same as in Europe.) :))) Of course, to be sure, he also targeted some bad guys in our world before working for our Government. Americans are so innocent. They think their country does not kill on contract. What a joke. It's a great country but so spoiled. I love it here. BTW, the real danger is China, not Muslims. China will rule the world.

I digress. This is to introduce myself, and I'll write to you on a regular basis at some point in time. Then, if you wish, we shall meet, and I'll add to your stories.

Best wishes, Sasha.

I would not hear from any of them again. I decided at that point that it was best to drop the project—at least for the time being.

30

Attorneys, discoveries, and lies

Time passed. I swallowed my pride. I had excitedly told family and friends about my book's impending publication, sure to be a best seller. Now I had to say to them that it wasn't going to happen as planned. Many scoffed and concluded I had been naïvely duped by Frank; that it was all his doing, a joke to him, though even the doubters could not comprehend why Frank would have created such an elaborate, time-consuming, hurtful hoax. To what end? I stood my ground. I acknowledged that there were many lies blended with the truth the four were supposed to be imparting, but that the vast majority of the stories were true, that the friendship and love among the four were real. Still, there was nothing to be done at that point, so I turned my attention to my life prebook. It was a life filled with the many blessings of family and their love and regained health. My daughter pointed out that at least I could say I wrote a book, something few can claim, published or not. The glass was more than half-full regardless. I was happy nonetheless.

Almost a year passed, and the manuscript gathered dust, literally and figuratively. Then slowly, I noticed the feelings of injustice and unresolved conflict resurfacing. I needed to get to the bottom of this bizarre episode in my life. I needed closure. I wondered again if I could publish my manuscript without Sean's legal reprisal, changing the names of all the others involved to spare them any possible anger, pain, or embarrassment. I sought the advice of a literary attorney. After I described the situation as succinctly as possible over the phone, I was asked to make an appointment. When I arrived, I was stunned to see that not one but four of the firm's top attorneys were in the room. They were fascinated to hear more. I felt a combination of pride and intimidation, not being used to such scenes. As stated in the prologue to this book, however, each time I relate the story in simple terms without having my audience read the manuscript, it comes across as the story of a too trusting woman having been duped by a very eccentric supposed friend.

They fired at me the questions I was so accustomed to being asked, the ones whose answers always sounded, frankly, lame. Yet they did not laugh at me, and for that, I was very grateful. They asked if at any point someone had asked me for money—absolutely not! I would have known better than that. What they told me, in conclusion, was that since all of my communication with all of them except Frank had been through their Gmail accounts, there was no way to trace the sources of the emails. Therefore, I could not prove that they indeed came from four different IP addresses and that one of them belonged to Sean Connery. I learned sometime later that computer geeks can trace Gmail IP addresses but that it is complicated and time-consuming. The attorneys suggested that I write to Frank and Loretta's children for confirmation that, first of all, Frank was dead, and also if there had indeed been a friendship with the Connerys. Barring that, they told me that Sean probably could sue me. Moreover, they explained that no reputable publishing house would take on such a manuscript without permission from Sean. Once he passed away, though, there would most likely be no issue with the publication, so patience was a possible option.

Still curious after I met with them, the law firm decided to run a Lexis Report on Frank and Loretta and send it to me. I had never heard of such a report, and when I saw all the information it contained, I was frankly shocked to see how much personal history could be dug up on someone so quickly. The addresses Frank and Loretta had mentioned in their stories generally jived with the report. There was, however, one entry that stopped me in my tracks, that made me want to scream and cry simultaneously. The attorneys explained:

01/11/12 at 10:19 AM
We are forwarding the Lexis Report we ran with every possible contact information for Frank, Loretta, and their children. This report indicates that Frank is deceased. However, the WARNING symbol is by that entry, meaning that that information cannot be taken as accurate without further investigation. No one in this office has ever seen that symbol on a report of death. The rest of the report would indicate that Frank was alive as of 2 weeks ago, living at the listed address in Salt Lake City, Utah. Mark ran a social security database search, and there is no indication that Frank has died. Therefore, our conclusion based on this information is that someone may have told people that Frank has died, but he has not.

A month spent in confusion, disbelief, and anger passed. Then, the familiar feeling of needing closure and wanting to know the truth came creeping back. I had to know. I sent friend requests on Facebook to both of Frank and Loretta's children along with a private message explaining my reasons for writing. One accepted my friend request but with no response. The other, the one living in Utah, never responded. The message was as follows, with the children's names omitted:

Dear ****** and ***,
This is Lynda Graham-Rowe. I was a friend of your father's from Lincoln High School. I hope that you will read and respond to this message as I need (and I believe I deserve) to know the truth, and I now know that you are the ones who can help me in this quest. I think you know that in November of 2008, Frank told me of his long-term friendship with Sean and Mickey Connery and that Frank, Loretta, and the Connery's began sending me stories of their times together at that point. A few months later, they asked me to write a book about their story, and I accepted, trusting that, as they continuously promised me, soon the retainers and "enough money to buy a villa in Paris someday" (to quote your mother) would be in hand.

Over the next year and a half, the four sent me hundreds of pages of emails. Then, in the fall of 2010, I received an email from Loretta that your father had passed away the night before in his sleep, that the cremation would take place the next day, and that he had requested no service. When Paula told me that you had said he was still alive and moving to Utah, your mother told me that that was not true and that you were not handling your father's death well; that he was not alive. At that point, I had no reason to believe Paula and every reason to trust your mother, and so I mourned your father's death. It was a tough time for me.

Next, in October 2010, I was told that you, the children, had decided you did not want the book published. I was again devastated and said to the three that I could certainly change the names to ensure your privacy – that the only critical real names were Sean and Mickey's. They responded that they had made a compromise with you and I could still write the book but that they would no longer help me. I agreed. I spent every free moment for 2 ½ years writing this book, which is titled "Love, Truth, Death, and Sean Connery – The Untold Story." In April of 2011, I finished the 1st draft and wrote to Quentin to see if he would help me find a publisher. The response came from Sean and said I could not use his (or their) names in any publication for reasons he could not explain and that I wouldn't want those from Frank's "other career" to appear on my doorstep. That was the last time I heard from any of the four.

Last month, I finally decided to speak with an attorney and see what rights I had in this matter as far as publishing goes. He informed me that it appeared as if your father had moved to Salt Lake City when you told Paula he had and that he is either still alive or only recently passed away. I have been reeling ever since from the news and trying to make sense out of all this. I didn't ask to write the book; they asked me, and I did it out of love for them and trust in them that they would make good on their promises for financial compensation.

So, I am pleading with you to speak with me and tell me the truth. I thank you in advance for your willingness to help me in this matter. I would never put you or your family in any situation that made you uncomfortable, just to be clear. My sincere thanks! Lynda

Another month passed with no news. Then one afternoon, as I was in my classroom preparing to head to parent-teacher conferences, my school phone rang. After my hello, I heard a very deep, almost sinister-sounding male voice say, "This is Frank Mitchell." It would be the most bizarre, eerie conversation I had ever had, and it will most likely keep that top ranking for the rest of my life. I would not be exaggerating to say I felt faint. I started trembling. I tried to concentrate on breathing as naturally as possible. Words were failing me, yet I had a hundred things I wanted to ask him, to tell him. Since he then said he couldn't talk long, I chose to mostly listen. He said, in a frighteningly icy monotone, "Please don't contact my children anymore!"

His son, he continued, had thought my Facebook message was some kind of joke or hoax, so I surmised that he hadn't been in the loop about the book all that time. He didn't mention his daughter's reaction, and I knew she was aware it existed since, at times, she had asked her dad to have me print some of the stories for her. Frank then said that I knew all along things might unravel at some point. I countered, "But Frank, I wrote for two-and-a-half years!" He told me I could still publish the book, but not with their names. So I said, "Are you telling me I can use Sean's name then, just not yours?" He replied, "Oh, I see what you mean, no, he won't approve that..." He went on to tell me that so much had happened since 2009. Loretta had been diagnosed with Alzheimer's disease seven years ago, but it had gotten much worse beginning in 2009. He said she could no longer distinguish time, as in future from past, etc. I then muttered, "Loretta told me a year and a half ago that you had died! I was devastated and heartbroken. I mourned your death, Frank!" His response was simply, "And I thank you for that." He added that he did not know that Loretta had told me he had died. This seemed farfetched to me, though I chose not to contradict him. Much later, I would realize that Sasha had written to me expressing how deeply she missed Frank now that he was gone and that she was in Malibu helping to care for the other three. Given their relationship, clearly, she knew he was still alive and that neither he nor Loretta was in Malibu. Frank also said that those in his other career had said "no" to the project. I asked how he was fairing, and he answered that he was OK but wouldn't be around much longer. Of course, he had already far surpassed how long he had said the doctors believed he had, but I know that can happen with cancers sometimes, thankfully. Frank said he needed to go, so I somehow managed to wish him well, and then I said, "Tell me, Frank, are you really friends with Sean Connery?" He said simply, "Yes." I told him I hoped he'd contact me again, and he hung up. I'm not sure how I made it through talking with parents for three hours after that, but I can state that I was badly shaken.

Conclusion

When I next saw Paula, I apologized for not having believed her and confessed that Frank had phoned me. She was kind and understanding yet worried about me; worried, I guess, that I was still operating under the assumption that the story's essence was true. She had no explanation as to why Frank would have done this to me, but she didn't seem to believe that any of it was true. However, we managed to inject some humor into our unusual conversation and ease the strain that had been between us. She also gave me an update on Frank and Loretta's situation. At that point, they were both, in fact, in Utah, staying with their son. Later she would tell me that Loretta remained in Utah, but Frank had returned to Lincoln to end his days there with his daughter.

I can only surmise that as Loretta and Frank both deteriorated, the children deemed it best that each care for one of their parents. I can certainly see how one of them caring for both parents would have been extremely difficult, if not impossible. I thanked Paula for her help and friendship and asked that she keep me informed since she remained connected with Frank and Loretta's daughter. Following our talk, I imagined what the devastating parting of the four must have been like, the painful conversations during which it was necessary to admit that things could not continue in the status quo. Mickey and Frank especially needed increasing levels of nursing care. That could have occurred in Malibu and all together, but Loretta could no longer be left alone, was no longer herself, was increasingly confused and obsessive. They had to part ways. Sean and Mickey were still quite capable of living happily and peacefully on their own, but not with Frank and Loretta in their world. The finality of their parting must have been excruciating—what a tragic, gut-wrenching end to their relationship. My heart went out to them.

As for me, I had crept closer to the truth but was still hungry for more. At the end of August 2012, I decided to try another angle to perhaps finally make sense of this whole insane adventure. I wrote an actual letter to Sir Thomas Sean Connery and sent it registered mail to his publisher's address as it was listed online. In it, I introduced myself as if Sean would know exactly who I was, making references to our friendship, the manuscript he had asked me to write, his nickname for me, and the Gmail address he had used to write me. I also mentioned that I was now aware that Frank was still alive, that Loretta was suffering from Alzheimer's disease, and that the two were in Utah. I ended by saying that since they had stopped writing, I missed them deeply, that I would like to continue our friendship and discuss the manuscript once more. Perhaps we could publish a shortened version that omitted the parts they found troublesome. I also asked that he kindly respond, leaving my email, mailing address, and cell phone number. I signed it, "With love, Frenchie."

My line of thinking was that if Sean and his publisher had absolutely no idea who I was and read this letter, they might be intrigued enough to contact me and say essentially, "Who the hell are you, and what are you talking about?" If Sean did know who I was, he probably wouldn't respond since he had wanted to end all contact and didn't want me to have any proof that he had written to me. Someone did sign the registered letter, but I never received a response.

The next time I saw Paula, which was in the fall of 2012, she asked me if I had heard that Frank had actually passed away. How strange to need to word the news that way. I had not. She gave me the few details she had. She had been notified and invited to his funeral but had been out of town, so had not attended. Loretta remained in Utah with their son and had deteriorated further. Though it was still quite sad to hear of Frank's death, for me, it was his second death, if you will, a déja vu of sorts, and my emotions centered more around closure and the finality of it all. I had shed many tears when Loretta told me he was gone, and I had missed him intensely for quite some time. Now I had become accustomed to his silence, to not being able to call him or write to him. I still missed him, of course. I always will. But it was on a more distant, mostly subconscious level.

In the days following my conversation with Paula, I began recalling all the details of "The Plan" the four had so meticulously laid out. I then started comparing it to the stark reality of how their lives were ending. It appeared that little had gone according to their wishes. I also tried to understand their silence toward me. They had made me feel like part of the family. I had felt their love and caring. But when their lives and plans began falling apart, I had been suddenly shut out; perhaps not forgotten, but certainly unwelcome. My emotions shared similarities with those felt during a divorce, I noted with a hint of humor. My friends had divorced me without explanation and were giving me the silent treatment. I may have smiled at the analogy, but the pain was real.

Several more years flew by, and from time to time, I would entertain various explanations as to why the story had played out as it did. I contrasted my fictitious epilogue with their reality as I knew it and wondered how Sean and Mickey were fairing, just the two of them now. I had heard nothing concerning her passing and wondered how she could still be alive so far past the supposed eighteen months the doctors had given her. A miracle remission? Yet another fabrication? The words *deception* and *lies* began to figure prominently in my mind. Should I somehow incorporate them into the title of the book? I still maintained, nonetheless, that love and truth were appropriate as well. I began to wonder if Mickey's purported terminal illness was to be added to the growing list of lies. Could she honestly have been blessed with such a lengthy remission? Why would they, or Frank alone, have invented such a horrific scenario as Mickey being terminally ill?

From time to time, I would check online for articles announcing Mickey's death. One would think that such news would make the headlines—"Sean Connery's wife died today..."—and I wouldn't need to search, but I looked regardless. I found no such news anywhere. I did find in several online articles that, interestingly enough, at the end of November 2015, Mickey was charged with fraud by the government of Spain. She was still very much alive. I also discovered that she and Sean were living in their home in the Bahamas rather than in Malibu at that point. Each of several articles said essentially the same thing.

Sean Connery's wife charged with Spanish property tax fraud
Friday 27 November 2015 09.37 EST
Sean Connery's wife has been charged with taking part in an alleged plot to defraud the Spanish treasury of millions of euros in property taxes[...] A letter will now be sent to Roquebrune in the Bahamas, where she and Connery live, informing her of the court's decision and ordering her to appoint a defence lawyer. The trial will take place at a criminal court in Málaga; the date is yet to be set.

Another confounding piece of news had now been added to this already bizarre tale. I noticed that there was no mention of Mickey being gravely ill. I surmised that had she been so, the

290

articles would have stated such as fact—"Given her age and frail condition she will be given special consideration..." for example, but no. It had now been more than five years since Mickey's eighteen more months to live had passed. The inconsistencies continued. My profound confusion, faced with what I still considered to be the truth, and the many bald-faced lies discovered in hindsight, was growing with the passage of time rather than lessening. Truth was drifting further from my grasp.

If Frank Mitchell was the sole author of all these tales of fantastic adventure, why not simply write the story himself? Why go to insane lengths to write me hundreds of pages? Why create different personas expressing different points of view on the same scene? And finally, why make me promises of success and riches when our entire friendship was based on both of us having cancer? One clear fact is that Frank was not a sadistic or vindictive man. He was warm and sweet and loved by all whose lives he touched (excepting his marks, of course). He was unique and, yes, eccentric at times, but I have great difficulty accepting that all of this was his invention, despite the many inconsistencies discovered over time.

Though I have no answers to these questions, I do have a theory, and when all is said and done, I prefer to believe that the foundation of this story is true. The intent of the four was initially sincere to my way of thinking, but far more was revealed than they ever fathomed would be, and Frank's former employers got a bit nervous. To compound the difficulties, instead of Frank and Mickey passing away on the timetable foreseen by the doctors, leaving Sean and Loretta to finish out their days peacefully in each others' arms as they had discussed in "The Plan," Frank and Mickey kept managing to cheat death somehow. Meanwhile, Loretta was succumbing to the devastating debilitation of Alzheimer's disease, gradually at first and then with alarming speed.

Loretta's period of rapid decline seemed to coincide with her reliving of "The Year." During that period, the others had noted her inability to return to the present and leave her horrendous past behind. Instead, her "Year" became an obsession. Whether revisiting the year exacerbated her already fragile condition or not would be a question best left to the psychiatrists who examined her. In addition, a few months later, Mickey would talk with Loretta and ask her if she realized that she was essentially ignoring Frank, giving all of her attention to Sean as she had in the early days of their relationship, another indication that she had become unable to distinguish past from present. This seemed to be confirmed when Frank called me at school and told me of Loretta's confused state. Such a tragedy!

Citing family concerns as a reason for telling me the story would not be published makes more sense when considered in that light. The four were likely overwhelmed that what they had envisioned as their final days was unraveling before them. The lighthearted fun of recounting stories turned painful as Loretta's condition worsened. As to the supposed warnings from Frank's former employers, declaring him deceased and telling me there would be no book, would be a simple way to end their contact with both Frank and Sean. The decision of the four after that—a very poor one in my opinion—was to invent and to lie, then to disappear from my life, all the while knowing I had no proof of anything beyond the existence of one Frank Mitchell.

As I end this story, I still have no answers. Sean, the legend himself, sadly passed away in his sleep on the thirty-first of October, 2020, following a battle with dementia. I cannot imagine his despair as he lost more and more cognitive function. Such a strong and commanding figure fading before his own eyes as well as Mickey's. He hoped to die peacefully in his sleep, and his wish

292

was granted. In their beloved Bahamas, with Micheline and other family at his side, the great Sir Thomas Sean Connery left us at ninety years young.

As for my story, no irrefutable truth has been uncovered. Perhaps it never will be, but I will never regret having been taken on one of the most amazing roller coaster rides of my life! As Frank would say, it's simple: "Believe it or don't!"

About the author

Lynda Graham-Rowe is a retired teacher who has always enjoyed writing. When she met an extraordinary substitute teacher who was close friends with the original 007, stories started flowing, and he asked her to tell his story—her way.

Made in the USA
Middletown, DE
18 May 2022

65813145R10184